What others are

"A delightful summer romance with a cozy Christmas feel! A Bavarian Summer is a sweet, yet beautifully deep, story about two people willing to go the distance for love, and learning a lot about themselves and each other in the process. If you're a fan of romcoms and inspirational stories, you will love this book!"

~ *Jennifer M. Bleakley, author of the best-selling* Pawverbs *devotional series and many other inspirational animal tales*

"Katie Reid has gifted her readers with another vividly written book to enjoy no matter their literal or figurative season of life. Similar to the first installment of this series, A Very Bavarian Christmas, Katie has written another relatable, yet inspiring story, that gives hope to readers familiar with the great pangs of insecurity, rejection, or inadequacy they experience as they seek to find their true love or life's purpose.

The last page will leave readers smiling—helping them to believe in God's timing; reminding them to trust that when faced with the challenges of life, His love will be with them every step of the way. Like the main character, Holly, readers will discover the view they behold at their final destination is pretty spectacular—making its beauty worth the pain and time it took to get there this side of heaven."

~ *Tracy Steel, Speaker, Women's Minister, and Author of* A Redesigned Life: Uncovering God's Purpose When Life Doesn't Go As Planned

"Katie's exquisite detail at every turn has you not only moving in step with the characters but transports you to the idyllic settings in which they reside. You can imagine yourself strolling down the main street with a waffle cone in one hand and a German pretzel in another. Your heart will both ache and rejoice as you take the journey through a long distance relationship with Holly and Nik. This heartwarming read will have you longing for a cozy Christmas in July even if you are reading this on the beach!"

~ *Dina Deleasa Gonsar, author of* At The Kitchen Sink Cookbook & Devotional, *speaker, and television personality*

"Katie M. Reid won my heart with the charming setting. *A Very Bavarian Summer* will appeal to fans of Kimberly Rose Johnson."

~ *Angela Ruth Strong, Author of the award-winning* Love Off Script Series

A Very BAVARIAN Summer

A Very Bavarian Summer

A Novel
Book 2 in the Very Bavarian Series

by

KATIE M. REID

MBI

A Very Bavarian Summer
Published by Mountain Brook Ink
White Salmon, WA U.S.A.

All rights reserved. Except for brief excerpts for review purposes, no part of this book may be reproduced or used in any form without written permission from the publisher.

The website addresses shown in this book are not intended in any way to be or imply an endorsement on the part of Mountain Brook Ink, nor do we vouch for their content.

This story is a work of fiction. All characters and events are the product of the author's imagination. Any resemblance to any person, living or dead, is coincidental.

No AI training

Scripture quotations are taken from the King James Version of the Bible. Public domain.
ISBN--978-1953957-63-4

The Author is represented by the literary agency of WTA Media LLC in Franklin, TN, www.wta.media

© 2025 Katie M. Reid

The Team: Miralee Ferrell, Tim Pietz, Kristen Johnson, Cindy Jackson Cover Design: Indie Cover Design, Lynnette Bonner Designer

Mountain Brook Ink is an inspirational publisher offering fiction you can believe in.

Printed in the United States of America

Dedication

Teresa: Thanks for summarizing the books for me in our college English classes because I didn't finish reading them. I hope you read until the last page of this one. :-)

Jenn Hand, Lisa Troyer, and Shari Braendel: Your belief in the Bavarian series is the whipped cream on my frozen cocoa. Enjoy, friends!

Contents

Chapter One: What's your next move?
Chapter Two: What are you hiding?
Chapter Three: What is your favorite childhood memory?
Chapter Four: What makes you snort laugh?
Chapter Five: What do you dream about?
Chapter Six: What makes you cry?
Chapter Seven: What if you had a million dollars?
Chapter Eight: What lights your fire?
Chapter Nine: How can I lighten your load?
Chapter Ten: What would a perfect day look like?
Chapter Eleven: What do you run to?
Chapter Twelve: What's my best feature?
Chapter Thirteen: What are you second-guessing?
Chapter Fourteen: What are some of your pet peeves?
Chapter Fifteen: What's your most embarrassing moment?
Chapter Sixteen: What do you want to save, and what do you need to toss?
Chapter Seventeen: What's one of your biggest fears?
Chapter Eighteen: What makes you angry?
Chapter Nineteen: Why do you love me?
Chapter Twenty: Where do you see yourself in five years?

Author Letter
Book Club Questions for A Very Bavarian Summer
Acknowledgments

CHAPTER ONE
What's Your Next Move?

THE DISTANCE BETWEEN HOLLY AND HER boyfriend was 2,167.3 miles. Almost a three-day drive by car, over five hours—and hundreds of dollars—by plane, or a few seconds by video chat. Holly couldn't smell Nik's cedar spice cologne through cyberspace, but the latter option of connecting with her boyfriend was better than nothing, yet still not ideal.

It had never been clearer than it was at this precise moment that Bavarian Falls, Michigan, where Holly Noel Brigham currently resided, was nowhere near Leavenworth—the quaint town in Washington state, not the military prison in Kansas—where her boyfriend lived. Although both towns were German-themed, with charming storefronts that almost looked as if they were clothed in dirndls and lederhosen, it felt as if an ocean lay between them.

At thirty-two years of age, Holly had experienced her share of unfair. Her beloved dad suffering from an aneurysm when she was young and never being the same, a failed community art space in the city that resulted in a move back home, to being single longer than she planned. But now, five-ish months into a long-distance relationship with her oh-so-handsome boyfriend, Nik Beckenbauer, the distance between them felt unfair. Holly had waited a long time to be wrapped in the arms of the one she adored and who adored her, and now those strong arms were out of reach. Nik's steely-blue eyes had a way of seeing into her soul—in a good and not creepy way—yet the pixelated phone screen didn't offer the same effect.

Holly couldn't imagine what it was like, back in the day,

when all you could do was send a postcard to your long-distance beau and hope it made it to him and he'd write back soon. Or if you had to limit your words to the space on a telegram, like Rolf and Liesl in "Sound of Music."

04 JUNE
DEAR NIK - (STOP) -
IF I STRIKE GOLD, I'LL HITCH A RIDE ON THE 1ST WAGON TO LEAVENWORTH - (STOP) -
I MISS YOU TERRIBLY - (STOP) -
YOUR ONE AND ONLY,
HOLLY
- (FULL STOP) -11:45AM

At least Holly's updates and playful sentiments could be received within seconds by text, which was usually a positive thing, unless of course she didn't check auto-correct and hit send too soon and "Hey, whatcha up to, hot stuff?" actually read, "Hey, watch out, too hostile!" *Big difference.* With the swoosh of a quick text message, Holly could accidentally start a fight with her boyfriend when she intended to flirt. Ah, the perils of twenty-first-century dating.

The catchy tune from the beach scene of the second "Top Gun" movie blasted from Holly's phone.

She picked it up, swiveling in her desk chair. "Talk to me, Goose."

"Gosh, I miss you, Hol." Nik's warm baritone voice made her feel at home, despite the distance.

"The feeling is mutual." Holly pressed the cellphone harder to her ear, imagining Nik settling into his desk chair as he surveyed the snow-capped mountains from his office cubicle.

While Bavarian Falls could easily win a prize for most Christmas spirit, it could not boast the panoramic views surrounding Leavenworth. Holly hoped to see its stunning peaks in person instead of vicariously, like last week when Nik briefly video chatted before his work day started. According to Nik, the postcard-like setting through his office window showcased the beginning of the Stuart range of the Washington Cascade mountains.

Outside Holly's office window, a crowd lined up to sample bits of hazelnut fudge from the shop next door. The fudge's aroma wafted through the air like Bavarian Falls' signature perfume. While Leavenworth enjoyed fresh mountain air, Bavarian Falls produced a sweet and savory aroma all year round.

Holly and Nik were trying to figure out who would visit whom and when, this summer. Nik had a few weeks of paid vacation time built up, and he could also see his Aunt Claire while he was in town. Not to mention it would be fun to visit a few of the landmarks that marked the beginning of Nik and Holly's unexpected love story.

"Hang on," Nik said. It sounded as though he muffled the receiver as he offered a garbled, "Wait a sec…yes, it's her…I can in a bit. No, that hasn't been disclosed yet. Give me five?" When he spoke again, the words were clearer. "Sorry about that. Where were we?"

"Professing how much we miss each other." Holly smiled. "This place is not the same without you. Chase asked about you the other day when he was at Music Keys for choir practice. He's afraid you'll never come back."

"Aw, I miss that kid. Can you give him our secret handshake when you see him next?"

"I'll do my best to remember. Hey, did HR get back with

you about your vacation request?"

"Yeah, about that…"

The minimal background noise on Nik's end crescendoed as the work day was soon to begin for him. Holly slid her thumb up the side of her phone to increase the volume so as to not miss a syllable of Nik's response. She tried to keep her breathing steady and light. Her pulse quickened in anticipation of seeing him in the not-so-distant future. She was more than a little eager to plant a big 'ole kiss on Nik and finally enjoy quality time and close proximity again.

"I want to be there, but work is not making things easy. With this new account and tourist season upon us, I'm not sure it's going to fly for me to leave as planned. I'm working on it, but I don't…"

Nik's soothing voice was interrupted by Holly's, like the scratch and screech of an album halting on a record player, "Wait, what? Surely, you're joking?"

Holly paused for the punchline. None came.

A few minutes later, after some clumsy, strained chatter, she hit the red "X" to end her call with Nik, so he wouldn't be late for his meeting. He was on Pacific time and she on Eastern, the three-hour difference making it tricky to chat during the week. The end of their phone conversation had been an awkward dance as Holly had tried to downplay her disappointment that Nik hadn't yet solidified his plans for his much-anticipated visit to Bavarian Falls.

Holly knew relationships took work and time. Having a disabled father and a well-meaning but opinionated mother had taught her that. She was thankful she had moved toward healing with her parents and not given up when it felt like too much to face. Yet she hadn't expected that she and Nik would be out of sync. It threw her off, like a skip in a record during a favorite part of the song. The thousands of miles between them were proving to be more challenging than expected.

Holly took a swig of water and then turned over her water bottle to let the rest of it dribble into the viney succulent on her desk. A clothesline hung against the brick wall of her quaint office space at the Music Keys building. Clothespins held works of art from her students, like proud parents displaying their children's most recent creations. Holly wished Nik were here to see firsthand how the Heart Turn program was currently flourishing from its modest roots. She had tried her best to describe the growth to him over the phone and show it through the screen, but that didn't do it justice. He needed to experience it up close and personal.

Nik had been around to witness the success of Music Keys, the non-profit that helped individuals with disabilities unlock their potential through music therapy, spearheaded by his ex-girlfriend, Lena Albrecht. But now, his current girlfriend, Holly Noel, was making her mark upon the community with her own artistic flair. Maybe he had a type, although Lena and Holly were different in almost every way. Besides, Lena was long gone, helping others around the country start up their own non-profits, like she had done in Bavarian Falls.

Holly pushed open the ornate, wooden door at Music Keys, and headed to her Prius parked on the street—the car with the dented bumper. The humidity coating the June afternoon made Holly feel as if she'd stepped into a sauna as she left for her lunch break. She pulled at her athletic shirt with the colorful heart screen-printed on it—designed by one of her clients. Her thick, brunette hair was piled on top of her head in an effort to relieve her neck of the heat.

It had been almost a year and a half since Holly founded Heart Turn, a program that brought students and senior citizens together for art classes—overseen by Music Keys and housed in their building. What began as heartbreak due to her reluctant return to her hometown, morphed into a fulfilling outlet for her passion for art, children, and making a difference. Thankfully, the job paid enough to cover her bills and leave a little room for fun.

Even in summer, Bavarian Falls was outfitted with Christmas decorations. Velvety red ribbons hugged the historic lamp posts that lined Main Street. The downtown fir trees were still adorned with ornaments, but sea shells, sand dollars, and burlap ribbons had temporarily evicted Santas and snowmen. Instrumental versions of classic holiday carols rang through the thick air as tourists, dressed in way less than was typical in the colder months, licked drippy ice cream in freshly baked waffle cones from Sugar Shock.

Holly wiped the sweat beading on her forehead with the back of her hand, willing the AC in her vehicle to cool her off faster. She was running late for a lunch date with a friend who had a way of lifting her spirits. As she snaked through the noon traffic of her small yet crowded hometown, Harry Connick, Jr. crooned from the radio. She and Nik shared an affection for his music. Holly sighed, hoping she and Nik could talk again later and figure things out after he finished work.

Holly pulled into the mammoth parking lot at Neumann's, the mile-long Christmas store—her place of employment before Heart Turn where she'd clocked umpteen hours hand-painting custom ornaments during the holiday season. Once Holly was inside, she passed Station 8, where she had spent most of her time. Her previous co-worker and good friend, Andy, waved as she rushed past. Holly mouthed to him, "Betty Jo awaits!"

"Go get 'em Holly-girl." He offered a head nod and bearded grin.

The tantalizing aromas of freshly baked German pretzels, steaming sauerkraut, and almond stollen flooded Holly's senses as she neared Stocking Stuffers' Eatery. The hubbub of the café located inside Neumann's was a mix of lively conversation. An announcement over the loudspeaker interrupted a peppy version of the "Sleigh Ride" song: "Leslie, please report to Section 16 for a Code Icicle." Holly smirked, knowing that no-nonsense Leslie from customer service would not be happy with this announcement. A Code Icicle usually meant that a glass ornament or two or twenty had broken and needed to be cleaned up in order to keep everybody safe. Usually the culprits were adorable toddlers who ignored their parents' warnings not to touch the sparkly glass ornaments within reach.

Holly spotted Ms. Betty Jo Wilson, the store manager, nestled in a booth. She was enjoying what looked like the café's frozen cocoa, complete with whipped cream and a cherry on top.

"Holly No-el! Yoo-hoo, over here!" Betty Jo stood and flung her arms open, ready to envelop Holly.

"Hi there, good to see you too," Holly said.

Betty Jo rocked her side to side in a grandmotherly embrace.

After they situated themselves in the booth, Holly noticed remains of whipped cream clinging to Betty Jo's upper lip as she grinned widely. Holly wished Andy was there to witness her fluffy white mustache. They always thought Betty Jo would make the perfect Mrs. Claus—although at present she could give Santa a run for his money with her jolly enthusiasm and edible facial hair.

"Do tell, Holly dear. How is your man?" Betty Jo offered her infamous snort laugh. "He sure is dreamy, isn't he?"

Holly nodded. "My mom once pointed out, rather awkwardly, that he's not hard on the eyes. I can't argue with her assessment." Holly scooped a bit of frozen cocoa out of the glass in front of her. She took a small bite, trying to avoid a brain freeze. "Oh, but he's so much more than his good looks. The way he cares for others is equally attractive. He's thoughtful and a hard worker to boot. And the way he looks at you. My oh my, that one is a keeper."

"You've got that right. Although, I'm starting to think his job might not sign off on his long-overdue vacation days. We were supposed to see each other in a few weeks, but HR isn't cooperating." Holly indulged in another bite of the chilled deliciousness.

"That must be tough to be so far away."

Betty Jo's offer of comfort carried weight, hemmed with a tinge of regret, based on her past confession to Holly during last year's staff Christmas party.

"I hope you get to see each other soon." Betty Jo patted Holly's hand across the tabletop, her creamy skin contrasting Holly's sun-kissed tan.

"Me too. We don't often fight, but we were close. Well, at least I was. I don't do well when I'm taken off guard." Holly squeezed Betty Jo's hand.

"You have some good reasons for that. But I'm afraid much of life is unpredictable. I think that's why I'm such a fan of Christmas. It comes every year, at the same time, offering a thrill of hope for weary hearts."

Holly lifted her gaze from her hands to the manager's kind eyes.

"In situations like this, my mother often quoted Friedrich Heinrich Wilhelm Körte," Betty Jo said, releasing her hands to cup her drink. "That's a mouthful. Reminds me of a children's book my mom used to read to us. The child's name had more letters than I could count. Do you remember that crazy custom ornament order Andy received when I worked here?"

"Which one?" Betty Jo chortled.

"That long one. I'll never forget it. The customer wanted 'Matilda Jenaye Gertrude Perry-Harrison' hand-painted on an ornament for her goddaughter."

"Oh my, that's ambitious." Betty Jo raised her penciled-in eyebrows. "Now, as I was saying, my *Mutter*, in her thick German accent, would point her finger right down her nose in my direction, look me square in the eyes—usually because I was getting lazy with practicing my violin or trying to avoid washing the dishes after supper—and she would say, '*Anfangen ist leicht, beharren eine Kunst.*' Basically it shut me right up. How could I argue with that?" Betty Jo snorted again.

"It's embarrassing to admit, but my German is not exactly top-notch. What was she saying…in English, please?"

Betty Jo winked, pointing her finger down her nose and looking deep into Holly's brown eyes. "To begin is easy, to persist is an art."

Holly let the profound statement sink in. As an artist, she knew this to be true. During her schooling, at work, and even in her spare time, she did not rush her art. It required dedication, along with confronting the voice in her head that called her an imposter and tempted her to call it quits *about every twenty-eight days.*

"Wow, I don't think I'll be forgetting that any time soon."

"Holly, you and Nik go together like peanut butter and jelly."

"We're not that boring and predictable, are we?"

"You're right, I stand corrected. You two are more like corn beef and sauerkraut. You make sense. But it seems you're at the stage and circumstance in your relationship where you need to fight for one another instead of fighting each other. *Persist*, Holly dear."

"How'd you get to be so smart?"

Betty Jo presented her German mother's scowl and finger pointing again as she answered, "*Mutter* knows best!"

"Nik and I are committed to this long-distance relationship, but it certainly is no picnic. It'd sure be nice if we were together, having a romantic picnic in the park, sitting by the river on a gingham blanket with a wicker basket full of Spundekäs cheese, soft pretzels, and juicy strawberries from the Farmer's Market. We could watch the riverboat go by, or maybe hit up Klingemann's Tavern for karaoke, or even splurge and go for a sunset carriage ride through historic downtown."

"Now, that does sound nice and it's making my belly rumble. What'll it be, Holly? Get whatever your heart desires— my treat."

Holly enjoyed the casual conversation over fruit salad and Schnitzel. Nearing the end of the meal, Betty Jo's demeanor changed slightly as she leaned in and lowered her melodic voice half an octave.

"I probably shouldn't disclose it here," her eyes darted to and fro as if searching for a lurker nearby, "but I want to run something by you. It's only an idea, but I can't shake it, and I fondly recall how you, Frank, and I helped Andy make an important decision around one of these tables a while back, so it feels right."

Betty Jo took a deep breath, puffing out her well-endowed chest as if revving up to blow out sixty-ish candles on an invisible birthday cake.

"What is it, Betty Jo? You can trust me."

"To the grave, right? You won't utter a word of this to anyone? Except Nik, of course, as long as he doesn't spill the beans from across the country."

Holly shook her head. "He wouldn't."

"I'm, oh, it feels so bold to even whisper this, but I'm thinking of...retiring from Neumann's." Betty Jo released her breath with force.

Holly's eyes widened. Although Betty Jo wasn't getting any younger, she was as much a part of Neumann's as Baby Jesus #1, the life-sized ceramic figurine right outside the entrance that held the key to unlock the storehouse. Both were iconic centerpieces that represented the values the Christmas store held dear. Both had put in decades upon decades of faithful service to the millions of customers that visited Neumann's each year.

"Really? Is everything okay? Is Frank driving you crazy?" Holly bit into a juicy strawberry.

"Oh no, I'm fine, really. Don't worry, Frank has nothing to do with it. You know, I think Nik is wonderful and all, but when you first started working here, I would have placed my bets on you and Frank. Of course, I'm not the gambling type. He was quite smitten with you though. Imagine you ending up with the boss's grandson. You might still be working here if that was the case." Betty Jo snorted again.

"I see what you're up to. You're trying to divert my attention away from the zinger you just dropped. Please tell me, what brought on this thought process of..." Holly leaned in and whispered the final word, "retirement?"

"It may sound silly, but I'm confiding in you because, truth be told, you inspire me, like when you didn't give up on your dreams when everything went belly up with your community art space in the city. I know it wasn't easy for you to regroup and move back home, but you stuck it out and started Heart Turn—which would have never happened had everything gone according to plan. It's like you made frothy frozen cocoa out of that which was bittersweet and out of season."

On cue, Betty Jo sucked the last drop out of her fountain glass, making a loud slurping noise. She grabbed her napkin to dab her lips. *No more mustache.*

"As I was saying, even though I adore this place, I don't want to kick the bucket before I check a very important item off of my bucket list. I've stayed put and comfy for most of my adult life, even missed out on a chance for love because of it, but the time has come to stop procrastinating and take the plunge."

"The suspense is killing me. Where are you plunging?" Holly thumped the tabletop with each syllable.

Before her former manager could respond, a familiar voice interrupted the pair. "Never fear, Frank is here! I got you, Betty Jo. I'll handle the plunging while you finish lunch with my favorite Holly."

The voice belonged to the boss's quirky grandson.

"Not that kind of plunging." Holly clarified, eyeing Betty Jo, who was now the shade of Rudolph's nose. Her coloring was less likely a result of the misunderstanding about plunging toilets and more likely because the boss's grandson might have overheard the news about her possible retirement—assuming he didn't already know, which was a reasonable deduction, given Betty Jo's blotchy neck and the way she was fidgeting with her brass name tag.

"You're saying my ninja-plunging skills are not actually needed?" Frank demonstrated a karate chop move.

"Ding, ding," Holly said.

"Carry on then, ladies. I'll take my five-star services elsewhere." He aimed a playful finger gun at Holly and tipped an imaginary hat to Betty Jo upon his exit. Classic Frank—over-the-top, thoughtful, and moderately obnoxious.

"That was close! What do you think, Holly? Could this place get along without me?"

"It definitely wouldn't be the same. I'm happy you want to try something new, though. What is this new thing exactly?"

"It's not set in stone. I'm still waiting to see if a spot opens up, but I applied to attend the top-rated Kris Kringle Academy. Their next class is in the fall. You may be looking at the new Mrs. Claus of Bavarian Falls!" Betty Jo struck a cheery ta-da pose, jazz hands included.

"That's fantastic. You're made for that role." Holly couldn't wait for Andy to discover that their hopes and dreams for Betty Jo were coming true.

"You think so? My grand plan was to get trained as the best Mrs. C I can be and then approach Mr. Neumann to see if I can use my training right here in the store—come the day after Thanksgiving, of course. That way I'm not totally leaving this smorgasbord of Christmas cheer, only spreading my wings a bit."

"I think it's perfect. When should you hear?"

"Any day now. And don't you worry, Holly dear, you will be the first to know."

After her eventful lunch with Betty Jo, Holly finished her shift at Heart Turn and met her best friend, Elaine, at the park on Main.

They tried to fit in exercise a few times a week, in the evenings, when the summer tourists were inside enjoying the local cuisine from Edelweiss Inn or Engel Haus. The friends circled the historic park as they caught up on what had transpired since their last walk.

Holly recounted her and Nik's tense phone call from earlier.

"Girl, you've got to figure things out. You and Nik are made for each other. Whatcha gonna do to smooth things over?" Elaine adjusted her crimpy ponytail on the top of her head.

"Smooth things over? He's the one who seems too busy for me. Oh brother, do I sound like a possessive girlfriend? That's the worst."

"I cannot confirm or deny your claim." Elaine shrugged.

"I'm determined to prove others wrong, that long-distance relationships can work. But right now, it stinks. I think I'm whining. Gosh, I like Nik so much and was looking forward to face-to-face time."

"Ha! I think you mean mouth to mouth." Elaine laughed.

"That too." Holly's face warmed.

"What's the game plan, boss? You're creative...paint an alternative."

They rounded the corner and passed the stately fountain filled with coins from secret wishes tossed into the crystal-clear water.

"I'm not sure. Any ideas? You watch so many of those rom-com movies all year round. Surely, there's an idea about how to fix this in one of those shows?"

"You've got a point. Hmm, let me see. What about stealing an idea from *Lottie Wins the Lottery*? You buy a five-dollar lottery ticket, win the jackpot, and use your earnings to relocate Nik's entire office building to Bavarian Falls?"

"That's what they did? The heroine moved her man's place of business to her hometown, so they didn't have to live and work apart?"

"No, that's not exactly what happened. But it could work."

"Elaine, I'm losing faith in your abilities."

"Wait...I've got it! In *A Fixin' Kind of Love*, the main

character, Everleigh Rae, and her high school boyfriend, Cash, have a shotgun wedding, followed by a set of twins and a third child in rapid succession. Between working two jobs to keep them afloat and taking care of a fixer-upper farmhouse they inherited, they have to grow up fast. Everleigh and Cash are like ships passing in the night as they attempt to manage it all. When their kids are finally grown and they've survived bankruptcy, they finally finish the farmhouse, transforming it into a B & B. But they realize they don't really know each other anymore. They have operated in survival mode for so long they haven't stayed emotionally connected through the craziness of it all."

"Wait, what are you saying? That Nik and I are drifting apart?"

"Hold on. I was getting to the good part. Cash and Everleigh are on the brink of divorce until their elderly neighbor, Ms. Ida Devine, gives them an idea about how to reconnect. When she was a young bride, her husband was drafted for war. They wrote letters to one another to stay connected, taking turns asking questions and responding back with the answers. Then Ms. Ida wrote out, in near-perfect cursive, the same twenty questions that she and her now deceased husband asked one another. She cut them into thin strips, dropped them into a decorated Mason jar, and presented it to the struggling owners of the B & B. She added a label to the jar that read, 'Twenty Questions IOU'. She instructed Cash and Everleigh Rae to pull out a few questions a week and take turns answering them. After a few months, the couple connected emotionally and physically because surprise! They had a bonus baby on the way and rediscovered why they fell in love in the first place."

"What in the world, Elaine?"

"I realize it's farfetched, but ya have to admit it's endearing, right?"

"No, not that—I mean, yes, far-fetched, aren't they all? But it makes no sense."

"What doesn't? Cash and Everleigh Rae and their restored home as the backdrop for their restored love? It's priceless."

"No, no, that's fine. I'm talking about what Ida put on the mason jar, 'Twenty Questions IOU?'"

Elaine offered a friendly wave to a passerby.

After the Midwest pleasantries were taken care of, Holly said, "Let me guess, IOU was an acronym for Interesting, Outlandish, and Unique, as in, don't offer any boring answers to my questions, Cash, because we need to spice things up before our love grows cold and our money runs out?"

Elaine remained silent as Holly's agitation grew. She was convinced one of Elaine's hobbies was withholding information so that Holly looked the fool as she tried to figure things out.

"You don't pay somebody back with a question, you pay them back with a good old-fashioned answer. Why did Ms. Ida call the whole questions game 'Twenty Questions IOU?' Give me an answer or else doesn't sound romantic. That's all I'm saying. If I'm going to buy into this, I need more info, pronto."

Elaine chuckled. "What you're saying is I owe you an answer?"

Holly rolled her eyes. "You don't owe me a question, that's for sure."

"IOU stands for an Investment Opportunity in Us. Twenty Questions to deposit wealth into the relationship. That's what it was all about," Elaine said, a tad smugly.

"Why didn't you say so in the first place?"

The two friends rounded their third lap around the park.

"You know, that's actually really beautiful." Holly's steady voice was in stark contrast to her frantic interrogation a few moments prior.

"Isn't it? It's not an 'I have to,' like I owe you this. It's an opportunity. It's an 'I get to,' because I believe what we have is worth investing in."

Holly was surprised by her friend's profound observation. "That's one of the most romantic things you've ever said."

"I guess the rom-com marathons are paying off."

"Apparently."

"I need a pit stop before the next lap." Elaine entered the Bavarian-themed bathroom facilities.

Holly drew near the fountain. The copper and silver coins reflected through the water as they caught the floodlights and appeared to dance. She dipped her sweaty palm into the cool, aqua-marine water and delicately traced an invisible figure eight under the surface. Like a watercolorist softening the saturation of paint before putting brush to paper, a thought crystallized in her mind. "If you want the interest to keep growing, continue to feed the investment." Holly smiled, equal parts surprised and satisfied by the fountain-side revelation. "Thank you," she whispered as she plunged her hand deeper to retrieve one of the coins.

"I know money is tight, but really, Holly? Stealing from the fountain?" Elaine had jogged over.

"No one will miss it. Besides, it's going to help me remember something." Holly slipped the coin into her pocket.

"While I was in the bathroom, I remembered another thing about *A Fixin' Kind of Love*. But, shoot, I forgot again."

They left the fountain area and headed around the park loop for their final lap.

"How on earth you recalled all those details from the movie in the first place is beyond me. Don't they all run together? I usually fall asleep after the first fifteen minutes when you force me to watch them. I do think you might be onto something, though."

"You're going to open a B & B?"

"Ha, no. But I think the twenty questions thing might help. It won't get Nik here faster, but I think it might help us feel closer than five states away."

"See, my marathon movie watching isn't all bad," Elaine teased. "Now, let's try to find it on-demand, so we can write down those questions."

"Would you look at the time?" Holly pointed to the lighted clock in the park. "How about you do that. Then text me your findings and I'll type them up—maybe even add a fun illustration to them."

"Oh no, you're twisting my arm. I *have* to go do something I enjoy." Elaine mocked. "I'll re-watch the movie and type up the questions so you can't peak at them ahead of time. You concentrate on decorating the mason jar to house them."

"Sounds like a plan. Thanks for being a good sport and for putting up with me."

"No prob, friend. You and Nik are worth it."

"What about you? Anything to declare in the guy department?"

"Hmm, not sure how to answer that." Conveniently, Elaine's watch beeped several times. "Gotta go!"

"Where are you headed?" Holly wanted Elaine to 'spill the tea' about any romantic developments that might be percolating beneath the surface of her easy-going exterior.

"Frank and I are going to shoot hoops at the community center tonight." She checked her watch.

"Oh, really?" Holly's voice lifted as she raised her eyebrows.

"Brigham, don't push it. Hey, I remembered what the first question was that Everleigh drew out of Ida's jar."

"Oh yeah, what was it?"

"What's your next move?"

"Next move? I've finally come to terms with living here in Bavarian Falls for a bit, not planning to move anytime soon, thank you very much."

"No, I'm not asking you. I'm telling you that was the question, 'What's your next move?'"

"That's a weird one. What did it mean? Did Cash and Everleigh play chess as a hobby?"

"I think it was meant to help them get on the same page. Like, where are you headed so I can decide if it's where I want to go too?"

"Sounds risky," Holly blew her bangs off her forehead. "What if they weren't headed in the same direction?"

"Love is risky, my friend. Now, it's been real, but I'm going to be late for the pick-up game if I don't leave soon." Elaine bent down to tighten her shoelace.

"Your next move is on the b-ball court?"

"You could say that. And you?" Elaine stood.

"I'm going to wait to see if Nik calls back. Hopefully, he'll be game for the Twenty Questions thing you suggested—I mean, it's worth a shot, right? But what if he thinks it's too cheesy, or it annoys him, or, worse, it drives him away?"

"If he gets any farther away, he'll land in the Pacific."

As Elaine jogged from view, Holly prayed that Nik's next move would be an airline ticket to Bavarian Falls.

CHAPTER TWO
What are you hiding?

NIK AGREED TO HOLLY'S PROPOSAL OF a few intentional "IOU" questions per week in an effort to grow their relationship. They hoped that two of those weeks would be spent in person. They were not able to video chat as long as Holly would have liked. Nik had to get up early the next day for a last minute work meeting.

Before Nik hung up that evening, he answered the first question Holly asked, "What's your next move?"

"At this moment, I'm headed to "Ginger's Cookies in a Snap" to pick up a dozen cookies for the meeting tomorrow. But I'm guessing you're not asking that quite so literally?" Nik teased.

"No, but gingerbread cookies are a delicious choice any time of year," Holly said.

"As you know, I'm not the best at having things all figured out or put into a solid five-year-plan, but right now my job is enabling me to save up for things that matter, so I'm willing to stick it out. Maybe I'll even get a promotion so I can help more people."

Classic Nik—hard-working, generous, and selfless. Plus, more than moderately good-looking—but not so ridiculously handsome that people were uncomfortable to be around him.

Nik was supportive of Holly's goals and her biggest fan when it came to her art, second to her adoring niece, Claudia. She wanted to return the favor and not hold Nik back if Leavenworth was the best place for him, but trying to fit their communication into the margins of their work days and only gazing at each other on a screen was getting old. Holly wasn't getting any younger.

"What I'm hearing is, you're heading up the ladder at work in an effort to reach your goals?"

"That sounds quite corporate, but I guess that's accurate. My goals aren't solely my own though. They include you, Holly Noel Brigham."

"Is that so? I'd like to hear more about these goals, Beckenbauer." Holly's defenses lowered, her cheeks warming. Holly wished Nik could save up, reach his goals, and help people closer to her current zip code, *and in closer proximity to her lonely lips.*

"Oh you will, but before I go, it's your turn to answer—what's *your* next move?"

"Tomorrow I'm headed to the library. Claudia is coming over while my sister-in-law has an appointment. I promised my mom I'd go with her and Claudia. She's growing up so fast. As far as my goals go, I'm pretty content working at Heart Turn, but I wonder if there's more I could be doing with my art. Don't get me wrong, it's fulfilling to help the young and old connect through art, but I've always been a dreamer, and I haven't given up on wanting my art to reach further. Does that sound prideful? I hope not. Since I was young, I've felt this pull to travel and see the world and for my art to be viewed by the masses. Oh never mind, this isn't coming out right."

"Holly, don't brush it off. It matters. I want to hear about it."

Nik had a way of taking her, and her art, seriously, and she loved that about him. She wondered when he would finally say 'I love you' to her. Holly was strong and independent, but she was also *moderately—but not ridiculously—*a fan of old-fashioned romance. Therefore, she was stubbornly waiting for her man to be the first to declare his love.

Holly tried to recall Nik's previous sentence so as not to let on she was fantasizing about a pronouncement of affection like the one between the German professor and Jo March at the end of the 1994 movie version of *Little Women*.

"As far as you and I are concerned, I hope we're headed to an in-person visit where we can talk more about these goals of yours and how we're going to make this relationship work long-term."

"Is this not working, Hol? I mean I know it's not easy, but we're okay, right? It won't be like this forever."

"I'm ready for a change."

"Like what?" Nik's voice tensed up as if he was wondering if Holly's commitment to him was waning.

Holly clarified, realizing that Nik might be having a flashback to the hurt he experienced when his former girlfriend, Lena, wanted a change—as in them breaking up for good.

"For starters, a change from this long distance thing would be nice. Like being able to walk hand-in-hand with my boyfriend around town, enjoying summer, together. We only have in-person memories in winter. You realize that, right?"

"We shall have to remedy that, now, shan't we?" Nik's poor attempt at an Irish accent caused her to laugh freely, momentarily forgoing her frustrations.

"We shall. Where do you want to go for our first summer date in the Falls?"

"How about a boy and a girl and a little canoe with the moon shining all around—that sounds like a pretty good start, doesn't it?" Nik chuckled as he quoted the catchy camp song.

"Sounds good to me." Holly's imagination stirred then swirled as she envisioned the hues and textures that would work for the artwork emerging in her mind's eye. Maybe she would call it "A Midsummer Night's Kiss." She'd select a deep sapphire shade for the sky and fling tiny diamond stars into it. A sliver of moon would illuminate the silhouette of a couple in the canoe below. Flowing brushstrokes for the dark river would signify movement as the canoe meandered down the river toward whatever was around the tree-lined bend.

Nik stared at her tenderly. Holly willed herself back to the present, pausing her vivid imagination before they went their separate ways. He to his cookie errand and she to Greta's Grocery to replenish her fridge—a far cry from the romantic date he had just planned and she had all but painted.

"I'll try to contact HR again, right after my meeting tomorrow, and check the status of my vacation request." Nik said.

"Regardless of what happens next, I hope we're headed closer together, not further apart."

"Me too," Nik paused before quietly adding, "I'm planning on it."

Holly studied Nik as he stared at her through the screen. They stayed that way for a moment, before Holly broke the silence, "When should we do the next question?"

"Umm, let's see, can I get back to you tomorrow about that? It's going to be a crazy day with the early meeting kicking things off."

"Sure thing. Elaine should have the rest of the questions sent over by the end of the weekend. Don't forget the gingerbread."

"Shoot. Hope I'm not too late. Talk tomorrow?"

"Tomorrow." Holly nodded before ending the video chat.

Holly grabbed two of her cloth grocery bags before heading out the door of her studio apartment in the heart of Bavarian Falls. She passed the blank canvas positioned on her easel. "A Midsummer Night's Kiss" remained unpainted, for now.

The next morning, Holly pulled into the driveway of her childhood home, 725 Kühn's Way. As an adult she had spent a lot of time, money, and energy trying to make it elsewhere, doing whatever it took not to return as a resident to the town that felt too small for her big dreams. It had been about a year and a half since Holly moved back to Bavarian Falls. Thankfully, she was no longer living in her childhood bedroom. Through observations from, and conversations with, Nik and Betty-Jo, Holly discovered she could use her artistic abilities in her hometown after all. Her hand-painted ornaments were displayed on Christmas trees during the holiday season, in homes across the country, and even some internationally, as a result of her time working at Neumann's. Merchandise created by her art clients was available for sale online in an effort to support the Heart Turn program. These were a far cry from seeing her art in a museum, but Holly had made peace with life not always turning out like she had envisioned...almost. The chasm between her and Nik's current coordinates didn't exactly flood her with peace.

"Auntie Holly is here." Claudia ran to bear hug Holly in the doorway.

"Oh my goodness. My Claudi-boo has disappeared and been replaced by—"

"Claudia the Unicorn!"

Holly's boisterous niece pranced around the hallway in her unicorn pajamas, complete with a tail and a headband horn.

"Where have you taken my niece, fair unicorn?"

"To the pot of gold, under the rainbow!" Claudia zigzagged around Holly.

"Watch out now, darling," Holly's mom, Anna Brigham, semi-scolded her granddaughter as the galloping unicorn nearly knocked a plate of egg bakes from the platter in her hand.

"Hey, Mom, those look delicious."

"Thanks, Honey."

Holly kicked off her sandals before the energetic unicorn could charge her from behind.

"You'll need to change into your big girl clothes before story hour." Holly's mom reminded Claudia who was twirling near Holly's dad in the living room.

"Hi, Dad!"

In the place of a verbal greeting, Holly's dad smiled from his recliner. Daughter greeted father with a peck on the cheek.

Unicorn Claudia demonstrated a lop-sided somersault for her captive audience.

"Ta da!" She raised her hands in victory.

"You've got a front row seat to all the action." Holly patted her dad's shoulder.

A gentle voice interrupted the lively shenanigans in the living room, "I'm headed out now, I can't thank you enough for helping."

Holly turned to greet her sister-in-law. Monica's long ginger hair was styled in a loose side braid. Her sunglasses were on, keys in hand.

"Come here, sweetums, give mama a hug before I go." She knelt to receive her daughter's embrace.

Monica fixed her daughter's headband, and whispered, "Now, you be good for Grandma and Auntie, okay?" She rested her head against Claudia's curls and pulled her closer, as if breathing her in.

"Where are you off to?" Holly tilted her head.

"Um, an appointment." Monica stood. The sunglasses proved a barrier as Holly tried to search her sister-in-law's hazel eyes for clues about this mystery appointment. Monica fidgeted with her keys.

The unicorn let out a "neigh," trotting toward the blueberry crumble muffins her grandma had placed on the kitchen table.

"Thanks again for keeping an eye on this ball of energy."

Holly sensed there was more Monica might say if her parents weren't within ear shot.

"Go wash your hooves, before you dig in," Holly's mom instructed Claudia.

Monica offered a slight wave before leaving.

After breakfast, Holly's mom convinced Claudia she needed to dress in actual clothes to leave the house.

Holly cleared the table, including her dad's tray.

"I'm ready!" Claudia emerged from Holly's old bedroom. Her pajamas had been replaced by a flowered skirt and a glittery t-shirt.

Dad's respite worker arrived and then three generations of Brigham women headed to the library for their Saturday outing. The youngest grabbed her unicorn headband from her book bag, securing it back in place.

Holly opened the heavy doors of Storybook Library. Claudia skipped inside, holding her grandmother's hand.

"Take me to the fairy books, pu-lease, Gram."

As they continued on, Holly paused. Inside the vintage building a mix of musty books and lemongrass cleaner transported her back to days gone by. Holly could almost hear the childhood laughter of her and her older brother, Gabe, as their Grandma Bea lovingly reminded them to use their "library voice." That only worked for a second or two. The siblings soon squealed with delight, catching a glimpse of the bulletin board showcasing the book for that week's story time. On the colorful area rug, sheltered by a life-sized play tree house, children sat, hungry to hear the new book and taste the themed snack that awaited them, if they were good listeners.

Almost every Saturday morning, when Holly was a girl, Grandma Bea took them to the library. It was there that teddy bears had picnics, mischievous monkeys stole caps from a sleeping salesman's head, Tikki Tikki Tembo fell into the bottom of the well, and Narnia became real. The engaging artwork and captivating stories of her favorite tales transported Holly into another world, one that was kinder and more carefree than her own. The library outings distracted Holly from the dread she often felt at home in the aftermath of her dad's brain injury. In the company of beloved books she felt temporarily shielded from the harsh elements of pain and loss. Storybook was a respite of sorts.

"Nice to see you here, Holly." The welcoming voice of Nik's Aunt Claire, brought Holly back to reality.

Holly collected her lingering thoughts as she steadied Claire's teetering tower of books.

"I don't know why I check out so many at once. I'll never get to them all before they're due back, but they feel like new friends and I don't want to hurt their feelings."

Holly grabbed the top book as it started to slip off the edge of the stack.

"There you have it, I'm not a crazy retired cat lady, I'm a crazy retired bookworm."

"It doesn't sound crazy to me. It sounds pretty wonderful." Holly walked Claire and her book pile over to the librarian's desk for checkout.

"How's my favorite nephew treating you?" Claire winked.

"Nik is good…and he's swamped with work." Holly said.

"All the more reason he needs a vacation. When does he fly in?"

"Not soon enough, that's for sure. Although nothing is set yet."

"Let me know as soon as you hear. I miss him. I'm sure you have a lot planned when he visits, but I'd love his help with a few things on my fix-it list. Come over with him, I'll feed you takeout from Edelweiss Inn as payment. I'll be sure to order the famous club sandwich without bread because of your gluten sensitivity and all. I think they do lettuce wraps now."

"Oh, I love the Inn's bread." Holly grabbed a tote bag for Claire to use for her books.

"But won't it upset your stomach, dear?"

"Not me." Holly reassured Claire she did not have a gluten issue.

"Are you sure? Nik mentioned it several times on our call a few weeks ago."

Holly was thoroughly confused why Nik did not remember she adored bread, and why on earth he told his aunt otherwise.

The librarian was almost finished scanning Claire's stack 'o books.

"Oh dear, you know what? Nik was talking about one of his co-workers. He mentioned her several times and I think I got you two mixed up." Claire offered a sheepish look as she found one more book in her purse. She slid it to the librarian.

Holly would make a terrible spy. Her emotions acted like puppet strings, twisting and turning her face to reflect exactly what she was feeling inside. Thankfully Claire was busy chatting with the librarian while Holly tried to temper her scowl and assure herself she was overacting. Her suspicious thoughts reared, her rational thoughts tried to wrangle them.

Why was Nik mentioning a co-worker several times on the phone to his aunt? He's never mentioned her to me!

Calm down, Brigham, I'm sure there's a logical explanation for this.

Like what? He seems too busy for the IOU questions, he's vague about work.

Jealous girlfriend is not a good look on me. I'm sure it's nothing.

Think of all that time he spends with his co-workers instead of you. Who wouldn't enjoy his company? How would you know if something shady was going on?

Stop it. I'm trying to believe the best. Nik has never given me reason to doubt his commitment to me.

Oh yeah? Like how HR hasn't been able to help him sort our his visit to Bavarian Falls.

"Auntie Holly, come on. Can you read me this one?"

Holly's mental battle continued as Claudia approached.

We'll continue this later, but you need to behave yourself. You're a grown woman not an insecure 7th grader who passed a "Do you like me, yes or no?" note to her crush and is nervously awaiting his response. Nik is my boyfriend.

"Aunt Holly, are you okay?" Claudia's doe-like eyes made contact with Holly's. She tried to act normal and not let on she had been interrogating herself over whether Nik could be trusted with her tender heart.

"I'm fine. What'd you find?"

"This one! It's about becoming a big sister." Claudia beamed.

Holly's expression flipped from conflict to elation, "Are you making my day with the best news ever—without your mom's consent?"

"Huh?" Claudia adjusted her drooping unicorn headband. "Is your mom expecting? Is that what her mysterious appointment is all about?"

"Is my mom expecting what? Me to behave? She did say I could have a lollipop if I was a good listener today. Have I been a good listener?" Claudia hugged the picture book.

"You bet...now, why did you pick this book?"

"I asked mom for a baby so I can have someone to play with at home, *besides* my parents. I want to be the best big sister ever! I don't like sharing my toys very much so I need to practice. One of the nice workers helped me find this one. Will you read it to me, puh-lease?"

"That is a great goal to have. I'd be happy to read this to you. Where should we sit?"

Ten minutes later, nestled on the wooden bench in the kids' section, underneath the play tree house, Holly turned to the last page of the beautifully written and illustrated book Claudia had picked out. Her niece's head rested on her arm as she read her the ending quietly, "All my practice using gentle hands, all my practice using a hush-a-bye voice, and all my practice sharing my favorite things—like my toys, my room, and even my mom and dad—prepared me to be the best big sister I could be. But all that practice did NOT prepare me for the feeling of my heart bursting into a hundred tiny butterflies of joy when I held my baby sister for the first time. I'm glad I get to practice loving her forever."

Holly brushed her hand over the last page as if it were a cozy blanket wrapped around a sleeping baby. She let the beauty of prose and page linger in the air. The hush-a-bye moment didn't last long with Li'l Miss Energy ready to take flight.

"Thanks for the story, Auntie Holly. Now, I'm gonna find

Gram. Do you know where she is hiding?"

"My guess is she's lost in the mystery section, trying to locate the latest Louise Penny novel. It's right up the stairs, near the fish tank."

Claudia dashed off.

"Don't run!" Holly whispered-pled as her niece exchanged her sprint for skips.

Holly remained on the bench, returning her attention to the open treasure on her lap. She studied the whimsical art of the last page's spread, noting how it appealed to children and adults alike. She moved her lips slowly, repeating the last line of the book, as if trying it on again for size, "I'm glad I get to practice loving you forever."

Holly let out a contented sigh.

Just right.

"Kids' books, huh?"

Startled, Holly looked up, automatically closing the book in her lap. She was relieved to see the source of interruption was her friend, and former co-worker. Andy. His son Oliver was by his side.

"Hi, guys. You caught me. The kids' section is still my favorite." Holly put her hand over her heart.

"*Big Sister Practice*? That's an interesting title. We really do need to catch up, don't we?" Andy joked.

Holly blushed, "Let me assure you, my mom is *not* expecting a baby. I was reading this to my niece. She ran off to find her definitely-not-pregnant grandmother. What are you guys up to?"

"We're here to sign up Ollie for the summer reading program, although he is less than thrilled." Andy said.

Oliver looked from his shoes to his dad, "Why can't they have a summer gaming club? That's something I'd sign up for."

"What is your favorite video game?" Holly quirked a brow.

"Gaming as in, hunting…like turkey, squirrel, rabbits." Andy chuckled.

"But, of course, that's what you meant. A summer *gaming* club. With a hunting aficionado like your dad, I'm not sure why I assumed you meant video games. Although, I don't think I've heard of a hunting club associated with a library before."

Oliver sighed.

Holly empathized with his frustration. She had felt that way about her hometown, most of her life, until recently. Not that she wanted a gaming club growing up, but she had longed for her small town to house a fancy art museum or a resident artist who would mentor her in out-of-the-box techniques. It wasn't that she hadn't gotten to do neat things with her art, right here in Bavarian Falls—from a downtown mural to personalizing ornaments at Neumann's to developing the Heart Turn program. She saw the beauty in those things now, but she probably would never experience a swanky gallery show featuring her artwork, while sipping champagne and rubbing elbows with art collectors, while on the arm of a drop-dead gorgeous, rich city boyfriend—probably named Sterling, Preston, or Zane. Then again, those kinds of things only happened in the movies, like the ones Elaine guzzled by the gallon.

"There's a first time for everything." Holly tried to lift Oliver's spirits.

He kicked the carpet square at his feet.

"Son, we talked about this. I promised your mom you'd read more this summer, but she doesn't have to know you're reading about hunting gear and tracking strategies."

One side of Oliver's mouth lifted slightly, "I guess. But I'd rather be out in the woods than reading about it."

"There'll be time for that, but this will kill two birds with one stone."

"Two birds with one stone? Now that sounds fun!" Oliver grinned.

"Like father, like son," Holly said.

Andy's smile revealed his approval of her observation. Holly knew the pain of Andy's divorce had taken its toll, especially with his ex-wife's recent marriage to her boyfriend, Bill. But Andy was a great dad and was excited to have more time than usual with Oliver this summer, while Tammy finished up her nursing degree.

"What's new with you, Holly-girl?"

"Oh you know, occupying the children's section of the library on the weekends, holding down the fort at Heart Turn during the week, and counting the days until Nik comes to visit."

"What about karaoke? You and Elaine still going strong at Klingemann's?" Andy pulled his library card out of his wallet.

"With all the tourists flooding the streets and packing the local businesses our karaoke game has slowed a bit."

"I saw Elaine at the Community Center last week when I picked up Ollie from the summer sports program." Andy fiddled with the card.

"Miss Elaine is cool," Oliver nodded. "And good at basketball too."

Holly nodded as Oliver offered up a spin move, followed by a shot into an imaginary basket. Andy handed his library card to his son.

"I don't know how she does it, working at the Inn and working at the Center. She's pretty remarkable." Andy rubbed the side of his beard.

Holly tried to keep her face neutral as she took in what Andy said. She was caught off guard by two things:

#1: *Elaine working at the Community Center? Why didn't she tell her that?* Holly knew she played basketball there on the co-ed team. *Why would Elaine hide the fact that she started working there too? She had explaining to do.*

#2: Was Holly imagining it or did Andy put an emphasis on the "pretty" before he said "remarkable" when referring to Elaine? Holly was probably overreacting, or over-eager for Elaine to find a man, so they could double date with their boyfriends this summer. But Holly never considered Andy as an option. If he did emphasize "pretty," why was Holly feeling weird about it? Andy was like a big brother to her, wasn't he the same to Elaine too?

Holly couldn't picture any interest there, on either side, especially since Elaine hardly mentioned Andy in conversation. Then again, Elaine hadn't mentioned she was working at the Community Center to her *best friend*. Besides, stranger things were possible…like Holly falling for Nik—Lena Albrect's ex-boyfriend. Never had Holly thought she and Lena were in the same league. Holly tried to collect herself before the awkward pause between her and Andy became an awkward minute.

"Elaine sure is remarkable," Holly gushed. "Although the same could be said about you. It's not everyday someone gives away a house to help a single mom and her kids." Holly play-punched Andy's bicep, recalling his generous act of kindness to their co-worker, Teresa, at Neumann's.

Andy shifted uncomfortably, turning his attention to a group of kids gathering under the Summer Reading Program sign.

Shoot! Why did she forget that Andy hated attention being drawn to the whole house thing.

Holly wasn't sure if it was because Andy didn't want a fuss made out of his extreme generosity or because he once had a crush on Teresa but it never panned out beyond friendship.

"Better get going before the line gets too long." Andy pointed his thumb toward the sign-up area.

"Happy reading."

Oliver rolled his eyes.

"And happy hunting." Holly patted his shoulder.

Oliver's eyes twinkled, "Now that's what I'm talking about."

Andy smiled, "See you around, Holly-girl."

"Auf Wiedersehen." Holly curtsied.

⁂

Holly left the children's area of the library, texting Elaine while she meandered up the staircase toward the general direction of the mystery section.

Are you a spy? Holly cut to the chase.

I've been meaning to tell u, but... Elaine responded.

Yeah right, and I'm an accountant. Holly typed back.

...then I'll have 2 kill u. ;-)

Elaine, be serious. Why didn't you tell me about working at the Community Center?

Is this another one of your infamous interrogations? Wait, are u a spy?

It was weird to hear it from Andy of all people...about my best friend's business. Holly admitted.

Which is definitely not an accounting business.

Definitely not.

I didn't know I had to run it by you, Mama Brigham.

Of course you don't, just felt weird.

Ok.

Anything else to declare?
A little indigestion after lunch, but that's getting a little personal.
What about Andy, any interest?
Can't a single gal live in peace around here?
Can't best friends share all the deets of their lives? Holly insisted.
Are you trying the twenty questions thing on me now? I pass.
Sorry. I'm feeling a bit off while visiting the library today.
That library will sure do a number on you- ha! What's up?
Stirred up some stuff, about a co-worker of Nik's, childhood memories, my sis-in-law, and…sorry gotta go, Nik's calling.
I see where I rank. :-)
You're irreplaceable, Elaine. But no more secrets, k?
I cannot confirm or deny. Ya know, the whole spy thing? Ha!
Later, Bestie. Elaine signed off.

Nik apparently butt dialed Holly, because when she picked up all she could hear was muffled voices and the distant tapping of computer keys. She tried getting his attention with loud whispers as she perused the art magazine section of the library. No luck. Holly tried to look at the bright side, at least she was likely the last person he had called.

After their library excursion, Holly, her mom, and Claudia enjoyed lunch at the local deli downtown before heading home. Monica was due back in a few hours so Holly decided to hang out at the house until she arrived. Maybe she'd be more receptive to an interrogation than Elaine had been, although Monica was quite reserved. She and Gabe balanced each other out nicely. Claudia was soon occupied by a cartoon, sprawled out on the plaid couch. "One more show, then it's story time with Gram. We've gotta get through that stack before your mom gets back." Holly's mom instructed her granddaughter, looking on from a standing position, alternating between lifting five-pound weights and doing squats. Holly's mom had never been accused of being idle or lazy. She was the queen of multi-tasking. Holly, on the other hand, liked to focus on one thing at a time in an attempt to avoid being overwhelmed.

Holly excused herself, exiting through the sunroom to the serenity of the backyard. She climbed into the navy-striped hammock, shaded by the two oaks trees she scaled as a kid. She texted Nik to see if he was available to video chat. Nik said he had to run into the office and it'd be easier to talk on the go instead of dealing with the spotty video signal due to the mountains.

Holly tried to stay calm as she and Nik talked. The gentle sway of the hammock served as a tangible reminder to not rock the boat, or capsize it. She didn't lead with, "Who is this mysterious female co-worker of yours with the gluten allergy? The one you talk about to your Aunt Claire but haven't ever mentioned to me?" She didn't even ask, "Anyone else going to be at the office with you on Saturday? Since when did you start needing to go to the office on Saturdays?" But after a bit of small talk, she did jump in and ask the next IOU Question, which basically, and eerily, covered the above mentioned concerns. "What are you hiding, Nik?"

Nik, who had been explaining, in great detail, about the new Bavarian pretzel shop that opened in Leavenworth, stopped mid-sentence, "What did you say? Hiding something? Nope, I think I told you all there is to know about Bertha's Bavarian Pretzels, probably more than you wanted to know, come to think of it. But I know how much you like bread."

"It's our next question, on the list." Holly said tightly, "But regarding my love for all things bread..."

Don't do it. Stay cool. Deep breath.

"I bumped into your Aunt Claire today at the library and..."

Whoa, girl. Nice and easy, sway in the hammock—don't flip your lid. Sway, breathe.

"Was she checking out *more* books? That's quite a hobby she's picked up in retirement. I guess it's a pretty good one, as long as she keeps track of them all and doesn't rack up library fines on her fixed budget." Nik cleared his throat.

"She got me confused with one of your co-workers." The smell of fresh cut grass filled Holly's nostrils as she breathed in.

"How'd she do that? She doesn't even know my co-workers."

"I don't really either." Holly said.

"They're pretty great but none of them are as great as you."

Holly wanted to believe his words, yet decades of disappointment left a thin layer of doubt. It really wasn't Nik's fault, he hadn't disappointed her, except for the recent ordeal with his visit to Bavarian Falls. But disappointment had been her default for so long, such a familiar companion, that it was tempting to fall back into that habit of assuming and expecting the worst. Elaine lovingly teased Holly about her cynicism, her mother labeled it recovering perfectionism. Holly's counselor, Nina, explained it was likely a trauma response—fight or flight—from the aftermath of her dad's aneurysm. While Holly had gained a lot of ground in the healing department, it was still difficult to expect the best. Guarded hope stood courageously around the walls of her heart while past hurts threatened to barge

through with a battering ram of speculation.
Sway, breathe...sway, breathe.
"I think you're great too. Now, how 'bout answering the question?"

"Ladies, first?"

"Convenient. But I'm more stubborn than that. You first." Holly gripped the edge of the hammock with her free hand.

"All right, I'll go...but you're not gonna like it. I've been hiding the fact that HR has denied my request for time off. Even though I have time saved up, there is a huge account we're trying to land, which would do wonders for Leavenworth's tourism revenue. That's what the meeting is about today, trying to tighten up our plan to woo this company our way."

"Can HR do that?"

"They said I could go, but without pay. But I can't do that right now, with all this hanging in the balance, and my goals—"

"When did you find out? Why didn't you tell me right away?" Holly sat up in the hammock abruptly, nearly losing her balance.

So much for trying to stay positive and believe the best.

"I'm really sorry, Hol. It stinks. I didn't know how to break the news to you. I'm totally bummed. I miss you so much."

"Apparently not enough..." Holly muttered, equal parts fuming and disappointed.

"That's not fair. You know I'd come if I could."

Holly had lots of words to say in response to her boyfriend dashing her summer plans in one fell swoop. She willed herself to display some restraint. After all she was in her thirties and not three, or thirteen. *Baby steps.*

"I know it's terrible timing but my co-worker just pulled up. I don't suppose you want to share anything you've been hiding before I have to go?" Nik asked.

Holly took a beat, resisting the urge to ask, "Is your co-worker a he or a she?" She planned to deliver a snarky answer with the execution of a stealth bomber. But at the last minute she deflected. She laid back down in the hammock, determined to return to a more tranquil state.

"I've been hiding the fact that…Betty Jo is going to retire from Neumann's."

"No way. Can we have Christmas without Mrs. Claus?"

"Funny you should say that—"

"Shoot, Hol. I'm sorry, I want to hear more, but Marina needs help unloading her car. You should see her trying to juggle it all. I better intervene before there's a cookie catastrophe."

"Marina?"

"Yeah, I'm sure I've mentioned her. She hasn't been here long, but she's proving to be quite the ally in this whole ordeal."

"Let me guess, she has a gluten allergy?" Holly rolled onto her side, propping up her head up with her arm, anticipating Nik's response.

Thud. Static. Indistinct chatter.

"Nik, are you there?"

"Sorry, what did you say? Almost dropped my phone trying to do too many things at once. I missed that last part." It sounded like Nik was fumbling with the receiver.

Convenient? Or coincidence?

"It's nothing, just a hunch," Holly said.

"Let's talk later. I want to hear about Betty Jo, and anything else you're hiding."

"Same." Holly offered with a slight bite to her tone.

"Sorry we got cut short."

"Yeah, me too."

Click.

Click.

CHAPTER THREE
What is your favorite childhood memory?

HOLLY STAYED IN THE HAMMOCK. SHE slowed her quickened breathing.

She had not planned on a tense phone call with Nik. She *had* planned on taking time during the weekend to decorate a mason jar to house the IOU questions Elaine had sent over, putting one set of the questions in a jar for herself and sending another set to Nik. It felt more romantic that way. However, after the bomb he dropped about not being able to come visit, her motivation was waning. She was willing to see this little experiment through, but it didn't seem like their communication was improving, more like getting worse.

Holly swiped to one of the questions Elaine had sent over to see if the next one might be a bit more upbeat than the last.

"What is your favorite childhood memory?" Holly read out loud.

She often felt transported back to childhood when she visited home. At the moment, beneath the oak trees, she felt like she was back in sixth grade, reeling from a misunderstanding with the cutest boy in school. Not a favorite memory, but a vivid one.

His name was Duke Bentley. In the middle of science class, he passed Holly a crumpled note. Their hands met for a second under the table as he delivered it. At his touch, her stomach flip flopped. Holly kept her eyes on the teacher, willing her to speak louder so she could open the note undetected. She was finally able to read it when the teacher passed out papers on the other side of the classroom.

In messy cursive it said, "Are we going out?"

Holly had had a crush on Duke since third grade. She couldn't believe he passed her a note and that its contents would change her status from single to spoken for, if she would only respond with a brave "YES!"

She stole a glance his way. Duke's beach blond hair framed his tan face. His mischievous green eyes looked at her in anticipation.

"Are we?" He flicked his hair to the side.

Holly nodded. "Yes" she whispered, offering a shy smile.

She tried to concentrate on the worksheet in front of her but it was a lost cause.

At recess she told Elaine the news. Turned out the school gossip overheard their conversation and reported it to Duke's best friend who confronted Duke. The school gossip told Elaine what had actually happened, who reported it back to Holly by the end of recess.

"Oh, Holly, I'm afraid you were never Duke's girlfriend. He was asking you if we were "going out" for recess today? He came late to school because of an orthodontist appointment and wondered if recess was still on or not because he was gone during announcements. Since you were sitting near him, he passed the note to you, and…"

Holly's stomach was instantly in her throat. She felt like she was in one of those anxiety dreams where you forget to get dressed before getting on the school bus. Except she was dressed, head to toe, in humiliation. She stood on the edge of the tennis court, trying to keep her balance as the horizon swayed. Elaine steadied her, "I'm sorry, Holly. This is terrible."

"I'm an idiot," Holly sighed. "I read the note the wrong way."

Elaine steered her best friend away from gawking onlookers

and toward the safety of the tree line, "One day you'll go out with a guy who is crazy about you. And Duke Bentley will realize he missed out, big time!"

"Please tell me we'll laugh at this one day because right now, I feel sick."

"I don't know if we'll laugh, but we'll never forget it, that's for sure." Elaine said.

Still on the hammock, Holly shook off the sting of the pubescent rejection. She searched for a more pleasant thought to soothe her after the disappointing blow Nik offered—he wasn't coming to visit this summer.

A butterfly landed on the black-eyed Susans in the backyard. Their beauty begged to be noticed. Holly watched the butterfly work gracefully before it flitted away.

Holly's view from beneath the trees, looking up through their leafy curtains with the blue sky and cotton candy clouds as the ceiling, stimulated her artistic eye. She recalled a more pleasant childhood memory. She was transported back to another classroom, during an art lesson for the summer program for gifted students after her sixth grade year. The teacher taught about the importance of perspective by having each student paint a replica of a bouquet of flowers, positioned on a table, in the center of the room. She instructed one student to paint from a tall stool, another to paint from a seated position on the ground, another to sit at eye level. Each student painted the bouquet, but from a different vantage point. Once they were done the students revealed their artwork. "Oohs and aahs" filled the room. Same bouquet, varied perspectives. It was a lesson they would not soon forget.

Modern-day Holly followed the trunk of the oak tree to its full height, its branches swaying gently with the summer breeze. She recalled the countless hours she spent near the top of these trees, as a child. From that bird's eye perspective she dreamed of flying away from the hurt of home. Often her paintings as a young girl were of the sky and the tops of trees looking toward the horizon, longing for escape. She saw things differently than others did, and her art reflected that. Sometimes her perspective drew others in and other times they didn't get it. Sometimes she got a painting just right and other times it didn't translate well from thought to execution.

Holly hoped that Nik not coming to visit wasn't like the ridiculous situation with Duke Bentley. Maybe she needed to look at things from a different perspective and put herself in Nik's size eleven shoes. He obviously cared about her. He obviously was a hard worker. At that moment, across the country, he was putting in extra time at the office for his company, alongside mysterious—and probably intelligent and exotically gorgeous—Marina.

Sway, breathe...sway, breathe.

An hour later, Holly's brother, Gabe, arrived at the house to pick up Claudia.

"Daddy!" Claudia ran to him for a hug. He swung her around, her feet barely missing the recliner.

"Where's Monica?" Holly closed her magazine. She had moved from hammock to couch, intent on a lazy Saturday, and maybe a bowl of ice cream later from her mom's not-so-secret stash in the garage freezer.

"Hi, son, this is a pleasant surprise," Holly's mom set down her laundry basket to hug Gabe.

"Monica is waiting in the car. Hurry up Claudi-o, mom and I have a special stop planned."

"Are we going to the Christmas store to get that new

ornament, Daddy?" Claudia tried to wink but closed both her eyes instead.

"Funny time to be buying ornaments, but I guess Christmas in July is coming right up," Mom laughed.

"Let's not forget that Neumann's provides a mile of Christmas joy for every girl and boy," added Holly. The store's slogan was forever etched in her brain after hearing it umpteen times while working there.

Holly had a sneaking suspicion this new ornament would say something like, "Baby's 1st Christmas." She was 95% elated at the thought of being an aunt twice over and 5% deflated that a baby of her own was likely years down the road. Heck, she wasn't enticing enough to sway her long distance boyfriend to come for a visit.

"It was sure nice of you to drive up, especially with the outrageous gas prices. Can you stay for dinner?" Mom picked up a stray sock that had fallen out of the laundry basket.

"Hey, Mom, normally I'd say yes, but our little family of three needs time alone before we head back."

"I see," Mom said.

Holly recognized the growth in her mom. In the past she probably would have laid the mama-guilt on thick, saying, "You can be together anytime you want, at your home, *hours away* from us. Can't you spare a few hours for your dear old mom? I guess we'll try to enjoy our quiet dinner here." But she didn't. Her disappointment was apparent, but she no longer said everything she thought. *Progress.*

"Are you driving back separately?" Holly set down her magazine.

"I hitched a ride with a buddy of mine who was headed up north. He dropped me off at Monica's appointment, so we can ride back together."

"At least let me pack a snack." Mom busied herself in the kitchen, channeling her disappointment into productivity.

"I'll text Monica and let her know we'll be out in a few minutes." Gabe typed on his phone.

Peculiar. Maybe Monica was determined not to give away her exciting news prematurely, so she was going to sit in the car, in the driveway, and not come in?

Holly recalled how her brother and sister-in-law had waited to announce their pregnancy with Claudia until Monica was through her first trimester. She sort of understood why people did that, yet she couldn't imagine herself keeping news like that a secret for very long.

"Hey, bro, I have a question for you."

Gabe, who was helping Claudia collect her things from the living room floor, briefly made eye contact, then he continued his task. "Oh yeah, what's that?"

"What's your favorite childhood memory?"

Gabe flashed his easy-going grin, the one that had gotten him out of many a predicament. As kids, Holly had gone more inward as a result of her dad's disability, expressing herself with art over words. Gabe had amped up his antics and attention-seeking behavior, landing himself in the principal's office and earning himself volunteer hours at their church, St. Schäfer's Lutheran, after a prank that nearly ruined its ancient plumbing system.

Holly and her brother were quite a pair. Their shared grief, although contrasting in perspective and manifestation, drew them together in a way most siblings did not experience. That was one good thing about her dad's incident, perhaps.

Gabe proceeded to tell Holly a memory she could not recall

about their dad, pre-aneurysm. He assumed the position he had taken so many times growing up, planting his feet in front of the couch preparing to tell a compelling—slightly exaggerated—tale with sweeping hand motions.

"Let me set the stage for you. It was a balmy June night and Dad had been trying to surprise Mom." He bent at the knees and rubbed his hands together in anticipation.

"Which is nearly impossible." Holly said.

"Affirmative. But he enlisted his band buddies, Walt and Pastor Meyer, to help with a covert birthday party in the backyard of St. Schäfer's."

Holly's dad shifted in his recliner leaning slightly toward his adult children, his eyes still fixed on the TV. Holly thought she spotted a smirk.

"It seemed like a good idea to reenact a scene from one of Mom's favorite movies, "Back to the Future" but when Dad invited his band mates to back him up on a lively rendition of "Johnny B. Good," no one expected things to go down the way they did. Right Dad?"

"Daddy, what does back to the future mean? That doesn't sound quite right? Don't you go back—"

"Hang on Claudi-o, Daddy's telling a story." Claudia shrugged, wandering into the kitchen toward Gram who was packing a snack big enough to feed a family of fourteen.

"How did things go down?" Holly turned her attention to her brother.

"You know that part in the "Johnny B. Good" performance when Marty McFly starts hopping across the stage on one foot?"

"Of course, it's an iconic moment."

"With an overzealous kick Dad's pants split right down the middle. Pastor Meyer's wife almost passed out, and Mom screamed. She was definitely surprised. A glimpse of Dad's tighty-whities, contrasted by his black dress pants, was not easily forgotten. There was a mix of church folks, Mom's book club ladies, and his military pals in attendance and members of all three groups did not let Dad live it down, for years."

"Oh dear. What was going through your mind, Dad?"

Holly Dad's worked to add his two cents, "Gr...gr...great Scott!"

"Exactly." Gabe laughed.

"I don't think Ingrid Meyer has ever looked Carl in the eye again," Mom called out from the kitchen. "It was horrifying for all in the moment, but Dad recovered and kept his backside behind him the rest of the night."

"It's the thought that counts, right? Plus, it makes for a memorable story."

"Like Nik's misguided proposal to the wrong girl?" Gabe teased.

"Watch it, Bro. I've got dirt on you too."

Holly mentally retrieved her lengthy list of Gabe's shenanigans.

- When Gabe watched "Home Alone" one too many times and booby-trapped their grandparent's house. Grandpa Dale almost got hit in the head by a swinging paint can.
- When Gabe snuck out to meet his 9th grade girlfriend at the park but got drenched by the sprinkler system and chased by the mayor's dog.
- When Gabe accepted a dare from one of his buddies to place melted candy bars inside the stored diapers in the church nursery to "surprise" the workers on Sunday morning when they reached for a clean diaper. *Pastor Meyer's wife actually passed out that time.*

Gabe's smart watch alerted him to a message. He quickly scanned the message, his face blotching instantly. His eyes darted to each member of his family of origin until his frantic gaze landed on his prancing unicorn daughter. Her "paws" were already coated in the sticky Puppy Chow she had been munching on.

"Mommy's waiting, let's roll."

Holly studied Gabe's profile as he fist bumped Dad.

He gave Holly a rushed hug and his mom a quick peck on the cheek.

"Say good-bye. It's go time." Claudia waved to her aunt and Gramps and hugged Gram tightly, leaving chocolatey smudges on her apron.

"Don't forget your snacks!" Mom called after them. She rushed to catch them, with two overstuffed grocery bags in tow. They looked like they were about to split in two and expose all their contents.

Great Scott.

Holly returned to her loft apartment downtown, after dinner at her parent's house. She plopped down the heavy tote bag her mom sent home with her. A few snacks were tucked inside along with a few childhood keepsakes. Her mom went through spurts of purging. She definitely did not like clutter yet she valued nostalgic items from the kids' growing up years. Every so often she'd find some of these items in the basement to pass off to Gabe and Holly. Mostly Gabe and his family were the recipients of the prized possessions because Claudia was their first and only grandchild...so far. It hadn't gone well when her mom assumed it was okay to pass Holly's first art easel to Claudia.

Since then Holly and her mom had an understanding she'd

be asked before her childhood things were given away, or sold at a garage sale, or donated to the Community Center. Holly didn't want many things, but the easel was a beloved relic from B.C. *Before the Christmas* that changed everything. *Before the Crisis* that altered her father's brain, her family's normal, and her future. It was a memory she could hold on to remind her of favorite times with her dad. He'd encouraged her creativity. Holly's eyes tracked to the vintage frame she salvaged from her Grandma Bea's estate sale. It hung above her end table. A tarnished gold bolder and layer of glass seared a handwritten note her Dad had written before his last deployment. The one that changed everything.

It read:

Dear Holly: I'm no artist like you but here is my attempt at a flower bouquet. Don't laugh. Keep growing your gift, sweet girl. Water it, tend it, and see what sprouts. Who knows, maybe one day it will multiply like that field of wildflowers you like near Grandma's house? I'll be home before you know it, Brave One. I'll miss you every day.

Love, Daddy

Holly poured herself a glass of ice tea and plopped in a thinly sliced lemon and clipped a fresh mint leaf as a garnish. She situated herself on her second-hand Mid-century modern sofa and opened the book her mom had sent home with her. It was one of her favorite books as a kid. She had fond memories of her mom reading to her most evenings before bedtime.

Holly thumbed through the captivating illustrations, mouthing the story from memory.

She studied the page before her. She tilted her head to the left, trying to take in the beauty from a slightly different angle. Her thoughts swirled like the mint leaf on the surface of her cool drink. The nostalgia led her to recall the magical scene from the "Mary Poppins" movie where the Banks children jump into chalk paintings at the park—where carefree children could escape the harsh realities of burdens their tender shoulders might break under.

Lost in thought and delicious melancholy, Holly almost tuned out the low hum of her phone on the kitchen counter.

Before "hello" Nik jumped right in, "I know it stinks that I can't make it to Bavarian Falls. But what if you came here instead?"

Holly's jolted emotions needed a moment to find center.

"Hol?"

"Sorry, getting my bearings."

"Were you painting?"

"No, I wasn't. I was taking a stroll down memory lane. What were you saying?"

"What if you came to Leavenworth this summer instead? I know it wasn't the plan, but what if we make a new plan?"

"I haven't budgeted for a plane ticket across the country because you were going to come this way. And what about Heart Turn? I mean, maybe I could hand off some of my responsibilities to Shayla and her intern, but that would take convincing and quite a bit of preparation. And…I mean it'd be great to see you. I have wanted to see those mountain views you brag about."

"Right?"

"I need time to think it through," Holly said.

"Of course, yeah. "

Awkward silence.

"Got a question for me?"

"What's your favorite childhood memory?" Holly asked.

"That's an easy one. When I turned ten my dad took me on

a weekend camping trip. Since Dad often traveled for work, it was special to have that time with him. We hiked up a pretty challenging trail. I'm sure I slowed him down but he didn't let on. The scenery was incredible. Redwoods and ferns. Snow-capped peaks in the distance. We even caught our dinner in the river. Nothing like fresh fish over the campfire. We slept under the stars, in hammocks."

"Wow! Did you see any bears?"

"No bears, but a moose, a handful of deer and a rabbit that became the main ingredient for a stew we ate the second night."

"Ew, I can't even."

"I have to admit I was kind of grossed out but didn't let on. How 'bout you, what's one of your favorite childhood memories?"

"I already told you about one of them months ago. Remember "Saturday Workshop," when my dad would tinker in the garage with his tools and I'd paint on my little easel while we listened to big band music?"

"For sure," Nik said.

"But I thought of another one. I loved when my mom read picture books to me. Even though I'm sure she was tired from taking care of my dad after his incident, she made time to read at bedtime."

Holly could picture it…her hair still damp from her bath, her snugly cloud-themed pajamas, and the soft glow from her nightstand lamp as she nestled her head on Mom's shoulder. Holly would trace the sweeping strokes and tiny details of the illustrations with her finger while her mom's soothing voice narrated the story.

"Did you have a favorite book?" Nik's soothing voice put Holly at ease.

"*Where the Wild Things Are* was popular with Gabe and I, but for different reasons. I think Gabe was amused by the defiance displayed in the main character. I was mesmerized by the far-off land of imagination that served as an escape for the boy, at least temporarily."

"You are a dreamer, my Holly."

"Most likely to have her head in the clouds."

"Were you voted that in the high school yearbook?"

"No, but I might as well have been. Did you have a favorite book as a kid?"

"I was a fan of those, *I Spy* books. It frustrated my mom when she'd check one out from the library for me and I'd find all the items within ten minutes or less."

"Most likely to find what's hidden?"

"Something like that. Now, will you do a favor for me?"

"What's that?"

"Consider getting that head of yours in the actual clouds and fly out here this summer?"

"Nik, I want to see you, but I don't know how I can swing it financially with such short of notice."

"I know this wasn't our Plan A, and I'll be working quite a bit when you're here, but it's better than nothing, right?"

Holly wished Nik would have offered to pay for at least part of her ticket. But, to be fair, she hadn't offered to pay for part of his when he was planning to fly to her.

"Let me think about it, okay?"

"Of course. But not too long okay, this long-distance thing is quickly losing its appeal."

"Was there ever an appeal to it?" Holly teased.

"Not exactly, although it's helped us stay focused on our jobs and goals instead of me being distracted by your beauty, your brains and your…" Nik's voice turned hoarse and trailed off.

"And my what, Nik?" Holly lowered her voice.

"Um…I'll tell you sometime, but in person. Hopefully soon?" Nik cleared his throat.

"Perhaps."

"Big plans, tonight?"

"Oh you know, hunkering down in my makeshift art studio—a.k.a my messy antique desk with the supplies strewn about—while I sip lukewarm ice tea, listen to sad Norah Jones songs on my record player, and try to make money come from trees so I can leave on a jet plane to see my man since HR is holding him hostage."

"That's the spirit. Talk tomorrow? I've gotta finish up paperwork so I'm not the last one here."

"'Bye, Nik."

Holly plopped into her desk chair. Slips of paper from the IOU project slid around as she blew out a sigh. A photo of her and Nik stared back at her. There they stood under the giant mistletoe at Neumann's. Holly had a wide, surprised smile as Nik planted a kiss on her cheek a split second before Holly clicked her phone camera.

Holly spied a man who adored her but might be letting his "goals" of getting ahead at his job impede their goal of making this relationship work long-term.

CHAPTER FOUR
What makes you snort-laugh?

TODAY 10:00 PM EASTERN
    Holly texted Nik. If we're going to get through these questions, we might have to speed things up a bit?
    Today 7:00pm Pacific
    Nik replied. Speed dating? Count me in.
    I'm serious, Beckenbauer.
    I seriously like you, Brigham.
    ;-)
    Hit me up, what's the next IOU question?
    What makes you snort-laugh?
    Not sure I ever have? But it's cute when you do.
    You're deflecting. Holly grinned as she typed.
    You mean flirting?
    What makes you LOL for real?
    LOL? I think you're dating yourself, Hol.
    I thought I was dating you, Nikolaus.
    That made me snort laugh. Nik's reply seemed a little delayed.
    Did not.
    How would you know if it did or didn't?
    K, I'll go. I snort laugh when I watch "Nacho Libre".
    The 2006 comedy with Jack Black? Classic.
    That's the one. The one-liners run through my head on a steady loop. Case in point: "Get that corn out of my face!"
    We should watch that together.
    Deal. Your turn.
    I LOL anytime you mix up your idioms.

Ha! Whatever do you mean? Holly pretended she was surprised.

Oh you know…six in one, a dozen in the other…or you're the bee's elbows…or my personal favorite…a bird in the hand is worth two cats in the bush.

You may have a point. But you're meowing up the wrong tree with that last one. I've definitely never mixed up that idiom before.

Bark.

Huh? Bark what? Bark on a tree?

No, it's barking up the wrong tree. Not meowing.

Holly would bet Nik was laughing now. Oops!…I did it again.

It's cute.

Me mixing up my idioms. Final answer?

Locking it in.

That wasn't so hard.

Nope.

Thanks for humoring me with this whole twenty-questions thing.

Anything for you, My Lady.

…*typing, erasing, typing, pause…*

Hol?

Yes?

I'm proud of us. This long-distance thing isn't easy, but we're making it.

Aw, shucks.

I do have one more question though.

What's that?

Like it's a big question.

Hang on! Are YOU gonna pop the BIG question via text?!

Holly typed rapidly, her heart pounding.
    Me? No. I was going to say...
    Yes?
    When do I get to plant a big ole kiss on those lips of yours?
    Double shucks. ;-)
    Well?
    You know what they say...actions speak louder than words.
    Nice, Idiot...I mean idiom.
    We'll be lip locking sooner than later, I hope. I'm working on it, I promise. Gosh, I miss being close to you. The apricot shampoo of yours makes me weak in the knees.
    Same ;-) Holly tried not to giggle as she typed.
    It makes you weak in the knees too?
    No silly, I miss being close to you too.
    By the way...I'm glad you aren't a nun.
    Huh? That one almost stopped her from typing. Nun?
    Nacho Libre's crush was a nun.
    Ha, ha. Yes, she was. God bless Sister Encarnación.
    Was that an LOL or a snort laugh?
    It was an eye roll.
    Today 7:04pm Pacific
    Shoot, I gotta go. We're schmoozing a client at the country club and I can't be late. Talk again soon?
    Today 10:04 pm Eastern
    Yeah...soon.

CHAPTER FIVE
What do you dream about?

SUNDAY IN BAVARIAN FALLS, FOR MOST of the locals, included a church service at one of the most attended churches in town, either St. Schäfer's or at Blessed Epiphany, depending on where they landed theologically. Despite Holly's dad's accidental exposure of his undergarments to congregants at the surprise party decades ago, the Brigham family were faithful attendees of St. Schäfer's.

Pastor Meyer was partway through a series called, "Christmas in Every Season." When he first announced the series, the well-liked reverend was met with some opposition. Even though Bavarian Falls already looked, felt, smelled, sounded, and tasted like Christmas all year round, even the most devout residents grew fatigued from the day-in, day-out celebration. You can only hear "It's the Most Wonderful Time of the Year" so many times before you start twitching.

Holly recalled her conversation with her parents, over Sunday lunch, when the year-long sermon series was revealed, "I've never known Pastor to do a series this lengthy. The holidays are fun and all, but anticipating their arrival is what builds the excitement. If there's no break, it can lose part of its wonder and shine. But don't tell that to Frank's grandpa. He counts on millions of people wanting to celebrate Christmas all year round by shopping at Neumann's. His mammoth ornament inventory proves it."

"I'm sure Pastor Meyer's sermon series will be wonderful. Although it is hard to believe he has fifty-two different Christmas messages to give," Holly's mom put her cloth napkin in her lap.

"The word on the street, or from stall number two in the ladies' bathroom, is that he might have been approached by a publisher to write a devotional that combines scriptures about the Christmas story with inspirational stories about parishioners."

"Interesting..." Holly's mom reached for the butter.

"I hope it's more of a testimonial than a tell-all," Holly said.

"It's a good thing Ingrid hasn't been charged with the task."

"Holly."

"Come on, Mom, you and I both know that the pastor's wife has more dirt on us all than Farmer Schroeder's manure pile in spring." Holly helped herself to another helping of casserole.

Holly's dad smirked.

Holly's mom spread a thin layer of butter on her roll. "While Ingrid does like to be 'in the know,' you really are too hard on her. It's true, she and I have had our share of disagreements, but she has a heart of gold and does more for this town than people realize."

Holly's rumbling stomach alerted her back to the present as Pastor Meyer continued his sermon.

"Anna the prophetess was no spring chicken. She was older than dirt but was determined to devote herself to God. When she saw young Jesus with Joseph and Mary in the temple, she immediately recognized him. We don't know the condition of her physical eyesight, but her spiritual eyesight was spot on. Anna's daily routine of service and sacrifice prepared her to see what others missed. Luke 2:28 (NRSV) reads, "At that moment she came, and began to praise God and to speak about the child to all who were looking for the redemption of Jerusalem." In the original Greek, the word "looking," in this verse, refers to an expectancy of the fulfillment of promises."

Holly's doodle of a chicken wearing a Jewish head covering

was nearing completion, when Pastor Meyer's last words pricked her heart. "An expectancy of the fulfillment of promises."

Ouch. That was it, wasn't it?

Pastor Meyer gripped the pulpit and leaned closer to the stationary microphone, "Anna's rhythms of faith-growing activities tuned her heart to see the presence of redemption she had been longing for, and she couldn't help but tell others. She was a truth-telling, good-news bearer even in the wake of the difficulties life had dealt her."

I'm listening.

"I have a hunch that Anna's devotion to God and hopeful expectations in His promises kept her heart young. In the words of Franz Kafka, 'Jeder, der sich die Fähigkeit erhält, Schönes zu erkennen, wird nie alt werden.' In case you've neglected your German studies, I will translate before you're tempted to ask your phone to do the work for you, 'Anyone who holds on to the ability to see beauty never grows old.' Even in loss, in loneliness, Anna chose to worship and serve. God enabled her to see what others missed because her eyes were fixed on Him. In her singular focus, she was positioned to spot a promise fulfilled. She knew she was in the presence of the One who would usher in the redemption of Jerusalem, a promised baby who would make a way to bring beauty from ashes, restoration from rubble, and redemption from condemnation.

"Anna, in her twilight season, beholds the light of the world and prophesies what is to come. Isaiah 9:2-3 and 6-9 (NRSV) declare, 'The people who walked in darkness have seen a great light; those who live in a land of deep darkness—on them a light has shined. You have multiplied exultation; you have increased its joy; they rejoice before you as with joy at the harvest, as people exult when dividing plunder. For a child has been born for us, a son given to us; authority rests upon his shoulders, and he is named Wonderful Counselor, Mighty God, Everlasting Father, Prince of Price. Great will be his authority, and there shall be endless peace for the throne of David and his kingdom. He will establish and uphold it with justice and righteousness from this time onward and forevermore. The zeal of the LORD of hosts will do this.' Like Anna, may we fix our eyes on Jesus who came to fulfill the greatest promise of all. May we not miss Him because we thought He would come another way. Don't downplay the miracle of redemption and new life. The beauty of Christmas is present in every season. Amen?"

"Amen," answered the congregants, along with anther rumble from Holly's midsection.

Once a month, after church, most of the year-round residents of Bavarain Falls enjoyed a potluck at the Community Center, where Lutherans and Catholics alike intermingled, along with jello salad, corn beef and Mrs. Donna Rasmussen's famous German potato salad. Today was such an occasion.

Upon arrival, Holly's parents situated themselves near the door at the Center so her dad didn't have to shuffle through the crowded space. Holly scanned the room for anyone under forty. Before she could make a full sweep, Mrs. Rasmussen intercepted with her flashy white smile, "Do tell, Holly Noel, when does your hunky arrive?" She gestured toward the door with her French manicured nails.

Besides her potato salad recipe, Mrs. Rasmussen was also famous for being the dentist's wife, her expansive Christmas village collection—purchased at Neumann's of course—and her over-the-top affection for her four darlings—a.k.a her pure bred dogs. She and Holly had a rough start when Holly began personalizing ornaments at Neumann's and misspelled one of her darling's names.

"Looks like his visit is a no-go."

"Trouble in paradise?" Mrs. R. asked.

"I don't think so. He wants me to come out to Leavenworth instead. But—"

"When do you leave?"

"I'm trying to figure it out, I'm not sure I can swing it with my non-profit salary on such short notice."

"Have you asked Santa?" Mrs. Rasmussen nodded toward Dr. Rasmussen who was serving the corn beef to a long line of starving-after-the-church-service children.

Dr. R. often played Santa at Neumann's during the holiday rush. The children pushing in line at the community center wasn't much different than what he experienced at the mile-long Christmas store. In both cases he was their ticket to the treasure they sought, whether the most coveted dish at the potluck or the most popular toy of the season.

"He is in high demand per usual. Plus, I think it's poor taste for a thirty-something to ask Santa to fulfill her grown-up Christmas list…six months early."

"Charge it then. That's my motto. Doc and I are headed to Banff soon, courtesy of all the reward points I racked up on my credit card. Thankfully, I found a pet-friendly chalet so my darlings can be close by. Wait until you see the matching get-ups Betty Jo made for them. Their photo shoot is all lined up—"

"Excuse me, Donna," Ingrid Meyer scooted past the pair with a loaded paper plate in hand. "Had to grab Pastor food or he'll never eat."

Holly turned to see Pastor Meyer cornered by Father Clark from Blessed Epiphany. Holly spotted Elaine behind them wiping down tables.

"Hope you have a great trip, Mrs. R."

"I hope you find a way to fly to Leavenworth, even if you need to borrow Santa's sleigh." Donna gave Holly an optimistic smile.

"It might come to that." Holly shrugged.

Ingrid Meyer looked as if she was going to say something, but stopped and kept walking toward her husband.

That woman overheard more than the FBI. She always seemed to be in the right place at the right time to nibble on the latest piece of juicy town gossip.

"They've got you working here on Sundays too?" Holly leaned over as Elaine picked up a glob of stray Jello—with a gloved hand—from under the table.

"You know they frown at working on Sundays in our fair village, but somebody has to man this place before a debate breaks out about which wine to use for communion."

"I'd place my bets on Mrs. Meyer winning that one over Mrs. Rasmussen."

"I don't know, have you seen the length of Donna's nails? I think she'd win in a cat fight."

"Or dog fight."

"True, true." Elaine laughed as she wiped the corner of the table with a damp rag.

"Nik and I are on question #5 today."

"Oh yeah, how's that going?"

"It's going...I mean, it's good to get to know each other better and be more intentional about it, but I feel like we're digging up dirt along the way, which is making things a bit messier."

"Ooh, is he secretly a twin with a single brother who's even cuter and smarter and ready to settle down?" Elaine nudged Holly, which almost caused her juice to spill. Holly steadied her glass.

"No, but it feels like…I don't know…like he's keeping something from me."

"Maybe he has two jobs like me and doesn't feel the need to disclose every detail to Ms. Holly Noel who wants to keep tabs on his every move."

"Ouch."

"We're at that stage in life where a bit of a mystery is a good thing. Which is why I've decided I'm going with a tankini over a bikini this summer. Ya know, to keep things a bit of a mystery."

"Fuller coverage never hurt two single, Midwestern gals who enjoy Bavarian baked goods all year long." Holly shrugged.

"But my dear Bestie, you're not single anymore. Remember?" Elaine dipped the rag into a red pail of sudsy water, then wrung it out.

"Oh my gosh, I've been identifying as single for so long it still rolls off the tongue. Also, having a boyfriend who is almost never seen on my arm makes it easy to forget."

"Out of sight, out of mind?" Elaine started wiping the table again.

"Every once in a while, but not because I'm not crazy about him."

"Look who it is, two of my faves from the Falls." Frank strolled up, resting his lanky arms on Holly's and Elaine's shoulders.

"Let me finish up for you, Lainey Lay-up, so you can shoot the breeze without worrying about spilled fruit punch." Frank took the washcloth and pail from Elaine and semi-bowed. "My lady."

"Normally I'd protest, but have it your way Frank. I'm starved."

Holly and Elaine hurried through the crowd and slipped in line before the ravaging teens elbowed their way in for seconds.

"Lainey Lay-up, huh?"

"Cringey, right? Frank started calling me that on the basketball court. I'd prefer Dunkin' Divine or something like it, but I guess Lainey it is."

"How about Hottie McShotty?"

"You can't be serious...you're so cheesy, Brigham."

"Who me? I think it has a nice ring to it." Holly smiled, quite pleased with herself.

"Oh boy, I know that look in your eye. Stop playing matchmaker for two seconds and focus on the eats."

Betty Jo Wilson was serving the dinner rolls, "What'll it be lovelies, two or three?" She wore a ruffly apron that read, "Santa likes my cookies best."

"Only one for me, thanks," Elaine said.

"I'll take two and..." Holly lowered her voice, "We need to continue our conversation about *you know what* soon."

Betty Jo nodded and winked, leaning over the pile of potato buns.

"No new developments, but I'm watching my mailbox like a hawk. *Like a hawk.* Caw! Caw!" Snort-laughed Betty Jo, flapping her arms, clicking the tongs still in her hand.

Holly couldn't imagine Neumann's without their beloved store manager and her infectious energy and sincere devotion for all things Christmas.

Once they made it through the potluck line, Holly and Elaine, with plates piled high, found seats in the corner. Mid-bite Andy approached with his son Oliver in tow.

"Mind if we join you, ladies?"

"Mmm, hmm," Holly said as she chewed.

"Make yourself at home." Elaine patted the seat beside her.

Holly wondered if Elaine was simply good natured or if

there was more there.

Andy obliged.

"I see you've trimmed down the lumberjack beard since we're officially out of hibernation." Holly bit into her buttery potato bun.

"It was getting a bit unruly." Andy reached for the salt.

"Dad, can I go sit by the kids?" Oliver said.

"We're not cool enough for you, is that it?" Elaine cocked her head.

"Oh, you're pretty cool, Miss Lainey, but not quite as cool as my friends."

"Fair enough, Ollie."

"Go ahead, son, mind your manners. I'll find you afterwards."

Oliver bounded off while the adults continued their conversation over lunch.

"Am I the only one who didn't know you go by Lainey now?" Holly laughed.

Andy piped in. "Anyone who hangs out at the Center calls her that. But you're hardly ever there, Holly girl. Not that we blame you…we blame your art…and we blame Nik for pulling you away." Andy playfully raised his full eyebrows.

"Guilty as charged. Since I have a captive audience, at least until they serve dessert, can I ask you guys a question?"

Elaine shot Holly a *behave yourself, Brigham,* look.

"I'm all ears." Andy took a bite of potato salad.

"*Lainey* here is helping Nik and I stay connected across the miles with intentional questions to spark deeper conversation and the next question is, what do you dream about?"

"Like bagging a 12-point buck with two drop-tines off the back forty?" Andy offered.

"Why am I not surprised?" Holly shook her head.

"Or that I actually got the basketball scholarship I was counting on post high school," Elaine added softly.

"They were idiots. I know it was years ago, but I still can't believe they gave it to someone else."

"Yeah, my biggest rival. But really I'm fine. Every once in a while, it stings a little. But it's fun helping out here, playing pick up and helping the kids get better."

"You're great." Andy leaned slightly closer to Elaine. His shoulder and elbow touched hers.

Holly witnessed her friends make eye contact briefly. She not so discreetly watched them like a hawk.

Caw! Caw!

"Hey party people, room for one more?" Frank wiped a stray crumb by Elaine's other elbow before he sat down beside her.

Andy cleared his throat and Elaine tightened her ponytail.

Holly's eyes widened. Let the games begin: Team Andy or Team Frank?

It wasn't that long ago when Holly had been a contestant herself, except it was Team Nik or Team Frank. Or to put it another way—Mr. Mysterious or Captain Obvious. She chose mystery, obviously. But even Holly had to admit that "what you see is what you get" with Frank, and there was something comforting about that.

Andy leaned over farther to ask, "What do you dream about my man?"

"That's getting kind of personal isn't it? I mean I use to dream about—wait, is this like one of those conversation starter things. Did Betty Jo put you up to this?"

"Answer the question." Elaine waved a hand at him.

"I'm not usually a man of few words, but in this case I plead the fifth…considering present company." Frank winked at Holly.

Holly swallowed the last bit of her sickening sweet fruit punch.

Oh, Captain Obvious, surely he didn't still dream of them married with children while they carried on the Neumann family business?

"Since Frank is passing, you're the only one left, Holly girl." Andy, Elaine, and Frank sat on one side of the table, all eyes on her, waiting on her answer.

"This feels like an interrogation. I'm not sure how I'll answer it with Nik, but here's how I'll answer it for you Three Amigos."

"Oh…I see…we get a censored answer." Elaine threw her hands up nearly hitting Frank and Andy.

"I didn't mean it like that…oh never mind, I'll spill it. Lately I've dreamed about becoming a children's book author and illustrating the book too. I know it's silly, but kids' books still speak to me."

"I saw it with my own eyes in the library, the other day. It's a good dream."

"Probably unrealistic…but that's kind of my specialty, isn't it? Trying to attain things that are out of reach."

"Like Nik," Captain Obvious said. "He is definitely out of reach right now. Ya know, if you change your mind, I'm the first in—"

"Frank, I swear," Elaine hollered. "Besides this is not exactly the place for your go-to karaoke lyrics."

"No swearing at the church potluck." Andy chuckled.

"I meant that Nik is living in Leavenworth and—"

"Better stop while you're already behind, my friend," Elaine said.

"It's fine, Nik and I are fine. Actually, we have a phone date and…"

"Holly, I'm sorry, I didn't mean it like that," Frank said.

"It's okay. Thanks all for answering the question. I better get going."

"You good?" Elaine mouthed as Holly stood up, collecting her empty plate and cup.

Holly nodded.

Elaine grabbed the washcloth from Frank. "I'll take this back over, Footloose Frank, but thanks for covering for me so I could sit and eat."

"Anytime, anytime."

Holly thought that was a fitting nickname. Frank's height and coordination often resulted in clumsy moves…on the b-ball court, in everyday life, and in the relationship department.

"See you on the court this week?" Elaine asked.

"Definitely." Frank nodded, patting her back briefly before making a beeline for the dessert table.

Elaine didn't seem phased. She wiped down Holly's vacant area at the table and wiped around Andy's half-full plate. He smiled up at her. Was it the summer heat or did Elaine's neck look a little flushed?

Advantage Team Andy? More life experience, less obnoxious. But quite a bit older with a bit of a complicated past. Hard-working and outdoor loving. Generous and maybe… Holly should help Andy spruce up his online dating profile. *Who was she kidding, he probably doesn't have one.*

Or is it possible Frank is the more desirable bachelor for my bestie? More quirky, less jaded. A bit younger, with no ex-wife attached. Heir to the Neumann empire one day, and although quite goofy, caring and sweet in his boy-next-door way.

"Tell Nik hi for us," Andy interrupted Holly's mental assessment of Elaine's potential suitors.

"Will do. Later, friends." Holly moved past them, threw away her trash and waved to her parents on her way out.

⌘

Holly put on her polarized aviator sunglasses she'd been using as a headband to hold back her wavy hair that had doubled in volume due to the humidity. She walked back to St. Schäfer's to retrieve her car. The stately church steeple led the way, an arrow shooting into the bright blue sky. A bird soared above the brick church. Holly followed its flight path until it flew out of view.

Mental note: Check the discounted airfare app later and see if the astronomical cost of a flight from a nearby city to Leavenworth went down in price.

The sun glimmered on the multi-colored stain-glassed windows as Holly neared the church. While her brother Gabe had spent his Sundays trying to make spit wads from his bulletin to project toward his buddies or in the direction of his latest crush, Holly got lost in the narrative art on either side of the pews. The stain-glassed mosaics had served as a storybook of sorts throughout her upbringing, at least on Sundays and the occasional wedding and funeral. Stories without words. Stories that spoke differently to her depending on her age, occasion, and season.

Even though Holly was prone to a melancholy mood at the slightest change of circumstances, she was also prone to incessant inspiration. She often slid her thin, mini journal into her back pocket to catch ideas before they vanished. Holly preferred pen to paper vs. finger to screen when it came to capturing creative ideas. Thankfully her ivory sundress housed delightful side pockets for said journal. She reached for it along with a fine-tip pen and began sketching as she neared the church.

She was accustomed to studying the intricacies of the colorful windows from the inside of the sanctuary. But from the outside, bathed in sunlight and a few shadows from the surrounding trees, the perspective shifted.

Holly sat down on a large rock shaded by a willow tree. She studied the stained-glass window closest to her. She could feel an idea bubbling and brewing. Its form wasn't clear yet. She kept sketching...tiny strokes, messy yet purposeful. She drew a portion of the intricate window and a semblance of the aged brick. She paused. She waited. She bit her lower lip and tilted her head. There, in the delicate space between trying and receiving, an idea rose up and floated down at the same time until *Pop!*

Clarity.

The stained glass above her, the unfinished sketch below her, the Franz Kafka quote echoing in her mind from the morning's service served as a three-footed stool holding up the idea. She couldn't wait to tell Nik.

As a creative, Holly had learned the art of letting inspiration interrupt her and the discipline of responding to it before it dulled or disappeared. It wasn't always convenient to drop everything in order to pick up the creativity that rose up or floated down, or converged in a *Pop!* But it was a part of her creative process and it had served her well. Except in math class or while driving. Holly's slightly dented Prius? Exhibit A, a continual reminder of that one time she had tried to jot down an idea while driving and had an incident with the mayor's mailbox.

"What do you dream about?" Holly pressed the phone against her ear, not wanting to miss a word of his reply.

"Besides you?" Nik said.

"Yeah, I mean—"

"Besides you here, with me?" Nik's voice lowered.
"Listen, I'm trying to figure—"
"I hate disappointing you."
"Nik, I...it's not that..."
"You had your heart set on it and I messed it up."
"You mean HR did, right?"
"Kind of. I'm sorry...it's a bit more complicated..."
"Nik?" Holly wanted him to explain further but Elaine's words about her keeping too close of tabs on her man, stopped her.

"Yeah?"

"You haven't answered the question," Holly pivoted the conversation toward connection instead of contention.

"The question?"

"If you could choose your own adventure—if time, money, or ability were no obstacle, what would you do?"

"Hmm, I..."

"No second guessing. No thinking about the expectations of others, including mine. What is the dream of your heart, Beckenbauer?"

"Do you want thirty-four year-old Nik to answer or sixteen year-old Nik?"

"You decide," Holly said.

"Teen Nik would have boarded a plane to Germany as an exchange student instead of backing out at the last minute."

"An exchange student?"

"Yeah, I took two years of German, apparently I was a natural. My teacher told me about the exchange program and encouraged me every step of the way. I was kind of reserved, but he saw more in me and pushed me to be a bit daring. I came up with lots of excuses, yet he kept at it."

"Why did you back out?"

"That's also complicated."

"Try me."

"My parents didn't have a lot and with my sister being sort of a dance prodigy, any extra went to her lessons. I was able to get a partial scholarship toward my flight, although I'm pretty sure my German teacher paid part of my way out of his own pocket. I did odd jobs around our neighborhood and scooped ice cream at the ballpark on the weekends. But right before the remaining balance was due and I was scheduled to fly, the transmission in our family vehicle went out. Dad was ticked. Mom was defeated. My sister was worried she wouldn't make it to her big dance competition five hours away. So I..." His voice trailed off.

"You what, Nik?"

"I rode my bike to the mechanic, paid for the repair with what I had saved up, and made him swear he wouldn't tell my dad."

"Oh, Nik, wow..."

"When Dad came home that evening he told Mom an anonymous person had paid for the repair in full. She fell to her knees right there by the couch, thanking God while she cried quietly, rocking back and forth. Dad looked so relieved but tried to play it cool. My sister started twirling on her tip toes over and over."

"What a sacrifice, and you never told them?"

"Nah. I knew if they found out they'd be embarrassed or upset."

"Or proud—like really proud of you—you decent human, you."

"As much as it was worth helping out, I still wonder what it would have been like to go to Germany. What would my host family have been like? Would I have made a new best friend? What food would I have enjoyed most? Maybe I'd have a different career because of my experience there?"

"Or maybe you would have fallen in love with Barbara from the 'for real Bavaria'?"

"Barbara?"

"Or maybe you'd own a Bratwurst stand in Bremen?"

"Or own a piece of land in a quaint village to pass down to my kids."

"You'll make the best dad."

"You think so?"

"I know so. If you're capable of sacrificing that much as a teen in the thick of stinky armpits and voice cracks…and I've seen you in action, caring for your Aunt Claire and volunteering all around town."

"Even you said it was excessive, remember?"

"I did…I'm just saying you have a generous heart, Nik. Which only makes you more attractive in my book."

"So, you like me for what I do, eh?"

"It's who you are, Nik. I'm sorry I've been so hard on you about not coming out to Bavarian Falls. I guess I felt like I wasn't enough…wasn't worth the sacrifice."

"Not a chance. I'm trying to make it, ya know? I don't want to be scraping by like my parents did. I don't want my future kids having to carry that burden. One time the power got shut off at home and Dad pretended we were camping…he created an elaborate set-up and…okay, I think that's enough vulnerability for me. Tag, you're it, Hol. What do you dream about?"

For the next fifteen minutes, Holly poured out her latest dream to her boyfriend, Following the thread from the kids' section at the library to the childhood books her mom recently sent home with her, to the potluck confession to her friends, to the stained-glass window revelation this afternoon.

"It's brilliant. That's all there is to say," Nik said.

"Did I bore you?"

"Not for a minute. My favorite pastime is watching you—or in this case, hearing you—burst with creative energy. Your eyes twinkle, your face flushes, your breath quickens, your voice gets higher. It's beautiful. You're beautiful and so smart."

"Why, thank you. That reminds me…today at church, Pastor Meyer shared this quote, 'Anyone who holds on to the ability to see beauty never grows old.' So to ward off your wrinkles and age spots I guess you better hold onto me." Holly semi-joked.

"Deal. To be honest, making out with you is my favorite pastime. But listening to your creative ideas is a close second."

"Yes, please."

"Soon."

"Soon?"

"Somehow it'll all work out."

"How can you be so sure?"

"Just a hunch."

"Let's hope that dream becomes a reality."

"Definitely."

Click.

Click.

CHAPTER SIX
What makes you cry?

SUNDAY NAPS ARE THE BEST KIND of sleep. Holly's window air conditioning unit provided sufficient white noise along with the muted voices of tourists parading the sidewalks on the Sabbath. Holly stretched her tan arms over her head and yawned.

She reached for her phone.

4:34pm Eastern, 1:34pm Pacific.

She replayed Nik's words over in her mind—somehow *it will all work out.*

Nik was optimistic by nature. Holly was equal parts skeptical and idealistic, a blend of predictable unpredictability. Yet Nik was a touch mysterious to keep things interesting and slightly frustrating at times.

Holly started humming. It took her a minute to recognize the tune.

"Leaving on a jet plane, don't know when…"

But how?

And when?

Holly was too old to start a Gofundme, too proud to try her hand at busking, and too sentimental to sell family heirlooms to underwrite her airfare to Leavenworth.

Their original plan would have been easier.

Holly had decades of experience with Plan A's not materializing, yet the familiarity of disappointment didn't give way to an affection for Plan B's, C's, or Z's. She was still pivot adverse, even though she had witnessed bright spots, and even peculiar beauty, in less-than-ideal circumstances.

She didn't know why she was caught off guard by this one.

Holly had enough years under her belt to recognize when being insistent—okay, stubborn—was counterproductive to the greater good.

Nik not sticking to the original plan of flying to Bavarian Falls, or HR not letting him, was unfortunate, especially because she had envisioned many of their dates here. But not having any in-person dates was worse than the dates not being in the Falls.

As Holly made room for the dim possibility of flying to Leavenworth, her craving for travel was fed. From a young age Holly dreamed of adventure beyond Bavarian Falls. This desire surfaced in her art, her Christmas lists, and her prayers. A hunger for more was etched into her DNA, not as an insatiable desire or chronic discontent, but like a dear friend was missing who had yet to be met, or a new dish with exotic flavors had yet to be tried. Beyond her reach, around the bend.

Instead of checking again on airfare, Holly indulged in her post-nap rhythm of watercolor painting. Watching the blues and greens expand in an unpredictable pattern of possibility soothed her.

Today she painted the ocean, and she hummed.

※

At Music Keys on Monday morning, Holly set up for her first class. Inspired by her weekend epiphany outside the church, she gathered the needed supplies.

After everything was laid out, she went to check on the coffee brewing in the lobby.

The front door jingled as her first client arrived.

"Ha-ha-hi, Miss Holly." Chase stuttered, his mom following him.

"Hello, young man." Holly welcomed one of her favorite clients. "Do you remember Mr. Nik? He asked me to do his part of your secret handshake next time I saw you."

Chase beamed, fist bumping Holly twice, flexing his biceps, then adding an exaggerated, "Oh, yeah."

Holly smiled, recalling the sweet friendship formed in this building between Nik and Chase, including their not-so-secret handshake.

"Enjoy your class, son. Remember the plan for afterwards?" Chase's mom smoothed down his cowlick.

"Yes. Ba-bye, Mom." Chase headed to the art room.

"I'll take that as my cue to leave," his mom laughed. "I can't thank you enough, Holly. Chase adores this place. It's a Godsend. A little breathing room for me while he's in such good hands, enjoying a hobby he loves with others who love him"

"It's our pleasure. Go enjoy your morning before the tourists wake up."

As Chase's mom waved goodbye, three more clients arrived, one of them being Walt, her dad's longtime friend who volunteered during the morning art classes.

"I brought the mail in for you, young lady."

"Thanks, Walt. I made the coffee nice and strong for you."

"Much obliged."

Holly sorted through the short stack of mail, two bills, junk mail, and an envelope with her name hand-written on it.

No time for that now, the rest of Holly's students were filing in the front door.

Soon, at the front of the classroom, facing elementary-aged kids and a handful of senior citizens, Holly described their week-long project.

"We can get inspiration from just about anything. Even things we pass by on a regular basis."

"Like the park's fountain?" One of the kids asked.

"Or this pretty flower I picked?" Another said.

"That is a lovely flower, where did you find it, Julie?" Holy said.

"From the garden in front of the bank. I thought it was free. But my dad said it wasn't. I tried to replant it, but my dad said it doesn't work that way. So I kept it."

"Oh dear," Walt said.

"Uh-oh, Commandment #8," Tony said.

Apparently Tony's parents had taught him the Ten Commandments, or he'd been paying close attention in Sunday School. Holly would have to fact check later to see if "Thou shall not steal," was indeed #8 on the list.

"You robbed the bank?" An elderly woman asked, who was hard of hearing.

Oh dear, indeed. Holly knew she better take charge quick before anyone else threw in their two cents about Julie's innocent mistake.

"It is a pretty flower. But yes, let's not take things from other people's property. The nice thing about inspiration is that it is free and totally fine to pick up whenever you go."

Julie nodded, clutching the stem.

"Is it ha-ha-heavy?" Chase asked.

Holly smiled at his innocence. "Inspiration can feel that way sometimes, but it also helps us feel light. As I was saying, the stained-glass windows at my church gave me ideas for a few projects. We're going to try one of them today."

Cheers erupted from the clients.

Holly went on to explain that stained glass is made by melting a mix of ingredients, sand, sodium carbonate and limestone, at a very high temperature.

"This is the foundation for the glass, then special

ingredients, called metallic compounds, are added to make colors like red, blue, yellow, and green."

"This is confusing, Miss Holly."

"I know, hang with me. The point is, it takes extreme heat to make the glass. It takes certain combinations of materials to make the pretty colors we see. Kind of like that flower, Julie. You enjoy the bright pink petals, but the flower had to go through a whole lot to get so pretty. It didn't look like that to start with. It needed to be buried, and watered, and experience the rain and the warmth of the sun to grow. Sometimes things heat up around us, like a fight with a friend or a loved one gets stick, or we feel misunderstood, or we lose something…or someone. But beauty can come from all the hard stuff."

Holly held up an example to show the class. "Stained glass is often held together by lead or copper frames. Who holds you up when you are mad or sad?"

"My dog!" One client shouted.

"My sweet Maria," an elderly class member said.

"Each of these colors can represent something we have been through in our lives…good things, hard things. Scary things, fun things. When we put it all together it creates a colorful piece of art, with a strong support system."

"Are we making stained glass?" Julie asked.

"Kind of. You will choose various colors of tissue paper to represent different times in your life. Then you will glue the supporting pieces of black construction paper to hold the fragile pieces together. It will be a paper stained-glass window. We'll put them up over there and enjoy how the light comes through them. Our broken pieces can work together to make us stronger."

"And more prettier." Julie sniffed her prized flower.

"Shall we get started?"

"Yes!" Holly's willing students cheered.

⊂≫⊃

After the last few students left the building, Holly swept the entryway. The next class would arrive soon. A few jingles from the front door caused her to stop mid-sweep.

"Hullooo, Holly. I'm glad I caught you." Betty Jo Wilson breezed in a bit breathlessly.

"Are you okay?"

"Not really. You're the only one who knows about my..." she glanced around to make sure no one else was around "...about my *retirement*."

"I've been meaning to ask you more about that."

"It turns out," she sniffed, "that I can't get into Kris Kringle Academy this fall because I accidentally filled out the wrong date on the form and it was notarized with the error. They returned my application because of the discrepancy."

"Oh, no. That doesn't seem very jolly to me."

"Right? It's such a competitive program. They can't make concessions for clerical errors because of the high demand. There's a waiting list longer than Rapunzel's hair. *So close*. I was *so close* to living out my dreams of becoming *The* Mrs. Claus of Bavarian Falls. Whatever will I do now?" Betty Jo burst into tears.

Holly led her by the arm, encouraging her to sit down on the love seat in the lobby.

"I'm so sorry. Any chance you can appeal their decision?"

Betty Jo reached in her blouse, retrieving a tissue from her bra strap. She blew her nose with a honk.

"Oh, Holly dear, I don't know. It's all so upsetting." She returned the used hankie to its holster.

"Is there anything I can do to help?" Holly sat beside Betty

Jo, her arm around her ample back for comfort.

"You're so sweet. Here you are with your own conundrum and yet you're willing to help me." She patted Holly's hand.

"Anything, say the word."

"I wish I knew. There's a lot of red tape over there. After all, they are the ivy league as far as Santa Claus schools go."

Holly bit back laughter. Christmas was serious business around here, even in summer.

"Oh my stars, I've gotta run. My shift at Neumann's starts soon. Mind if I freshen up quick in your powder room?" She stood, smoothing her full pleated dress.

"Right down the hall, second door on the left."

"Thank you, dear, I'm not usually so undignified." She smoothed humid flyaways back into her bouffant hairstyle. "But I've been dreaming about this new role for years—Ms. Betty Jo Claus." She emphasized each word with a sweep of her palm. "So close…" her voice constrained, "yet so far out of reach."

She dramatically turned, and sauntered toward the 'powder room.'

"I'll leave through the back door," Betty Jo hollered over her shoulder.

Holly shook her head. Never a dull moment with the store manager. She was disappointed for her friend and hoped she could help her, somehow.

Returning to the reception area, Holly remembered the stack of mail. She threw out the junk mail, placed the bills in their designated slot, and picked up the letter with her name on it. Dare she hope it was from Nik? Maybe the whole HR debacle was a cover-up and he was already here in Bavarian Falls? How romantic it would be if he had placed a clue in the envelope leading her to his whereabouts, reminiscent of his accidental scavenger hunt proposal to her. Or, if he had been telling the truth that he couldn't get away, then no address or stamp on the envelope meant the letter had to be from someone local.

She carefully opened the letter and gasped.

An instant stream of tears dotted the paper.

※

Holly tried to remain composed during her next art class, but she felt like she was trying to hold back a hole in the Hoover Dam with her thumb.

As soon as it was noon, she headed out the back exit of the building to try and catch Nik before he was too far into his work day to take her call.

"You're never gonna believe this." Holly blurted as Nik's gorgeous face appeared on the screen.

"What's that?" he whispered, looking over his shoulder. "Sorry, I sneaked away to take this, but they'll find me soon enough."

Holly switched her phone view so he could see the letter.

"Sorry, I can't make out what it says."

She flipped the view around again. "In not so many words it says that we'll be making out soon," Holly sang.

"It says that?"

"No silly, but it does say this:
Dear Holly:
Don't live with regrets. Go see your man and that glorious mountain range in Leavenworth. Your ticket cost is covered. Have the best time. No strings attached."

"Who is it from?"

"It's not signed. I'm pretty sure it's from Mrs. Rasmussen. She and I talked about my financial dilemma yesterday. She must have taken it upon herself to serve as my Miss Havisham."

"Huh?"

"*Great Expectations* by Charles Dickens?"

"Never read it, but I'm so excited you're coming for a visit. When do you leave?" Nik smiled wide.

"I literally just opened the letter. But when I get home I'll book the ticket."

"If you don't know who your benefactor is, how will they pay for it?"

"I left out an important detail. Inside the envelope was four hundred dollars!"

"Whoa."

"I'm beginning to think this twenty-questions thing is rigged, because today the question is, "What makes you cry?"

"Cry? But this is a happy occasion."

"Yes, but I cried happy tears when I opened the envelope, and the question doesn't specify what kind of crying."

She also filled Nik in on what made Betty Jo cry today.

"Oh, that stinks. Think you'll be able to help her?"

"I'm going to try," Holly said.

"What tempts me to cry is when I let people down. I hate it. I know me not coming let you down, Hol. I'm so relieved we can still have time together this summer though."

"You were right. I was doubtful, but you said it would work out, and it did, in a most surprising way."

"I'm gonna have to go, but let's talk details when I'm out of work. Things are crazy here, so let's see what I can move around so we can maximize our time together."

"See you soon." Holly lilted.

"Can't wait. I like you."

"Right back at ya."

Nik often ended his calls like that. Holly loved him and she longed for the day he changed 'like' to 'love.' But again, she was stubborn and old-fashioned enough to wait for him to initiate the 'love' word. She wouldn't let that blip on their relationship radar ruin her mood.

She was leaving on a jet plane, headed straight into Nik's arms.

Holly hadn't been in her apartment for more than twenty minutes when she heard a soft knock at the door. She wasn't expecting anyone. She peered through the peephole, shocked to see her sister-in-law.

"Monica?" Holly opened the creaky door. A sullen face stood before her.

"I'm sorry I didn't call first. Gabe is at your parent's house, but I couldn't face them."

"Come in. What's going on?"

Monica looked around slowly as if she had never set foot in Holly's apartment.

"I'm not sure what to say." She stared blankly.

"Sit down, sis. I'll grab us drinks." Holly would wait to share her good news. Something was off. The window unit whirred on, combatting the muggy air. She quickly assembled hospitality on a wooden tray, keeping an eye on Monica and on the knife she was using to thinly slice lemons.

Holly carefully carried over the tray, trying to evenly distribute the weight.

Soon the women were side by side on the couch, cupping iced-cold tea.

As Holly sipped, Monica, who was usually reserved, poured out her heart in fragments.

"We'd been trying to..." she tightened her grip on her glass,

"...and been poked and prodded. Calculating and praying. Pleading, really."

Holly tried to fill in the gaps to grasp the meaning, "Trying to?"

"But something's broken....and..."

Holly waited. The translation didn't come. She mentally counted to ten. Still no words emerged from the woman who had married her brother and mothered her niece.

"Help me understand."

Monica returned her glass to the tray, untouched. She breathed in unevenly and pinched out the words, "I lost....we lost. Barely the size of a speck but big enough to change everything." She grasped the couch cushions, as if drawing strength from them before continuing, "Oh the joy of that moment...and the terror of now."

Holly couldn't yet see the full picture through the shards of the story.

She started counting again. 1, 2, 3...*a flicker of fright stopped her.*

"You said Gabe is at my parents. But where is *Claudia*?" Holly's voice raised in a thrust of panic.

Monica, whose eyes had been boring holes in the planked floor at her feet, whipped her head toward Holly.

"No, no, no....not Claudia. She's fine. Alive and well. But...the baby...my baby...our baby is...is....gone."

Holly closed her eyes tight and breathed sharply. She put down her drink, her hand damp from the condensation. She wiped her legs, trying to dry them.

"Oh, sis...I am so sorry." Holly reached for her sister-in-law's shaking hand, determined to squeeze courage into her veins.

The women made room for silence to speak louder than any

formed words could.
Minutes passed, the hush of shared loss bearing down.
Mascara had long been washed away.
Shoulders slumped.
A whimper escaped.
Monica rocked slightly.
Hands clasped.
Heads bowed.
Holly's air conditioning kicked off.
No longer able to keep the grief contained, uncalculated sobs contracted from deep within Monica, pushing forth and out. The grief bearer inadvertently knocked over the iced tea precariously positioned on the tray. It toppled to the floor with a crash. Put-together Monica fell apart.
    Holly felt ill-equipped to pick up the pieces of shattered glass. She wrapped her arms around Monica and pulled her close. The spilled tea could be dealt with later.
    Sometimes what makes you cry is the delivery of the happiest news you could hope for.
    And sometimes it is the guttural groans of hope deferred.

CHAPTER SEVEN
What if you had a million dollars?

AFTER THE BROKEN GLASS AT THEIR feet was cleaned up, Holly carefully asked how Claudia had taken the news.

Monica sighed. "We weren't sure how to tell her. She was the only one we had told we were pregnant. I hadn't wanted to yet, *just in case*, but Gabe insisted."

Holly waited to see if Monica wanted to share more.

"I felt helpless to explain things in a way Claudia would understand. I didn't want to overburden her, yet I didn't want to minimize the depth of loss. She was so excited to be a big sister."

Holly grimaced, another wave of grief swelled. She imagined Claudia's trembling lip and brave face, the same combination of fear and courage Holly had displayed when she was around her age, when the worst news was delivered. Not a loss of a long-awaited sibling, but of a dad whose return she had long awaited.

Holly replayed the words and remembered how she hadn't fully understood what was being communicated in that moment.

An awful thing happened to Daddy's brain, Sweetheart. He's not coming home the same, but we're so thankful he's still with us.

At her young age, Holly had grasped what she could, and hid the questions she was afraid to ask.

Monica whispered her daughter's reaction to Holly, "Claudia said, 'Mommy, if the baby isn't in your belly anymore, where did she go? Did she move? Did she fly away? I want to go see her, please…right now.' Of course we didn't know yet if Baby Brigham was a boy or girl, but Claudia was insistent it was a little sister. Gabe stepped in, then he pulled Claudia up on his lap and did the best he could to explain that our baby, her sibling, was gone and not coming back. It was terrible, and tender, and...."

"Oh, Monica."

Holly had more questions like, "When did you find out you were pregnant, and when did you miscarry, and do they know why it happened and can, or will, you try again?" But she didn't ask any of those. She was familiar with well-intended people prying and saying the wrong thing in the wake of death. She swallowed platitudes and buried her curiosity, as she and her sister-in-law sat shoulder to shoulder. It was a terrible and tender situation.

Monica eventually drove over to Holly's parents to be reunited with her husband and daughter. Holly offered to accompany her, but Monica refused.

Between the whiplash of Betty Jo's disappointment, the surprise gift to cover her airfare to Leavenworth, and the shocking news of Monica's miscarriage, Holly felt out of sorts, unsure which emotion would win out—empathy, elation, or devastation?

She could try and wrangle her big feelings into action...helping Betty Jo, searching for a round-trip ticket to see Nik, praying for her brother's hurting family. Instead, she revisited the landscape she had painted —a cliff overlooking a swirling ocean of Aegean teal and cadmium. She held the art close. She studied the variations of watercolor in the sea, her hand gently grazing the surface as if she were reading Braille. Where there were swirls and dips, she saw layers of beauty and loss, of possibility and sorrow. She didn't fish for answers, she reflected. She waited for what might wash up on shore. She hummed. This time, a slow, sad rendition about leaving on a jet plane. Then she wept for the niece or nephew who was not coming back again.

The tears were her help, her search, her prayer.

Later that evening, after a phone call with her mom about the family's devastating news, Holly needed a reprieve. For what seemed like the hundredth time she pulled up her search for airfare out West. She gladly expanded her search since her budget had increased. She smiled as she scrolled, almost tasting the mountain air and Nik's soft lips on hers.

Nik was going to call after he got off work so they could finalize plans for her visit and she could book her ticket. She realized she had forgotten to mention the good news about her trip to her mom. Not that she had to, but she wanted to. It felt good to share when things were going well in her life. Not so many years ago, her mother might have responded with, "While I'm really happy for you, it's too bad someone had to cover the ticket cost for you. I know art has always been your thing, but I wish that—" Holly stopped the train wreck of her runaway thoughts with the more likely response of her mom now. She would probably say, "Ooo, that's nice, dear. I hope you have a great time out there. When do you leave? And I'm sure it goes without saying, but don't forget to write a thank you note to Donna." Which reminded Holly, she wanted to track down Mrs. Rasmussen and thank her for her thoughtfulness and generosity. Never would she have guessed the eccentric dentist's wife had paid such close attention to her plight. She had pegged her as more of a diva than a saint. But first, or fifth, impressions were not always accurate representations of character. She had found that out the hard way with Nik.

Nik's opening statement to Holly on their call was, "How's my favorite person on the planet? On a scale of 1 to 10?"

"That depends on what we're referring to. I'm an 8.5 about

my upcoming trip."

"Only an 8.5? I'm in the dog house, huh?"

"You know you're a 10 in my book, there's a lot to navigate before I'm there...seeing if Shayla or Walt can cover my art classes, checking on Betty Jo's morale, packing, borrowing Elaine's hiking boots, turning the vacation setting on my work email, and...I shouldn't complain about these minor things when it comes to trip prep. Remember me telling you about that woman who came into Neumann's and bought fourteen holiday figurines for her grandchildren, all from one family? Imagine what's it's like to get that crew out the door for a trip. Their mom deserves a gold medal."

"For real."

"You thinking mini cooper or mini bus?" Nik said.

"For a car rental? I thought you'd pick me up?"

"Oh, I'll pick you up all right, right off your feet, Holly Noel Brigham."

"Deal. Did you get a new vehicle and forget to mention it?"

"No, I'd tell you about most major purchases."

"Most, huh?"

"I was meaning do you want a small or large family one day, you know...hypothetically?" Nik explained.

"I prefer an actual family to a hypothetical one. I'm not sure, a few? I'm not getting any younger, but I want to feel good and ready, it's such a big decision."

"Do people ever feel totally ready to be a parent?"

Holly did not add, "Or a bride" because she was pretty sure she'd like to be one in the not-so-distant future. "Probably not. I guess that's where faith comes in. You go ahead and jump in, and figure things out as you go."

"I'm glad you were willing to take a chance on me, Hol."

"I could say the same. I'm no cake walk that's for sure. Me and my big feelings." Holly proceeded to tell Nik about Monica's visit. She normally was careful not to share family news that wasn't entirely hers to tell, but she hoped Nik would soon be family. But first they had to settle on which dates she'd travel so they could start dating in the same zip code instead of over Wi-Fi.

Nik expressed his sadness and offered comfort in just the right way, which only made him more attractive to his girlfriend.

"This is an awkward transition, but today's question is, 'What if you had a million dollars?'"

"Wow, that would solve a lot of problems," Nik said.

"Or would it give you more?"

"Always the pessimist."

"Am not. Well, sometimes, I suppose." Holly admitted.

"You already have your way paid for, so what else? If you would have asked me what I'd do with a million dollars a few years ago, I probably would have said I'd invest a substantial portion of it for my parents, to help make their retirement a bit more comfortable. But with the success of my sister's competitive dance studio in Arizona, which enabled her to build that *casita* onto her home for my parents, they're doing fine."

Holly had spent time with Nik's parents and sister, Alyse, briefly when they'd flown in for a dance competition in the city. Holly had met them for lunch. They were down to earth and kind. No red flags. Nik's estimation had proven accurate. His sister upstaged the conversation, whether she was trying to or not. She didn't come across as arrogant but in an I'm-wired-to-shine-and-help-others-shine kind of way.

"You're always thinking about others Nik, come on, be selfish for a minute. What would you do for *you*?"

"If you insist...I'd like to buy a cabin in the woods so I could escape from the pressure of work from time to time. It could be a place that family or close friends could use to get away as well."

"See, you're still thinking about others even when you have permission to be selfish. It's an endearing quality though. I hope some of it wears off on me."

"You being here will make that more of a probability," Nik teased.

"I'm counting on it. A cabin in the woods, huh?"

"Yeah, reminds me of those camping trips with Dad. Fresh air, open sky, a slower pace. No wifi, the wind blowing through the trees and open water for fishing or swimming. I can picture it now."

Holly's unedited response rattled around in her head, "No wifi would mean I'd be out of range when you're at the cabin, unless I became your wifey and am there with you. Gosh, she wished she were already in Leavenworth.

"What dates work best for you...for my trip?"

"Hold on there, missy. You didn't answer the question yet. What if you had a million dollars?"

"Oh, man, how do I narrow it down? Not that long ago, I would have said, fully funding that darned community art space in Chicago. A few months ago, I might have said investing into Heart Turn to help expand our efforts in connecting the generations through art. But with Lena recently landing that ginormous grant for the fall, we'll be set for years. Besides a tiny house for my personal art studio on property with an inspiring view, I'd have to say I'd love to travel more. If I actually do become a children's book author, I'd love to do a library tour, not only in the States, but also to places around the world, inspiring children to find their voice and write and draw their feelings, their findings, their questions, their discoveries."

"Any chance the tiny house could look like a cabin? Because if you think about our dreams, they seem to align there."

"As long as you promise not to decorate in evergreen plaid or silhouettes of bear and moose."

"Not quite your style, eh?"

"Far from it. Speaking of being far from it, let's nail down my travel dates."

Nik and Holly went back and forth trying to figure out what would work. They started with the practical but landed on the impulsive. Holly would leave in two days and stay for almost a month. Holly had a lot to do before she left, but it fed her sense of adventure and would enable them to have the most time together they could. If this was going to work they needed to put their best effort forward even when it wasn't convenient.

Holly was going to use two weeks of paid vacation time, and for the other two weeks Shayla, her supervisor, said she could receive a stipend by working remotely on a detailed plan to integrate the grant Lena had secured. The plan wouldn't be implemented until the fall, but Holly's efforts to document the most effective use of the funds would free up Shayla. It was the least Holly could do, since Shayla and Walt were covering her art classes in her absence.

"It's really happening, Hol. I'm going to see if HR will give me at least part of a week off while you're here. I know it won't be ideal for me to be tied up at work during the day, but it's better than nothing."

"Ah, come on, can't I come to work with you a few days? I could commission a piece for the office. Pro bono." Holly semi-teased.

"I don't think I could get any work done with your beautiful face at my workplace."

"At least a tour of the office then?"

"Of course. Make me a list of things you want to do while you're here, and I'll come up with some too. Or I'll ask Marina. She's lived here her whole life."

Holly chose to ignore the yellow flag that seemed to wave over the name Marina. While it was a lovely name, Holly couldn't help but wonder if a lovely face and a life-of-the-party, or a life-of-the-office, personality came with it. She would find out soon enough. For now, Holly needed to focus on what was good, right, and true. She would be in Nik's arms before this time next week. They would have the opportunity to answer their IOU questions in person, at last. They would be reunited under the banner of a Bavarian village across the country. Leavenworth or bust.

They didn't have a million dollars but they would soon have time together—actual face time—in the same time zone, in the same zip code.

Priceless.

CHAPTER EIGHT
What lights your fire?

TODAY WAS THE DAY HOLLY WOULD enjoy love in Leavenworth. Her flight left at noon and it was an hour-and-a-half drive to the airport. Her to-do list was not yet completed. The mound of clothes on her bed needed to be tried on. The half-packed suitcase begged to be reorganized. Not to mention the lesson plans that required submission. She would miss seeing her students and walking them through the next phases of their stained-glass project. The change in instructors would not be seamless, as many of them, young and old alike, thrived on predictable routines, but she knew they were in good hands.

Although she and Nik had full-time jobs, if their relationship was continually sequestered to the margins, she feared it wouldn't be enough to sustain them. That it might crowd out their couple hood. This trip was so important. It would be fun, but it would also be telling. Did they have what it took to make it? Would this next month draw them closer or would their quirks and different communication styles annoy each other and drive a wedge between them?

Holly swatted the negativity like a pesky mosquito. It was pointless to worry about what could go wrong with Mr. Right. She wanted to enjoy what she had. Which reminded her of the list she created once upon a time, recording all the things she didn't like about Christmas. Thankfully, she had replaced that lack list for a lavish list, which focused on what she *already* had, not what was missing.

She searched for a piece of paper Betty Jo had given her. She located it under a pile of art supplies on her desk. Holly held the treasure up to the light. Betty Jo had jotted down another quote her *mutter* used to say from German philosopher, Arthur Schopenhauer, *"Wir denken selten an das, was wir haben, aber immer an das, was uns fehlt."* The translation was written underneath. Holly could almost hear Betty Jo imitating her mutter's thick accent, "We rarely think of what we have, but always of what we lack." Holly resolved to appreciate the green grass under her feet—actually, it was planked wood, but you get the idea. She refused to give in to old thought patterns of happiness being "out there" instead of readily available in the moment. She knew this perspective shift didn't shield her from heartbreak, but it helped her not miss out on the joy of her right now life.

Soon Holly would have boots on the ground in the same town as her boyfriend. She had borrowed Elaine's hiking boots. They were a tad too snug, but Nik wanted to take her on a hike, time and weather permitting.

Holly directed her attention to the bathing suit options before her. One piece? Tankini? Bikini? She wished she would have exercised a bit more this summer. Or at least enjoyed a few less rounds of ice cream, in a waffle cone, from Sugar Shock.

She was doing it again, honing in on what was wrong instead of what was right. *Sheesh!* The mental gymnastics required to stay positive and upbeat was vigorous exercise in and of itself.

Holly threw all three bathing suits into her now overstuffed suitcase. She did one last sweep of her apartment, hoping she hadn't forgotten anything, like her razor, or the IOU questions and decorated jar. She double checked. Everything seemed to be there. She hadn't had time to look at the day's question. She was hoping to ask Nik in person, at last. She rushed out the door to finish her remaining errands before it was time to drive to the airport. Her first stop? Hunting down Donna Rasmussen.

Holly pulled into the parking lot of the dentist office. Her Prius looked dinky next to Doc Rasmussen's gleaming white Escalade that sported the license plate: 2TH DOC. Vanity plates weren't Holly's thing, but if it were hers would say: ART 4EVR. No matter where she lived, or what she did, art would be a part of it. It was her lifeline, her happy place, the language she used to communicate when words fell short. While she would have liked to bring her easel to Leavenworth, the extra cost and hassle deterred her. She had tucked art supplies in her checked bag though. She planned to draw or paint part of the time, while Nik worked. Her imagination was ready for fresh inspiration and mountain air.

Holly entered the empty lobby of the dentist office. As if it had been planned, she was met by the opening notes of a song her dad's band often played. Her steps toward the front desk were in sync with the beat. Holly's lips curled into a grin. She hummed along as Harry Connick Jr. crooned "A Wink and a Smile" over the office speakers. Leave it to Doc or the Mrs. to curate a playlist with as many mouth, lips, and teeth references as possible. The receptionist greeted Holly with a wave. She continued her phone conversation about a referral for braces. Holly took a seat in the white furry chair, shaped like a molar. Or was she imagining that?

At times, Bavarian Falls felt scripted or like the downtown area of a notable theme park. From the curated decorations to the quirky cast of characters, from the small-town energy to the steady stream of peppy music and sugary flavors pumping through the air. Which was one of the reasons Doc Rasmussen had done so well over the years. His clientele ingested more than their share of sweet treats since Christmas was celebrated all year round. Candy cane cavities and sugar plum fillings helped fund the Rasmussen's extravagant vacations and fancy vehicles with custom plates. They also gave back to the community by volunteering at Neumann's, as well as sizable and visible donations to their church, Blessed Epiphany, and their most recent project–funding an upscale dog park on the edge of town, predictably named "Hildebrant's Haven."

It wasn't that everything and everyone was happy all the time in the Falls, but the bright colors and Bavarian-styled architecture enticed the onlooker to enter into a kind of fantasyland. As if on cue, Mrs. Rasmussen walked through the office door. She had a potted plant in hand. She set it on the ledge of the front desk and fluffed it.

"Hi, Mrs. R. Glad I caught you."

Donna, decked in high heels, crisp white pants and a rose-colored blouse, turned her way. "Holly? Nice to see you. Most of the staff are on their lunch break. Are you scheduled for a cleaning with Doc?"

"Not today. I was hoping you'd be here though. I'm headed to Leavenworth soon and I wanted to thank you. It wouldn't have been possible without you."

"All I did was give you a little encouragement. No need to thank me."

"I'd say it was more than a little."

"It was nothing, really." Mrs. R pulled off a drooping leaf.

"It meant a lot to me...and Nik."

"You're welcome." Mrs. Rasmussen nodded and returned her attention to the plant which apparently needed a lot of fluffing.

An alert sounded from Holly's phone. She picked it up, unfamiliar with the tone.

Within seconds of scanning the notification, Holly gasped.

"Everything all right?"

"No, no, NO! This can't be happening. My flight is canceled due to a forest fire outside of Leavenworth."

"Oh, Holly, how disappointing. I'm sorry."

"Unbelievable! It's like something is trying to stop Nik and my reunion. Even the national forest is interfering."

"Surely there's another flight you could take?"

"If only it were that easy. The airline's website states it will refund the original cost of my ticket, but with everyone trying to rebook, the new ticket price is through the roof. It's almost double what the first one cost. I can't swing the difference with such short notice. I wanted to get there before sunset, Pacific Time, so Nik and I could enjoy it together. This is the literally the worst news."

Holly pinched the bridge of her nose.

Next up on the office playlist? "Smile" by Nat King Cole. Holly's Grandma Bea often played it on the piano and sang it over Holly when she was young. It was a sad tune that often paralleled Holly's mood as she drew her feelings, the notes reverberating from the keys and Grandma's vibrato.

If she was drawing her feelings right now, it would be scribbles of fiery red, not because of the wildfire alone but her fury at the injustice of it all. When happiness was within reach, unpleasant circumstances threatened to choke it out.

Holly's composure started to crumble.

"Now, Holly. Pull yourself together. We'll figure this out. Give me a minute to think." Mrs. Rasmussen clicked her heels over to the receptionist. She muttered under her breath and jotted on a notepad. Then she tapped her fingers impatiently as the receptionist frantically typed on her keyboard. It looked like they were plotting a covert operation.

Holly reread the notification, willing it to say something different. A wildfire was not on her radar when she set her itinerary. For once she hadn't allowed herself to think through worst-case scenarios about her trip. But a lot of good that had done. She started to text Nik about the terrible news, but was interrupted. Mrs. Rasmussen returned, grabbing her arm with her manicured nails.

"I think I've got it. Henry knows a guy who has a private plane. It's tiny, but it might be available. He's living offshore but he keeps the plane in a nearby hangar. If we can find someone with their pilot's license he might let us call in a favor. Henry did an emergency root canal for his famous wife a few years back. They owe us. Do you happen to know any pilots?"

"That's really kind of you, Mrs. R. But..."

The receptionist who was watching the drama unfold called Mrs. Rasmussen over and handed her a piece of paper. Once she read it, the dentist's wife clicked back over to anxious Holly.

"Eureka! I can't believe I didn't think of this right away. Pastor Meyer used to fly for the military."

"You're right. He and my dad go way back. They used to work side by side at—"

"Exactly. It's perfect. He'll drop you off in Leavenworth and that'll buy you time to figure out your return ticket. Unless of course you elope while you're there. At your age, you don't want to waste any more time. Marry before your cheekbones droop, that's what I always say. Although your mother would kill us both if she isn't invited to her only daughter's nuptials. *Never mind.* I need to focus. The pilot. I'll zip over to St. Schäfer's and talk to Ingrid and Pastor. Let's pray they're feeling charitable and adventurous today." Mrs. Rasmussen crossed herself as the Amen.

Holly lifted up a silent prayer that this crazy, spontaneous plan would work out and that Ingrid Meyer wouldn't choose to serve as chaperone on the cross-country trip. If the plane was anything like Holly imagined she'd need to knock herself out with an extra dose of motion sickness meds. She didn't want the pastor's wife keeping watch over her, singing, "Asleep in Jesus" while she snored and drooled her way to Leavenworth.

※

Within the hour, Holly was staring down Farmer Schroeder's makeshift runway in between his corn fields. If "Fields of Gold" starting playing from a speaker in sky, she would know for certain she had stumbled into a musical or a multiverse.

Between rapid-fire text threads with Nik, Elaine, and her mom, Holly caught everyone up to speed on her canceled flight and Mrs R.'s wild Plan B to help her arrive in Leavenworth before sunset, by way of the tiny plane in front of her.

Holly's mom had been concerned about her flying with the wildfire, but Nik assured her it wasn't as bad as the media and commercial airlines were making it sound. There was some smoke blowing his way, but there was enough visibility to land safely. It had been a controlled burn that got out of hand, but it was moving slowly, and containment was probable in the coming days. Holly's mom had tried to talk her daughter into waiting it out. Holly was done waiting. The Plan B, although not ideal, was thrilling, and slightly terrifying to the Bavarian Falls resident with a thirst for adventure—even if the chariot that would sweep her off her feet was not much bigger than a puddle jumper.

She coached herself under her breath, *You can do this. Nik is worth it. Pastor Meyer has decades of experience. Don't think about the fact he hasn't flown in a while and that the plane looks like a toy. Pastor M. is in good with the Big Guy. It'll be fine. I'll be fine. Before I know it I'll safely arrive and be reunited with Nik.*

Holly's pep talk sounded braver than she felt. She swallowed the two pills that would steady her equilibrium and whisk her into a deep sleep.

Mrs. Rasmussen looked out of place on the rural runway. She patted the back of the plane like it was an obedient dog. That's when Holly saw its name painted in black letters, "Stunt Double." She prayed the pastor-pilot wouldn't be inspired to try an acrobatic nosedive or anything like it.

Holly replaced her nervous thoughts with the quote she had read earlier from Betty Jo, "We rarely think of what we have, but always of what we lack." It was the motivation she needed. She refused to feed the fear and chose to focus on the love on display, there in the cornfield.

"How can I ever thank you, Mrs. R.? You literally saved the day...again. I owe you, that's for sure."

"How about custom hand-lettering on my darlings' Christmas presents for life?" Mrs. R. clucked.

"Anything!"

"I'm kidding, Holly. Really there's no need to thank me. Our receptionist handled the bulk of the details, I had the idea to reach out to an old friend, but she made it happen. I'm glad it worked out. Now, enjoy your time in Leavenworth." Donna held her short hair in place as a gust of wind blew past.

Pastor Meyer's wife was inside the plane checking to make sure everything was as it should be. Holly struggled to lift her bulky suitcase up to the door.

"Let me help you with that, dear." Mrs. Meyer reached for Holly's suitcase and secured it in the back of the plane. Pastor Meyer was already in the front seat, checking buttons and the flight path. Before exiting the small aircraft, Mrs. Meyer kissed the pilot on the cheek. She deplaned so there would be room for

Holly to enter.

"Ready?" She offered her hand to help Holly climb into the compact back seat.

"I'm sorry I won't be accompanying you, but you're in safe hands with Pastor. Enjoy your time with Nik. We look forward to hearing all about it upon your return."

Holly was certain she would not be sharing *every* detail of her trip. She was thankful she would be the only passenger aboard. No small talk required, but deep sleep to pass the time until she was awakened upon her arrival by true love's kiss. Okay, maybe it wouldn't go down like that, but a girl can dream.

Holly buckled her seatbelt. She waved to Mrs. Rasmussen and Mrs. Meyer from the window as they backed up into the corn for takeoff. What a strange day it had been. What started off as an errand to give thanks turned into a speedy rescue plan orchestrated by these two women—her benefactor and the busybody pastor's wife.

Holly retrieved a slip of paper from the front of her backpack. She had put today's IOU question there so it'd be handy when it was time to read it to Nik. Curiosity got the best of her and she peeked at it.

"Oh, you've got to be kidding."

"Everything all right back there?" the pilot asked.

"Yeah, no worries." Holly said.

The question in her hand only confirmed her suspicions that she was either a contestant in a reality show or her meds were already making her brain fuzzy.

What lights your fire?

What were the chances that today of all day's that was the question. Was it a sick joke or comedic relief? Did it mean:

A. What makes you mad?

B. What sparks your passion?
C. What materials do you use to start a literal fire?
Her answers?
A. Canceled flights due to wildfires
B. Art 4EVR
C. Depends on how fast I want it to start (pine needles, matches, or a blow torch)

She'd have to wait to hear Nik's answer in person. He'd never believe the question hadn't been staged.

"It's time for takeoff, little lady," Pastor Meyer said. Holly wasn't sure if he was talking to her or the plane.

Holly texted Nik once last time, letting him know she'd see him soon. She added the plane emoji even though a large bird emoji would have been a more accurate representation of the size of her flying chariot. She turned her cell to airplane mode. After a brief prayer from the pilot, it was indeed go time. Within minutes "Stunt Double" was in the air. Holly was finally headed to Leavenworth.

CHAPTER NINE
How can I lighten your load?

THE NOISY PLANE ENGINE MADE CONVERSATION taxing. Hugging her backpack, Holly settled in for the long ride. She put in extra hours at Heart Turn and a few late nights getting ready to leave on such short notice. She hoped her grogginess and the time change wouldn't impede the delight of her and Nik's evening under the same corner of the sky. Her heavy eyelids attempted to open from time to time as she flew across the country. Eventually she surrendered to the abyss of deep sleep.

"Holly."
She heard her name being called from a far off land. The voice was muted but persistent.
"*Holly. Holly!*"
She tried to determine if the voice was fantasy or reality. She was in the middle of the strangest dream about Doc and Mrs. Rasmussen being contestants in a televised tooth pulling competition. They had a limited time to complete their assignment and win a million dollars. They were competing against the owner of "Stunt Double" and his famous wife. Residents from Bavarian Falls, of all ages, were reclining in dentist chairs in the middle of Farmer Schroeder's cornfield. When a tractor honked, the residents—or victims—opened their mouths, ready for their tooth extractions. Except their teeth were corn kernels. Doc and Donna ran from person to person pulling out the golden "teeth" from their gums, stuffing them in a burlap sack.

"HOLLY, WAKE UP!"

Huh? Who? What the?

Holly's stomach flip-flopped, and she gripped the armrests for dear life. It felt like she had leapt off the high dive at the community pool, but the surface of the water was miles below. Her brown eyes darted, trying to gain context for where she was and what was happening.

"Wake up, missy. We're about to touch down in Leavenworth. Might be a rough landing."

Her pastor was the pilot? She rubbed her eyes, convinced she looked like a raccoon with smeared make-up. Maybe drowning herself in a double dose of Dramamine™ had been a mistake. Her head and heart were pounding due to the abrupt wakeup call. She accessed a tool she learned in counseling for fight or flight situations, like this one. She focused on slowing her shallow breathing in order to get more oxygen and calm her anxious mind.

Breathe in, 1, 2, 3. Breathe out, 1, 2, 3, 4, 5.

Holly turned her attention away from the bobbing horizon. She focused on what was directly in front of her. As her breathing evolved from gasps to uneven puffs and eventually to rhythmic input and output, it started coming back to the wildfire, the canceled flight, Mrs. Rasmussen paying her way and saving the day, her pastor knowing how to fly, and she was a willing passenger on this toy plane. She made sure her seat belt was still securely fastened.

Breathe in, 1, 2, 3. Breathe out, 1, 2, 3, 4, 5.

Her hands were shaking. Her head was spinning, but she was okay.

As Holly became less panicked and reacquainted with her surroundings, she realized her jaw was sore, probably from grinding her teeth while she was in la la land. She swiped inside her mouth to investigate, in case there had been an unwanted extraction or her teeth had turned to corn. They hadn't.

She felt something moist on the side of her face. She wiped it. *Eww, drool.* Her nap breath and matted hair were not the features she wanted to lead with as Nik laid eyes on her for the first time in forever. She had freshening up to do. But first "Stunt Double" needed to land.

"We're starting our descent."

Oh, thank heavens this will be over soon.

Sudden turbulence sloshed Holly around. The last thing she needed was barf breath. She was glad Nik wouldn't be waiting on the runway. She would dash to the ladies' room in the terminal to work some magic before they collided curbside.

The plane bounced, braked, and screeched as the wheels met the pavement. Pilot and passenger breathed a sigh of relief.

"The good Lord got us here in one piece. Not exactly smoothly…but safely. I'm sure Ingrid's fervent prayers had a lot to do with it."

"Amen." Holly took a moment to collect herself before unbuckling and retrieving her suitcase.

"Since it's such a small airport, we'll deplane by one of these hangars and be escorted over to the entrance. I'm going to hitch a ride downtown and visit the old stomping grounds before turning in. The Rasmussens' receptionist booked me a room at the Bed & Breakfast. I'll head back to the Falls tomorrow morning. How about you? Is Nik picking you up from here?"

"I was about to text him and let him know we're here." Holly turned off airplane mode on her phone, and within seconds her notifications bombarded the screen.

"Would you look at that? It's been too long." Pastor Meyer

pointed out the window.

Holly peeled her eyes from her screen. The plane had stopped, and she could finally take in the sights without heaving her cupcakes...no, tossing her cookies. *Pesky idioms.*

She didn't say it out loud, but she wondered what pastor was impressed with. Their surroundings weren't much to write home about. She imagined the airport would be decked out in its Bavarian best, but it seemed pretty ordinary. Almost abandoned.

Soon she exited the plane. At last she could stretch her legs and capture a panoramic view of her destination to send to Nik, indicating she had arrived.

Holly looked to one side. A river. She looked to the other side. Green trees for miles and miles. She looked up. And that's when she saw. The sign that spelled it all out.

"Ft. Leavenworth, Kansas? Oh you've got to be kidding me!" Holly shrieked.

Pastor Meyer, who had been checking over "Stunt Double" hurried over to his distraught passenger, "What's wrong?"

"Where is the mountain? Where are the dirndls and lederhosen? Where's Nik?" She spun around, her luggage hitting her ankles. "This isn't another corny dream, this is a living nightmare."

Pastor Meyer's expression shifted from confusion to revelation, "Oh, Holly. I'm afraid there's been a big mistake. The receptionist at Doc Rasmussen's made the arrangements and I carefully followed the flight plan. It all happened so fast. I'm definitely familiar with the airfield here in Leavenworth. I could have flown here on auto pilot. But if I would have stopped to think about it instead of springing into action immediately, I might have realized it was strange that your boyfriend was meeting you here. I assumed you were meeting halfway between the Bavarian villages. But Leavenworth, Washington, and Leavenworth, Kansas, are quite different, aren't they? Although there's a lot more to this town than the prison. It's really quite charming."

"Why does this always happen to me?" Holly flopped her head against the plane, "Ouch. Hopefully there's good cell service so I can alert Nik. He's never going to believe this terrible mix-up. Oh dear, I *am* grateful, Pastor. I promise. You dropped everything to help me. But, this is not the first mix-up Nik and I have had. Now I'm the one on the receiving end of a costly, misguided assumption. I'm beginning to think our summer rendezvous is not meant to be." She blew her long bangs out of her face.

"I'm truly sorry. While we sort it out, maybe a cup 'o Chamomile will calm the nerves? There's a lovely tea house downtown."

"Pretty sure this calls for something stronger."

"I didn't stow any communion wine, but how about an espresso? My treat."

"I should be treating you."

"I insist."

"Then I won't argue."

Holly tried to call Nik but the cell service was spotty at the airfield. She'd try again soon.

"I bet there's a better signal downtown. Hang tight."

Pastor Meyer located the airfield's overseer and arranged for them to ride into Leavenworth. Holly tried texting Elaine and her mother to update them on her whereabouts and the terrible, horrible, no good, very bad reality of her situation. She knew she was being dramatic, and probably childish too, but the cocktail of her pounding headache, empty stomach, and displaced hope were the right blend of ingredients for a grown-up tantrum.

Holly resisted unleashing the full weight of her feelings due to present company–Pastor and a beefy military man who was blasting Taylor Swift's "Anti-Hero" from the radio of his Jeep. The men in the front seat swapped military stories as the backseat occupant fought her own battle.

Midwestern air met Holly's lungs through the Jeep's window. She shut her eyes and opened them, open and close, back and forth, like wipers trying to clear off unexpected bird poop that blocked the view. She repeated the action again, determined to reset her mindset. They whizzed past glimpses of beauty on their way to Leavenworth, Kansas.

The military man delivered his passengers in front of "English Roses Tea Room." Its striped awning, fragrant rose bushes, and bright red door were a sign of welcome to the weary travelers. Pastor Meyer held the door open and Holly wheeled her suitcase behind her. A dainty bell signaled their entry.

"Welcome, welcome. Please take a seat. Tea's a brewing and a fresh batch of cherry scones are in the oven." The hostess's greeting was a strange yet charming blend of Midwestern and British dialect. The hostess's shape, countenance, and hospitable nature resembled Neumann's store manager, Betty Jo and Mrs. Potts from "Beauty and the Beast." They both exuded comfort and joy. Holly could use a double shot of that about now. She needed to check on Betty Jo soon. First, she needed to let Nik know about the most unfortunate mix-up. Holly reached for her phone. *Dead battery.*

She could have used Pastor Meyer's phone except she didn't have Nik's number memorized. She retrieved her charger from her backpack and located an outlet. Her cell phone looked out of place in the stepped-inside-a-storybook ambiance of the tearoom.

Pastor Meyer pointed at his phone, "Looks like the cell service is better, I'm going to call Ingrid and let her know what happened. Pick out what you'd like. Could you order an Earl Gray, one cream, two sugars for me, please?"

Holly surveyed the tea flavors from her seat. A framed sign hung above the counter:

"Let your decorum rise to the dignity of the occasion."
-Mr. Earl M. Lawson, Civil Rights Leader and Principal at Lincoln School

After eight minutes of steeping, Holly lifted the delicate cup, filled with lavender honey tea, to her lips. She sipped instead of gulped. Her circumstances were as disheveled as her post-flight appearance. Yet she ordered her despair to stand down, in order for decorum to rise. Pastor Meyer and Betty Jo's long lost British twin looked on with concern.

She took her first bite of the fresh-from-the-oven cherry scone. It melted in her mouth, soothing her shaken nerves. The comfort food sparked a bit of joy within her as she recovered from the whiplash of the landing—the bounce, brake, and screech of well-laid plans being hijacked by circumstances out of her control.

Holly blotted the corners of her lips with an embroidered napkin, an attempt to act dignified amid present company and the tea room's Victorian aesthetic. But as she pushed in her chair and retrieved her phone, she had a hunch the facade would soon crack like her mom's fine china plate when her brother, Gabe, threw it to her like a frisbee and she didn't catch it.

The dainty bell signaled Holly's exit. She situated herself on a bench outside the tearoom. A slight breeze drew the raspberry scent of the rose bushes her way. Normally Holly would have grabbed her sketchbook to capture the elegant details of the blossoms, but she was on a mission.

Nik picked up on the second ring.

"Are you almost here, Beautiful?"

At the sound of his voice, she was verklempt. It was then she realized he wouldn't have been worried yet because her plane wasn't scheduled to arrive until later. Leavenworth, Kansas, was much closer to Bavarian Falls than Leavenworth, Washington. While she had been panicking, he'd been obliviously awaiting her arrival.

"Oh, Nik, I wish I was," her voice cracked.

"What's wrong? Are you okay?"

Holly sniffed her way through the whole ridiculous situation.

"Oh, Hol, I'm sorry. This stinks. How can I help?"

"Funny you should mention that as our IOU question for today is…drumroll please…how can I lighten your load?"

"Seriously? I'm beginning to think you're making up questions to fit what's currently happening in our lives."

"Oh, it gets weirder. Guess what yesterday's question was?"

"How do you fly to Leavenworth when your commercial flight is canceled due to wildfires?"

"Almost. It was 'what lights your fire'?

"No way."

"Eerie, right?"

"So…what lights my fire? Like I said, it was a controlled burn that started the fire over here. However, what started the fire of my affection for you was seeing you blazing mad in the theatre at Neumann's, accusing me of all sorts of nonsense."

"It all started with Leavenworth, didn't it?"

"You have boots on the ground in the very place where your dad worked and where our history began."

"And almost never had a future. Can you imagine if you had not ever cleared the air about my big ole' assumption that you were a dangerous criminal?"

"Hurry and answer so we can come up with a place to teleport you into my arms. There's not a blue phone booth nearby is there?"

"You are a strange one, Nik, and I adore you. What lights my fire is art, but presently I am failing to see the beauty in this mess. I guess that phrase could mean what makes you angry too, right?"

"Sure?"

"This Leavenworth is much more than I realized…charming, hospitable, a place we should come back to some time, but I'm also thoroughly annoyed that this accidental detour is keeping us apart longer. Why is us being together in person so difficult?"

"I think it shows how resilient we are. We haven't let the challenges of a long-distance relationship stop us. We're facing another obstacle, yet we have an opportunity to get creative and figure out a way to get you here, ASAP. I happen to be dating one of the most creative people I know, and since I usually approach things in a level-headed sort of way, together, we're a perfect match."

Holly's tense shoulders relaxed. They'd figure this out. Whether by train, plane, automobile—or teleport—she'd get to Leavenworth, eventually.

"You're good for me and good to me, Nik. You naturally see the positive side of things, and this moody artist has all the feels and sees the complexities. You often lighten my load, but I seem to add to yours." Holly fished for ChapStick in the top of her backpack.

"You're not a burden. Don't be so hard on yourself. You've overcome a lot and you're still standing. We're still standing. Come wildfire or misguided flight plans, we're going to be okay."

"How did I get so lucky? You are a patient man, Beckenbauer." She applied the vanilla-scented ChapStick to her dry lips.

"I'm going to make some calls and see what I can work out. You see what you can do and we'll touch base along the way. Hang on, I'm getting a call. She's called three times since we've been chatting. I better see what's up."

"Aunt Claire?"

"No, my coworker, Marina. Sorry, gotta go. I'll call you back."

At the mention of "her" name, Holly's stomach lurched. *Breathe in, 1, 2, 3. Breathe out, 1, 2, 3, 4, 5.*

CHAPTER TEN
What would a perfect day look like?

THE JINGLE FROM THE FRONT DOOR of English Roses interrupted Holly's mental tale spin. Pastor Meyer exited the charming establishment and sat down beside her on the bench.

Holly imagined he would start quoting Jeremiah 29:11 at any moment, "For I know the plans I have for you, plans to prosper you and not to harm you. Plans to give you a hope and a future…"

But he didn't.

"I'm sorry, Holly." Pastor Meyer adjusted his collar. "You've been through so much, and not only today. Are you okay?"

Hmm, which option should she go with?

Option A: I'm fine. This is simply a little detour, it'll all work out. You know what they say, "Everything happens for a reason." Or…

Option B: I'm so stinkin' mad I could spit, or scream bloody murder, or throat punch someone, then they'll lock me up in the slammer—right down the road—for killing, not punching or spitting. Or…

Option C: I'm not sure which way is up or what to do next. How am I supposed to get to Nik's Leavenworth before dark? Why does *everything* about our relationship feel hard lately?"

She went with the last option.

Pastor Meyer waited, giving her space and time to process.

"Okay…not *everything* is hard. But still…"

He listened some more.

"Did they teach you that in seminary?"

"What's that?"

"The power of pause?" Holly's counselor had also used this technique. What usually preceded the pause was Holly spilling her guts...or at the very least digging deeper into how she was *really* feeling.

Pastor Meyer smiled. He slowly rubbed his knees which were probably stiff from riding in in the tiny plane.

"Any advice?" Holly tapped her foot, keeping time as the seconds raced by.

"I've been thinking about that."

Think faster, think faster.

"I don't think I can get clearance to fly into Leavenworth, Washington, today, on such short notice, but I talked to Ingrid and she had an idea—"

"No offense, Pastor, but I don't want all of Bavarian Falls to know my business or pity me." She was certain Mrs. Meyer might leak Holly's debacle to the local paper or blast it on the church's social media account in an effort to "help" Holly out.

"Maybe we can get you another ticket—"

"With all due respect, did you see the size of that airport? I don't think anyone else has flown in there since..." Holly stood, trying to take charge of her nervous energy, "Besides, I hate to bother Mrs. Rasmussen after her generous gift."

"What do you mean?"

"Whoops, maybe I wasn't supposed to say anything. Although Mrs. R. usually does things with a lot of fanfare, so maybe she doesn't mind. She bought my ticket here. It was quite shocking actually, but..." Holly paced in front of the bench, her hands on her hips.

"Holly—" Pastor Meyer said.

"I mean I know she's loaded, so that part wasn't out of the

ordinary, but her thoughtfulness sure was. I mean she's not selfish, but she's busy, not a busy body exactly, but she doesn't seem real in tune with the plights of us common folk, with her full social calendar and charity work and all." Mid-pivot, Holly noticed the tea shop owner, Betty Jo's lookalike, not-so-discreetly watching her animated monologue from the picture window. Holly felt like she was back in Bavarian Falls with well-meaning but over-involved onlookers. She turned toward the pastor. "Mrs. Rasmussen didn't make me feel like a charity case with the ticket though. It kind of reminded me of the time when my co-worker, Andy, gifted..." Holly would have continued her verbal processing, except the way pastor had his head cocked and kept opening and closing his mouth as if to speak but didn't, stopped her.

"The ticket, you say?" He stood.

"Yeah. my airfare to Leavenworth was completely paid for by—"

"My wife." Pastor Meyer said softly.

Holly sat down.

Pastor Meyer explained how his wife had overheard Holly talking to Mrs. Rasmussen at the community center, about how Holly could not afford airfare to Leavenworth.

"It brought her such joy to help you out. She had extra money saved up from her craft shows. She didn't want anyone to know about the ticket, but here we are."

"I had no idea." Holly scratched the base of her neck, trying to rid herself of the heap of guilt she was feeling from years of misjudging the pastor's wife.

"I have an idea. It's quite different from the one my wife had. Hers involved you on a cross-country trip with her cousin Wilma. Apparently, Wilma and her family are driving their

Winnebago from Tulsa to the West Coast for a camping trip and they could probably squeeze you in. It wouldn't get you there very fast and I'm pretty sure if would be reminiscent of the experience Kevin McAllister's mother had while riding in the back of the moving truck with a polka band in the first *Home Alone* movie. If it's okay with you, I'd like to pursue my idea and see if it'll pan out." Pastor Meyer reached for his phone, "I can assure you that it would get you there much faster than cousin Wilma's Winnebago. I can't really share many of the details because it's classified, and I need more time to try and pull it off. Can we meet back here in forty minutes?"

"Why not?" Holly shrugged.

She wished she could hear the idea first but what choice did she have? Pastor seemed fairly confident about whatever his mysterious plan was, and Holly hadn't thought of any viable solutions yet. Time was ticking away. She prayed Pastor would be successful in his endeavor. He had it in good with the Big Guy upstairs, so if anyone had a shot at phoning in a last-minute miracle, it was him.

While Pastor Meyer was occupied, Holly called her mother to update her on her predicament. She shared enough details to be truthful but painted the situation as positively as possible. It wasn't easy to spruce up her not-so-jolly reality. "Hey, Mom, my flight ended up in the wrong state and I have no real plan of how to get out of here, outside of Pastor working on some sort of solution he can't disclose."

Holly was hard enough on herself, she couldn't stomach a well-intended but cutting, "You know dear, if you had just done x,y,z, this might not have happened. Grandma Bea always said, 'If you fail to plan you plan to fail.'"

For most of her life Holly had longed for approval from her mother, as she was. But "as she was" hadn't seemed to match the color palette her mother envisioned for her. Holly colored outside the lines that had been drawn for her, not out of spite but because she had a sense there was more out there. Like a tune you can barely decipher on a gentle breeze, but swear you can hear as it dances past, Holly felt pulled toward "out there." Her senses were attuned to things others missed. The hint of a smile, the delicate veining on a violet leaf, the split-second flicker of disappointment from Elaine when Holly told her she was going to Leavenworth after all. And, sometimes, there were things she missed that others saw clearly. There was a lineup of embarrassing misunderstandings to serve as proof.

Thankfully, over the last year or so Holly and her mother had gained ground, discovering how to navigate their adult relationship with more sensitivity and mutual respect. While they had not gone to counseling together, they'd gone individually, and it had helped. The greatest breakthrough happened when Holly was able to shift her perspective from herself and try to see things through her mother's lens.

Holly used to hear only criticism from her mom. She now could, usually, interpret her mother's words as care, even if the method of delivery could use improvement. While on the phone, when her mom began to lecture and stopped, Holly could appreciate she was trying to change, instead of being annoyed she wasn't totally there yet. Holly was well acquainted with the feeling of "not yet arrived," in life and in this moment.

"If anyone can turn this around it's Pastor Meyer." Holly's mother assured her.

"Agreed." Holly walked slowly down the sidewalk, away from English Roses, lugging her suitcase with the squeaky wheel behind her.

"Is there anything you need? Do you want me to send money? You can pay me back whenever."

"That's kind, Mom. But you guys recently funded that big landscape project at your house. It'll work out somehow."

Holly and her mom had come a long way, but she still didn't find it easy to accept financial help from her mother. It made her feel fifteen again. The thought that she *should* get a job that paid more nagged her once more. A regular job felt like a life sentence to boredom and dissatisfaction. However, feeling needy and dependent on others to figure out a solution to her problem wasn't great either.

Holly wrapped up the short phone call with her mom.

Why hadn't Nik texted or called back yet? She commanded her runaway thoughts to behave themselves as she breathed in the humid Kansas air. She swallowed in an attempt to lubricate her dry throat.

While she waited to meet back up with Pastor Meyer, she texted back and forth with Elaine, who was at the community center getting ready for a basketball game. Holly filled her in on the crazy ordeal and mentioned how the IOU questions were eerily paralleling her circumstances.

Those twenty questions did work wonders for Cash and Everleigh Rae. Elaine texted.

But they seem to be driving Nik and I further apart...literally.

What's the question for today?

I haven't looked yet. Hang on...

Holly stopped walking. Holding her phone under her chin, she fished in her suitcase for the jar she was beginning to loathe.

You still there? Sorry, but gotta go soon, the guys just showed up.

Holly resisted the urge to ask if Frank or Andy were among "the guys."

Maybe I spoke too soon. This question is the exact opposite of what's happening right now.

Spill it.

It says, "What would a perfect day look like?" Definitely not like this. How cruel.

Hang in there, Brigham. This little exercise is bound to work. I know your life isn't a movie script or anything, but I believe you'll get to Nik one way or another. You might even laugh about this wild adventure one day. Don't hate me but even this plot twist has a bit of a romantic flair.

Typing, erasing, typing, erasing...

Too far?

You're lucky our friendship is strong enough for your tireless optimism.

Keep me posted on Pastor's plan?

I might have to kill you first.

Careful...you'll be charged with motive when they confiscate your phone for evidence. ;-)

I won't have to go far, slammer's right down the road. Kidding/not kidding. It actually is a sweet little town. I'll have to ask Dad more about living here when I get back.

You're a champ, talk soon?

Hopefully I'll be teleported to Washington within the hour.

Holly ducked into a local grocery store to get out of the heat. She refreshed her text messages. No word from Nik. She'd give him ten more minutes before reaching out. A blast of air conditioning coursed through her. She had a moment to think as she meandered past pints of ice cream and boxes of popsicles chilling in glassed coolers.

What would a perfect day look like?

If she was in Leavenworth, Washington, it might look like the postcard Nik had sent her in the first month of their relationship. A hot air balloon floating over an untamed landscape, at sunset, graced the front. Rich orange, deep navy, and evergreen were contrasted by bright linen clouds that served as a textured canvas. It seemed like the perfect way to spend the day, experiencing Leavenworth from a bird's eye view. Oh the art it would inspire, being privy to God's meticulous handiwork, from above the treetops. On the reverse side, Nik's messy script had made her heart soar:

Dear Holly:
This scene reminded me of you…and your art. Breathtaking. And no, not breathtaking because of the altitude. You help me see the world from a different angle, Brigham. There's no one else like you. How'd I get so lucky?
I know it stinks that we're separated by many miles now, but not always.
Yours,
Nik

But not always. Except they still were…far apart.

Holly was eye level with a pint of pineapple sorbet that was calling her name when her phone rang. It wasn't Nik.

"Hey, Holly, do you have a few minutes?" Holly's sister-in-law, Monica, was on the other end of the line.

Holly assumed her mother had spread her bad news to her brother, Gabe, and his family.

"Thanks for trying to call the other day. I wasn't up to answering." Monica said.

Holly waited. Maybe Monica didn't know…yet.

"There's no obligation to call me back. Take all the time you need…" Holly's voice trailed off.

"Thank you. I'm not used to these emotional swings. They come out of nowhere and about knock me off my feet. The hardest part is Claudia. She keeps asking where her sister is hiding. The other night we watched the second Mary Poppins movie, I sobbed into my throw pillow as soon as "The Place Where the Lost Things Go" song started. It practically, perfectly, unpacks the ache of this loss. Gabe tried to shield Claudia from my weeping, to protect her. But I'm not sure if it's protecting her or making it worse? There's no manual for grief."

"I'm so sorry, sis." Holly suddenly felt chilled. She left the freezer section and walked toward the canned goods.

"I think Claudia's too young to understand the song's lyrics and how they help explain the complexities of loss. I wish there was a resource tailored to her, to help her navigate her confusion about losing a sibling before she even met them."

Holly waited instead of filling the pause, as Pastor Meyer had for her.

"I'm scared to try again. Can my heart handle another loss? Maybe we shouldn't try anymore? Maybe Gabe should go in for the procedure, so I don't have to worry about the possibility. Is that terrible of me?"

"Monica, I'm not one for unsolicited advice. In fact I'm not a fan at all. But…"

"It's okay. Go ahead." Monica's voice whispered, unevenly.

"Could you wait a little longer before deciding anything permanent? Again, I don't know what it's like. But what if you wait?"

"Yeah..." Monica breathed in sharply. "I think I can...somehow. There's a support group Gabe found online. It's in the next town. I haven't wanted to go, but maybe I could. We'll see. I'm so tired."

"You're so brave, Monica."

Silence on the other end of the line.

"Is Claudia there? You okay if I check in with her?"

"Of course, give me a sec. Thanks for taking my call, especially with the time change. You're supposed to be enjoying your man, not taking calls from your weepy sister-in-law."

Holly didn't have the heart to tell Monica about her dashed plans.

"You're not an interruption, you're family."

"Thanks...here's Claudia."

"Auntie Holly! I miss you, I love you. I miss you. I love you. Are you back from your trip?"

For the next five minutes Holly's boisterous niece filled her in on her summer. Toward the end of her non-stop commentary Claudia asked this question, "Aunt Holly, do you think God is mad at me?"

"Oh, honey, why would you say that?"

"I prayed and prayed to be a big sister. And God answered my prayer, but only for a little bit. Maybe I didn't pray loudly enough? I used to pray when I took baths 'cuz my voice is real loud in there. Anyway, it seems like God changed his mind 'cuz Mom said the baby isn't coming anymore. I'm afraid it's my fault. Maybe I was too loud and bossy? I think I said please, but maybe I didn't?"

"Claudi-boo, I wish I knew why. But I don't. There's one thing I am sure of though, God didn't allow this because He's mad at you."

"How do you know though? Did He tell you?" Claudia's raspy voice lowered.

"Not exactly, but that's not how He rolls."

"He rolls?" Claudia rasped.

Holly and her squeaky suitcase neared an end cap shelf that housed local jams and jellies. She proceeded carefully, around the glass jars and her present conversation.

"Let me say it this way…there are many things in this life that don't seem to make any sense. But I've lived long enough to know God's ways often don't make sense to us, and sometimes life really hurts. But He specializes in making a way to help us, even when things look weird and feel like we might break into tiny bits of glass."

No words but noisy breathing was Claudia's reply.

"Can you trust me on this, Claudia Ann?"

"I'll try, but you might have to tell me again so I understand it a little better? It's time for my favorite show now. Bye. I love you, auntie!"

"Oh, I love you so much, sweet girl."

Claudia hung up.

After purchasing a bottled water, Holly left the store.

A wall of hot Kansas air met her as she trudged back to her meeting spot with Pastor. Holly's head and heart felt jumbled, but she didn't have time to process her conversation with her niece quite yet. She put a pin in her swirling thoughts, reminding herself to revisit the wisp of an idea that was forming.

She took a drink of crisp water before calling Nik.

Just then, a video call came through. Was this Grand Central station or small town USA? Holly ducked under an awning to shield her screen from the blazing sun.

She expected to see Nik on the other end, but it was a

weathered nostril instead.

"Hulllooo, Holly dear, are you there?" The caller's sing-song voice could not be mistaken for anyone else but Betty Jo. The woman, the myth, the legend.

"Yes, it's me."

Betty's Jo's nostril disappeared and her earlobe, complete with Christmas bell earrings, took center stage on Holly's phone screen.

"Um, Betty Jo, this is a video call not a phone call."

"Oh, dear, I do that all the time. Silly me. Let me get straightened out."

Rustle, thump. The phone, now on the floor, faced the ceiling of Neumann's and its rafters packed with Christmas lights and life-sized snowman, reindeer, and Nativity characters.

"Here you go Ms. Wilson," a familiar voice offered to help. "Holly Noel, always a vision of loveliness. Leavenworth looks good on you, my friend." Frank appeared on the screen, waving enthusiastically.

"Hey, Frank. I'll have Betty Jo fill you in later. I need to go soon, can you put her on please?"

"Anything for you, little darling," Frank drawled, tipping an imaginary hat her way.

"Sorry about the mix-up." Betty Jo snorted, her full face now in view.

"You have no idea," Holly said.

Before Holly had time to explain her plight, Betty Jo slipped into a supply closet and shut the door behind her. Everything went black until a single light bulb appeared over her head.

"Holly, I don't have much time. It's quite risky to call you from work, but I wanted you to know the latest development about Operation Retire...." Betty Jo looked behind her at the closed door then looked back. Her nostril was back, front and center, as she apparently leaned in closer to the screen. "I better call it Operation Sleigh Ride instead, in case Frank or his granddad have this place bugged."

"You never know," Holly whispered.

A few locals passed by Holly, smiling in a way that communicated, "You're welcome here, but we know you're not from here. Plus, we're really curious what you're up to."

Under the awning, Holly leaned against the cool brick wall, to blend in and cool off. No matter where she was, even here in Leavenworth, Kansas, the larger-than-life characters from Bavarian Fall, and their stories, found her.

"Here's the scoop…" Betty Jo said.

After Holly had heard the latest development about Operation Sleigh Ride and chugged the rest of her water, it was time to meet Pastor Meyer.

She called Nik as she walked. She should have asked if she could leave her suitcase at the tea house before traipsing around town.

"Sorry I didn't mean to leave you hanging. You okay?" Nik didn't sound out of breath, like she did, but he did sound concerned.

"I'm okay. You? Big crisis at work?" Holly asked gingerly, not trusting her foggy brain to send polite and pleasant words out of her mouth and into his ear.

"Not a crisis, no, but something pressing. I won't bore you with the details. We need to come up with a plan to get you here, ASAP."

Holly closed her mouth before saying, "You didn't take any of the last forty minutes to come up with a plan to help your girlfriend get to you?" Instead, she tried humor, so she wouldn't cry, or yell.

"Unfortunately, there are no donkeys or camels to bring me over. A train might be possible, but it takes days and waiting one more second feels too long. If Pastor Meyer's secret plan doesn't pan out there may be an option to hitch a ride with a relative of theirs...but that won't get me there soon enough."

Holly proceeded to tell Nik what she knew of Pastor's plan, which was basically nothing.

"I'm about to meet him now. I'll call again when I know more. But before I go, you'll never believe what today's question is."

"Wait, let me guess...it's something like, 'How do you prefer to travel cross country?'"

"Definitely not with cousin Wilma in a Winnebago." Holly tugged her staircase over an uneven section of sidewalk.

"Definitely not."

"But maybe by hot air balloon."

"That might be slowest of all...besides walking or riding a tandem." Nik said.

"It's that postcard you sent me early on. But you're right that wouldn't be much fun without you in the basket with me."

"You want me to ride in the basket of a bicycle built for two?"

"No, Nik. The basket of the hot air balloon."

"Gotcha. I'd choose a motorcycle with a side car for you, if you're nice."

"So generous of you."

"I'm teasing. You can wrap your arms around me and hold on for dear life."

"You won't let me drive?" Holly challenged.

"We'll see," Nik's voice lifted.

Holly repositioned her grip on her phone. She should have gotten her AirPods out long ago. Her out-of-sorts circumstances and the heat of the day weren't helping her think clearly.

"That wasn't really the question for today, was it?"

"No, it was, 'What would the perfect day look like?' But a hot air balloon ride near the mountains could be a part of mine."

"Like that post card I sent you?"

"Exactly. How about you?"

"It's definitely not talking on the phone with you—"

"Hey, now."

"Let me finish, please…I was going to say…it wouldn't be a perfect day only talking on the phone when we could be together in person, instead."

"Yeah, like we planned, and it all fell apart. Let's pray Pastor's plan works."

"Amen." Nik said.

"I call you when I know more."

"It won't always be like this." Nik said tenderly.

Holly imagined the feel of his breath on her ear. She closed her eyes.

"I'm counting on that." Holly whispered back.

"Talk soon?"

"Soon."

CHAPTER ELEVEN
What do you run to?

HOLLY DID NOT HITCH A RIDE on Santa's sleigh in order to land in Leavenworth, Washington, before dark. But Pastor Meyer had made an unconventional arrangement for her to arrive in haste, special thanks to the beefy military man who had driven them to town earlier in the day. Apparently, the military owed Pastor Meyer a favor, so he called it in. Before Holly knew it she was signing paperwork, including a disclosure policy, and being escorted onto a plane that didn't usually transport civilians.

It all happened so fast Holly barely had time call Nik back. Her call went straight to voicemail.

"Hi, Nik, can't say much over the phone, or much at all, but I'm on my way to you. I'll arrive fast and furious. I mean I won't be furious, I'll be ecstatic. I meant I'll be there soon. I'm rambling, sorry. For a minute I thought they were going to blindfold me, but I signed official-looking paperwork, so I won't reveal any of their secrets. Not necessarily my forte, but I really have no choice. Shoot! My message is going to cut off if I don't hurry. Can you meet me at the airport at 7:15pm your time? I should have started with that part. I hope you get this. I can't wait to see you. Soon."

Holly hung up.

The plane's massive engine roared.

"Ready, missy?" Beefy military man shouted.

Holly hugged Pastor Meyer before boarding, "Thank you for making a way. This is above and beyond anything I could ever imagine!"

"The Big Guy specializes in this kind of thing." He smiled.

"Who him?" Holly pointed to her burly escort.

"No, Him." Pastor Meyer pointed heavenward.

Holly grinned. She followed lower case 'big guy' up the massive ramp.

She was the only passenger of her kind...the only disheveled one, the only one not in uniform. Although her holey jean shorts, and buttery-soft tee were basically her uniform for the summer.

Holly carefully listened to the take-off instructions she was given by her traveling companion. She didn't dare tune out. She'd been given expedited clearance to ride along on a supply delivery. However, Holly was not privy to what exactly was being transported.

Before her suitcase was stowed, Holly peeked at the next IOU question coming up, "What do you run to?" As her escort and his small, uniformed crew were occupied with official looking pre-flight checks and cross-checks, she pondered the question.

Holly often ran to wrongful assumptions and worst-case scenarios. It was her default, yet she knew it was about as unbecoming as the mustard yellow, polka-dotted one piece—two sizes too small but on sale—that she had tried to squeeze into in the dressing room last week. She'd nearly split the seam in two.

When faced with inconveniences Holly wanted to rely more on her imagination than her irritation. She wanted to think differently, from the get-go. In the face of adversity, she wanted to be found more flexible, less doomsday. More Amelia Earhart, less Debbie Downer. Never would she have imagined her transport to Leavenworth would be this. Never would she have imagined she'd be gifted a second airfare. Never would she have dreamed that she'd be headed down the runway in this monstrosity.

"What do I run to?" Holly thought back on her life. In some ways, she ran away to art school when she graduated high school. Running away from the pain of home but lugging the baggage around with her just the same. She ran to the city after art school, in order to prove herself as she fought to open up a community art space. She did not run home to Bavarian Falls after her failure in the city, but she reluctantly returned, personalizing ornaments at Neumann's over the holidays.

After Holly had made up her mind to give it a try, she had run into her role as the founder and facilitator of the Heart Turn program. She and Nik did not exactly run into each other's arms immediately after his breakup with Lena, although it depends on who you ask. But they'd walked into a committed relationship over time, giving each other space to be sure this was the next right step and not a rebound move after Nik's breakup with Lena.

Holly wanted to be the type of person who ran more. Like literally, so she might be able to wear a one-size smaller bathing suit. But nothing too drastic, maybe a light jog here and there. She wasn't signing up for a marathon. She liked to look cute, but she had never been too wrapped up in her appearance. However, she wouldn't mind feeling a bit more confident at the beach. Maybe feeling more confident at the beach had more to do with her mindset than her suit size?

Holly wanted to point herself toward possibilities instead of predictable routines. To dare to dream again, like she did when she originally envisioned the community art space in the city. She wanted to resist getting tripped up by the practical and go for whatever was on the horizon.

The barge of a plane lurched forward. Holly was instructed to fasten her harness, not seatbelt. She closed her eyes tight, holding on for dear life.

The rest is classified.

Several hours later, a little before 7pm Pacific time, Holly was nudged awake.

"Stuart Mountain range, ma'am." Military man lifted the cargo net, revealing the window behind it. Light hit Holly. She gasped, then blinked.

Once her eyes had adjusted to the stark contrast, she surveyed the panoramic scene beneath her. A speck of an aquamarine lake, framed by evergreens and surrounded by mountain peaks jutting into the sky. There was a haze of smoke in the distance. According to her escort the wildfire was under control now and since the wind had changed, the air quality had greatly improved in the last few hours.

"If I had my binoculars, you might even be able to spot a mountain goat."

Holly pressed her nose against the window. "We're definitely not in Kansas anymore," she whispered. She was grateful there were a few more hours of sunlight left in the day, to gawk at the glorious scenery.

The bird's-eye view of the untamed landscape was overwhelming to Holly's senses in the best kind of way. No snapshot would do it justice. This beauty was meant to be experienced not exploited. She wished Nik were here with her.

Military man cleared his throat. Holly reluctantly turned from the majestic scenery to her uniformed companion. "Thank you, not only for the view, but for the ride here. I hope it wasn't too much trouble."

"Sounds like your pastor friend has some strong connections. Glad we could help." He nodded. "Now sit tight, we're about to land." He replaced the cargo net over the window and instructed Holly to put her chest harness back on.

Holly was relieved they weren't parachuting out. What an

entrance that would have made. Her ears popped during their descent from the altitude shift.

About ten minutes later, the sky chariot touched down with a mighty thud.

"One of our locals will give you a lift over to the main building." Military man unstrapped her suitcase and handed it to her. "Take care now."

"Thank you, you too." Holly cringed at her automatic reply, guessing the man before her was more than capable of taking care of himself and probably a few hundred troops too.

Holly headed down the ramp toward the vehicle waiting for her. The driver of a coyote-tan transport held out his credential badge. He led her to the passenger door and opened it. She slid into the seat. Her suitcase was secured in the back. Soon the vehicle raced toward the airport, Holly's hair flailing wildly. The toil of travel collided with the mountain air. Holly's imagination revved, blurring the lines between fact and fiction. She felt like the main character in a summer blockbuster. She resisted the urge to look back at the monster of a plane she had exited, in case it exploded with a blast while she was being whisked away from it.

Holly arrived safely at the main building of the airport. Despite her windblown hair and the fuzzy feel of her teeth, she grinned. Alpine-style architecture greeted her as rows of red, pink, and purple geraniums hung from the multi-level structure. A brightly colored "Willkommen to Leavenworth" banner flapped in the mountain air.

At last.

Her driver parked the vehicle, retrieved Holly's belongings, and led her to a side door. He swiped his badge, buzzing her in. He pointed her in the direction of the "damentoilette" (women's bathroom) and then he left. Holly climbed the stairs, her squeaky suitcase bumping behind her. Out of breath, she reached the upper level of the airport. According to the life-sized coo-coo clock overhead, it was 7:00pm on the dot. She had fifteen minutes to work some magic before her long-awaited reunion with Nik.

After her hair, face, and teeth were freshened, Holly took a moment to collect her thoughts after the tornado of a day. It was then she remembered to take her phone off airplane mode.

She scanned her screen for notifications.

Elaine: **Still in Kansas, Dorothy? Lemme know.**

Pastor Meyer: **I'm confident you arrived safe and sound. Enjoy your trip.**

Monica: **Thanks for talking to Claudia. She adores you. Tell Nik we said hi.**

Mom: **Give me an update when you can. My offer for the loan still stands.**

Nik: **Your cryptic voicemail sounded like you've either been kidnapped or rescued by a good Samaritan with a private jet. I'm hoping it was the latter. I'll meet you at 7:15 in the airport, by the alphorns.**

Holly made her way through the airport. She caught a glimpse of a floor-to-ceiling mural of a mountain scene. A painted waterfall came to life as real water misted from it. Tourists posed in front of the idyllic scene, as if they'd recently finished a high-altitude hike. One mother, whose family wore neon green t-shirts that said, "Leavenworth or Bust!" tried yodeling to get her less-than-enthusiastic family to smile for the group photo.

Holly kept moving, avoiding the mist and yodeling. She responded to the texts as she walked, trying to look at her phone screen and pay attention to where she was going.

To Elaine: **I'm over the rainbow...in Leavenworth, WA. More later!**

To Pastor Meyer: **Safe and sound. You're a saint! Thanks so very much for everything!**

To Monica: I have an idea brewing that might help our sweet Claudia, but I need time to think on it more. Love you all.

To Mom: It's a long story, but don't worry, pastor helped me get to Leavenworth and it didn't cost me anything. I meet Nik soon. Give Dad a hug for me.

To Nik: Leave the ransom money at home, your second guess was warmer. Not sure what alphorns are but I'll figure it out and meet you there.

Holly passed the Bavarian-themed food court, the savory aroma of sage and sauerkraut making her feel right at home. She thought she heard someone call her name. Holly whipped around, scanning the crowd for Nik. She walked backwards as she craned her neck. A blast of a brass-sounding instrument sounded as Holly felt her foot catch on something behind her. She started to fall, her suitcase rolling toward her.

"Help!"

Two strong hands reached out, blocking her fall.

It wasn't the first time Nik had caught her. Her heart raced from her near spill and because she was about to see Nik in the flesh again. Holly turned to greet and thank her man, who was still holding her up.

"Oh my! What? Who are you?" Holly yelped as she came face to face with an older gentleman dressed in Alpine garb. Good thing Holly had waited before planting a kiss on the man who had stopped her fall.

"One of the airport alphorn players, my lady. You tripped over the end of my buddy's horn, and I rushed in to help. Sorry if I startled you."

Holly took in the strange looking instruments, and the costumed men lined up, staring at her. "So that's what they look like."

"Eleven feet in length and made of spruce. No valves and it takes an immense amount of lung capacity to play these." The gentleman tipped his hat again to Holly. "I hope you enjoy your stay here in Washington's Bavarian Village."

"Thank you. Sorry I screamed. I was expecting someone else. I hope I didn't damage your friend's instrument."

"Don't worry about that. It's not the first time, and it won't be the last."

The man returned to the lineup of alphorns and joined in playing a festive sounding tune.

Apparently no damage was done.

Holly listened for a moment as she regrouped.

"Already causing a stir in Leavenworth, I see." A familiar voice called out behind her.

Holly spun around, dropped her suitcase, and ran into Nik's arms.

Time seemed to stand still.

She breathed in Nik's cedar spice cologne as he held her. She melted into his embrace.

"I can feel your heart pounding," Nik whispered.

"It's probably going to beat right out of my chest. I'm so excited to see you," Holly whispered back.

Nik leaned in closer. "I've been dying to kiss you, but can we wait until we don't have an audience?" He rubbed his fingers gently along the back of her buttery soft shirt, sending shivers up her spine.

"Definitely. But not too long, right?" Holly asked, her voice husky.

The band of alphorns crescendoed.

"Hungry?" Nik shouted.

"Starved!" Holly yelled back.

"I know just the place. Follow me."

CHAPTER TWELVE
What is my best feature?

ON THE SHORT DRIVE FROM THE airport to downtown, Holly filled Nik in—on what she was allowed to disclose—about her most unusual transport from Kanas to Washington.

"God works in mysterious ways," Nik shook his head.

"Right? I felt like Carmen Sandiego, being whisked off on a secret mission to a remote location to recover something stolen."

"Is this where I say…my heart?" Nik smiled.

"That works," Holly laughed.

They followed the Wenatchee River along Highway 2 and rounded a bend.

"Mood music, my lady?" Nik changed the radio channel to a station that played continuous German-band music.

Holly let out an involuntary squeal when she first saw it. Downtown Leavenworth was straight out of a storybook.

"Oh, Nik, it's darling."

"Is this where I say…no, you are?"

"Something like that."

Holly felt like a kid on Christmas morning, taking in the wonder of the toy-like village before her. She half-expected to see Hansel and Gretel skipping out of the faux candy-lined bakery with "Ginger's Cookies in a Snap" signage above the door.

Nik pulled forward, pointing out his favorite features of town.

"I realize this kind of thing isn't exactly new to you, Ms. Bavarian Falls."

"We definitely don't have mountains in Michigan…there's something special about this slice of paradise."

"Who me?" Nik laughed.

"Exactly." Holly leaned over to see out his window.

The white stucco buildings, contrasted by deep chocolate trim, boasted wooden balconies lined with overflowing flower boxes. Holly knew the rooflines by heart at home, but Leavenworth was new and exciting. Nik couldn't drive slow enough for her to soak it all in. The arched walkways, recessed windows, and colorful shutters were the backdrop of fairy tales. Time would tell if their storyline would be more Brothers Grimm or Hans Christian Andersen. For now, they were on the pages where you get to know the characters better and aren't yet anticipating looming peril.

Holly's stomach growled. Her body clock was still on Eastern time. She felt hungrier than a wolf. Beefy military man hadn't offered her any in-flight snacks and her scone from English Roses had been enjoyed and digested, long ago and far away.

"Contrary to the fit I threw when I moved back to Bavarian Falls to regroup as an adult, I liked its charming quality growing up. It sparked lots of creative play. You should have seen young Elaine and me prancing around the park in our jewel-toned dirndls, pretending we had discovered a lost treasure of gold in the not-so-deep waters of the fountain. But as I grew, my vivid imagination felt trapped by the smallness of my hometown. What started out as just right, became too small. What once felt comforting, felt confining."

"Now?" Nik applied the brake at the town's main stoplight.

"Bavarian Falls hasn't gotten any bigger, but it no longer feels like a cage, like it did when I was a teen. More like a fence…where I can come and go, stay or leave, and always feel welcome."

"I hope you like it here, as well. I've yet to get bored with the view."

"I don't see how anyone could. It's spectacular. I know Leavenworth is no metropolis, but the sky looks higher out here. Like there's no cap. Just space to explore, to wander…"

"And kiss under the stars?" The light turned green, and Nik rolled through the intersection.

"We're waiting until then?" Holly plopped her head against the seat. They were hours away from nightfall.

"Not a chance. But first…dinner." Nik grabbed the steering wheel to turn into a newly vacant parking space.

Nik escorted Holly into the bustling restaurant. Murals of German merriment graced the walls. Their table for two was tucked away in a dimly lit wooden alcove, in the far corner of the dining room.

They caught up on small talk, updating one another on the rising and falling action of the supporting characters in their family, work, friends. After that was out of the way and they were partway through their meal, Holly said, "I have a confession." With her napkin, she discreetly wiped off what was left of her lipstick, anticipating a future event.

"Oh yeah? Should I be worried? Or upset?" Nik took a swig of his beverage.

"You be the judge." Holly scooted her chair closer to the table. "I peeked at the next IOU question and prepared my answer already. Lame, I know. But it was a rough travel day and…now I'm making excuses."

"What you are saying is I should be the keeper of the questions from here on out?"

"I don't think that will be necessary." Holly reached for her third glass of iced water. Her cross country travels had left her parched.

"What was the question?" Nik lifted his fork to his mouth

and took a bite of his entrée.

Holly retrieved the folded piece of paper from her back pocket and slid it over to Nik, past her plate of half-devoured Schnitzel Cordon Bleu on Spätzle noodles and toward his plate of Bavarian Beef Goulash.

"What do you run to?" Holly recited as Nik silently read the words.

"I'm not always successful, but I try to run toward hope."

"Another co-worker I haven't heard about?" Holly teased.

Nik frowned.

"Kidding." Holly raised her hands in surrender.

Nik took another bite. Holly followed suit, so she didn't say anything else stupid. The breaded chicken and creamy Swiss cheese hit the spot.

After a few moments, Holly said, "That is true of you. You tend to look for the best in people and remain optimistic, even when things are tough."

"Why, thank you." Nik's canvased shoe tapped Holly's sandaled toes under the table.

"I, on the other hand, tend to see this." She held out her half-empty glass of water.

"I see what you did there." Nik laughed.

"Gosh, this is nice. Being on a date, not having to stare at you through a screen or glue my ear to the phone or peck out my affections through text."

"It's my favorite when you don't check autocorrect first." Nik winked.

"Hey, it happens to everyone right?"

"If you say so. Now, since you've had more time to prepare your answer, what do you run to, Holly Noel?"

Holly shared her thoughts with Nik about how she had run

away from pain and run toward art. She recounted her journey over the years of running from and running to.

Nik leaned his forearms on the table. His shoes moved toward hers again. Mid-sentence he playfully kicked off her sandal.

"You're making it hard to think clearly."

"Am I?" Nik smiled, reaching for her hands across the table. She willingly offered them.

"As I was saying...art is a refuge of sorts. Not the ultimate refuge, of course, but like a strong branch of an oak tree that shades you in the heat of summer, or the crisp waters of a river after a challenging hike. When I can't make sense of it all, I make a beeline toward my paints, trying to communicate what I can't express with words but can feel my way through and process on the page."

"And I love..." Nik squeezed her hands.

Is he going to say it at last? The three words I've been dying to hear and respond to.

"...that about you."

Holly bit her tongue. Thankful she had not automatically replied to what she thought he was going to say.

"We've got to make up for lost time. What's the next question?" Nik let go of Holly's hands as he reached for his fork and took another bite of goulash.

Holly retrieved the decorated jar from her bag. "I made you one too but I accidentally left it at home in the rush to get here. We'll have to share."

Nik shook the slips of paper toward the rim of the Mason jar. He retrieved one of the questions from the top. He opened it slowly.

Holly couldn't believe she was actually here, sitting across from her boyfriend at dinner, enjoying German comfort food and each other's company. This was the first of a summer full of dates. All around them tourists laughed and talked, while a few toddlers ran around as frazzled parents tried to wrangle them. Servers dressed in Bavarian garb meandered through the crowded dining room, refilling water and removing empty plates. Holly's gaze returned to the man she called hers. How did she get so lucky?

Nik had yet to read the question out loud. He raised his eyebrows and tipped his head to the side and waited…and waited.

"Come on, what does it say?" Holly blurted, offering a gentle tap to his shin, under the table.

Nik closed the paper in two and stuffed it in his pocket. "I'll tell you what. Let's save this one for an after-dinner walk. I'd like to answer this one elsewhere, where it's not so noisy. You ready?"

"Sure, let me run to the ladies' room first." Holly wanted to freshen her breath, plus her rehydration efforts were quickly catching up with her.

Never had Holly imagined she and Nik wouldn't have enjoyed several tender, or passionate, kisses yet. So much build up toward their reunion. And now? Was he stalling or trying to savor each moment together?

Upon exiting the bathroom, she popped a mint in her mouth, choosing to walk by faith and not by sight.

Holly, the tourist, was led by Nik, the local, down the sidewalks of the quaint village, her arm tucked in his. As the sun began to set, they strolled past shops, restaurants, and the local Nutcracker museum.

"The office is closed until Monday, but hopefully you can come meet my co-workers over lunch, early next week. I don't have to work this weekend, thankfully, so I thought we could explore a few of the gems this area has to offer. We won't try a big hike yet. You might need to rest more for that."

"Are you calling me out of shape?" Holly huffed, lightheartedly.

"Not at all, but the hike I have planned takes stamina." He pointed toward the mountain range in the distance.

"I'm choosing to believe you're simply being thoughtful in delaying our hike, due to the fact that I've had the longest and strangest travel day and need a good sleep." Holly gave him a playful jab with her elbow.

"Exactly," Nik led her toward a bench near the gazebo in the town plaza.

"That was the shortest walk ever. I think you underestimate me."

"Don't worry, our hike won't be short, but this IOU question is burning a hole in my pocket."

"You'd prefer to stare into each other's eyes while we answer the question instead of trying to navigate the crowded sidewalks while simultaneously pouring our hearts out to each other?"

"Something like that." Nik retrieved the day's question, before joining Holly on the bench. "What's my best feature?" He handed her the slip of paper. Holly slipped it into her pocket.

"That's an easy one. It's your steely blue eyes. I'll never forget the first time I saw them—at church of all places. There you were, being introduced to me by your Aunt Claire and I..." Holly looked away.

"You what?" Nik prodded.

"I quickly found out you were not single at the time, after my imagination got the better of me."

"We've come a long way."

Holly yawned.

"Boring you already?"

"Not at all, it's must be the jet lag talking." Holly wasn't entirely sure if it was jet lag or an involuntary deflection to the vulnerability of the moment. Or a bit of both. She repositioned herself on the bench.

"My favorite feature is your…" Nik leaned in, cupping Holly's face and pulling her in close. She opened her mouth slightly, not to yawn, but to receive the long awaited reunion kiss. The tender one. Not too quick, not too long. Just right.

"…it's your lips." Nik finished the sentence he had started before. "The curve of your smile…but not only that…it's the way they pout when you don't get your way and the way you bite the corner of your lip when you're concentrating on a painting, or on personalizing an ornament from Neumann's. It's the way they round in shock when you're caught off guard. It's…" He leaned in again for a soft, short kiss.

"My lips are your favorite feature?"

"I hope that doesn't sound shallow, I promise, it's not. They are the gatekeepers to your thoughts, your joy, your sorrow. I want to be a part of it all, Holly Noel."

No words formed, but a smile did.

"See, there you go again."

"Nik, did you read that quote somewhere?"

He sat back, "What the gatekeepers thing? Nah, that was an original." Nik ran his finger through his hair. Perhaps that was his form of deflecting the palatable vulnerability in their tender exchange.

If Holly sketched them on the bench—after the hug, the meal, the walk, the kiss—she would subtly add a word, carved into the bark of the tree branch overhead. This word, like a banner above them, encompassed Nik's expression and Holly's emotion in this moment—contentment.

The next morning, Holly sighed, leaning her head against the passenger seat of Nik's vehicle. She had given up trying to show restraint. Her senses were assaulted with pleasure. It was impossible to process all she was feeling in the moment as she experienced what she had only heard about.

"Nothing like it, huh?" Nik said, reaching for Holly's hand from the driver's seat.

Ever since he had picked Holly up this morning from her charming A-frame cottage set among Ponderosa pines, she had been drinking in the intoxicating landscape out the car window. Holly couldn't get enough. Delicate wildflowers carpeted open fields. Rocky mountain crags guarded them. Holly tried to memorize the details—the curves, the colors, the intricate handiwork from the Master Artist. She blinked, trying to reset her mind to simply enjoy the beauty of the moment instead of trying to bottle it all up.

"It's spectacular, Nik. Even better than I imagined." She turned from the addictive view toward her one and only. She felt like she was about to explode, surrounded by grandeur of the Pacific Northwest, and the good looks and good nature of the man she adored.

"I know this isn't the summer we had planned, but I'm glad it worked out like this. You have to see it to really understand all she has to offer." Nik squeezed her hand.

"We're talking about Leavenworth, right?" Holly teased.

"Who else?" Nik turned up the car radio, singing along to a 90's rock ballad. Holly joined in.

It couldn't get much better than this. Just the two of them, breathing the same air, experiencing life together, in real time. Nine a.m, Pacific, to be exact.

Holly had only been in Leavenworth for fourteen hours, but she was smitten, with the scenery and her present company. She studied Nik's jawline as he hummed. He kept his eyes on the road, an evident twinkle in them. She thought back to the night before: the hug, the meal, the walk, the kiss.

―――

"You ready for this?" Nik asked.

Holly was brought back to the present. The sweet memories of the night before could be replayed, or reenacted, later. The happy couple had arrived at their destination. It was time for their second date of the summer.

The decorative signage at the front gate read: Dasher's Reindeer Resort.

"Oh how fun!" Holly clapped.

"It was all Marina's idea, and I quote, 'What's more adorable than to pose with baby reindeer and enjoy a picnic lunch in the woods with your long-distance girlfriend?' End quote." Nik got out of the car and stretched.

Holly grabbed her tote and water bottle, following suit.

"That's what Marina sounds like? When do I meet her?" Holly put on her sunglasses.

"I'm not a professional impersonator or anything, but it resembled her enthusiasm. That girl doesn't miss a beat. She's funny, she's smart, she's…"

"Can't wait to meet her." Holly cut off Nik's glowing report of his co-worker, not wanting to hear another word about the office darling. She hadn't lied. She was eager to meet Marina— er, size her up and potentially throw her off a nearby cliff. Wait, Holly should be more dignified than that. She'd march right up and shake Marina's hand...right out of the socket.

"You okay?" Nik looked like he was reading her dark inner thoughts. She was certain annoyance was written all over her face.

"Fine, fine, I'm fine. You're fine. But you already knew that, right?" Holly fiddled with the lid of her water bottle. "I need a quick visit to Comet's commode before we strike a pose with the baby reindeer. Give me five?"

"Take all the time you need." Nik repositioned his Seahawks baseball cap. His dark wavy hair poked out around the edges.

Holly hurried down the path that led to a log cabin-styled outhouse.

She took care of business and caught a glimpse of her reflection.

Girl, jealousy is not a good look on you. Marina Schmeena is not here, so don't let her sabotage your date with Nik. Never mind that this date was her idea. Focus on the here and now, not the then and there. And for goodness' sake, throw away that insecurity. It's not your best feature. Enjoy today. Don't borrow trouble from tomorrow.

That last part was straight out of her Grandma Bea's go-to phrases for navigating life with your chin up and your dignity intact. Which reminded her...Holly quickly pulled up the picture on her phone she had snapped while in English Roses, to conclude her pep talk. "Let your decorum rise to the dignity of the occasion."

She nodded, then reapplied lip gloss to Nik's favorite feature of hers. Holly exited the facilities, determined to lead with dignity from here on out.

CHAPTER THIRTEEN
What are you second guessing?

DASHER'S REINDEER RESORT WAS DELIGHTFUL. HOLLY jumped in with both feet, avoiding the doo doo she could have found herself in, had she let herself think the worst of someone she hadn't even met yet—Marina with the gluten allergy and a knack for picking out fantastic dates for her good-looking co-worker and his midwestern girlfriend. Holly focused on the sights and smells before her, Nik's steely blue eyes and earthy cologne. Behind him, the high-definition mountain range was bathed in sunlight. The clicks and grunts of new antlered friends surrounded them.

Holly laughed as a young reindeer's velvety snout tickled her fingers, gobbling up the fresh willow she offered it, from the branch Nik had purchased at the gift shop.

"I see baby Blitzen is taken with you." An employee from the resort wandered over as Nik and Holly were feeding the reindeer. "Can I capture the moment for our social media page?"

"Sure." Holly said.

"I have a small favor to ask." The employee, likely a college intern, handed them a piece of paper that laid out the details of said photo shoot.

Fifteen minutes later, Nik and Holly were dressed in matching alpine garb. Holly's red knee-length jumper was detailed with embroidered flowers. A white eyelet half-apron tied around her waist and a felt Tyrolean alpine hat with a feather, completed her iconic look. Nik sported navy blue lederhosen. Underneath he wore a white highland shirt, partially laced with thin leather straps. When the resort employee offered to tie a red bandana around Nik's neck, Holly stepped in to do it. She didn't want anyone else intoxicated by the scent that drew her to him, especially up close and personal, near his neck.

"Why, thank you." Nik winked.

"My pleasure. Don't forget your feathered fedora." Holly handed him one to match his lederhosen. Nik wrapped his arms around Holly. She almost lost her balance. He dipped her.

"You two are the cutest. Ready to pose?" The employee positioned herself to capture candid photos that were totally staged...for the next ten minutes.

"My cheeks hurt," Nik said through clenched teeth.

"Lederhosen too tight?" Holly shifted her pose, leaning her head against Nik's shoulder while trying to pat the head of a reindeer who thought her apron looked like lunch.

"Not those cheeks. My face is numb from smiling."

"I had no idea what we were in for when I agreed to this," Holly mumbled, still trying to smile for their over eager photographer.

"You're lucky I like you so much." Nik spun her around.

The l-word again, but without the o-v-e ending.

"Let's do one more. Can you two do that again?" It wasn't the first 'one more' they'd heard from their sole paparazzi.

Nik spun Holly with a little too much oomph, which nearly landed Holly in the remains of the reindeer's lunch. Thankfully he didn't drop her.

"That's a wrap. Those were great. You guys are great. Who knows, you may even make it on the June spread of next year's Reindeer Resort calendar."

"Maybe we should have read that photo release agreement a little closer." Nik adjusted his fedora that had nearly fallen off during the over-zealous spin.

"You mean 'being a summer lederhosen model for a

reindeer resort' wasn't on your bucket list as a boy?" Holly curtsied to young Blitzen as they left the fenced area.

A perk of the photo shoot was a picnic voucher for two in the woods. Thankfully their alpine costumes weren't required attire for lunch, nor were more photos.

Under a willow tree, over corned beef sandwiches on rye, potato salad, and watermelon, Holly retrieved another question from the Mason jar.

"What are you second guessing?" Holly read.

"I'm second guessing my entire childhood." Nik leaned on his elbow, sprawled on the checkered blanket. "According to one of the placards along the trail, male reindeers shed their antlers in early December after mating season, but, get this, the females don't lose theirs. Santa's reindeer, minus Rudolph, are all females. My mind is blown. Who knew? What else did I believe as a kid that wasn't entirely true?" Nik took a bite of his sandwich.

"Far be it from me to crush your vision of sugarplums dancing in your head and let you know that Santa is not…"

"La la la…I can't hear you." Nik sat up, putting his hands over his ears.

"That's such a Frank move," Holly laughed.

"Frank, huh? How is he?"

"Haven't seen him a lot this summer. He's moving up in the family business at Neumann's, so now he has more responsibilities and less time to set up shenanigans."

"Do you ever second guess your decision to just be friends with Frank? He's lots of fun."

"Nik, are you being serious?" She couldn't tell if he was joking or not. Holly had never known Nik to be jealous. Maybe a tad when his ex-girlfriend seemed married to her work and didn't give him the time of day. But who wouldn't be envious then?

"All I'm saying is, Frank lives in your same zip code. He's financially secure. His future is planned out and there's never a dull minute when he's around..." Nik reached for a napkin to prevent an ant from reaching the last slice of watermelon.

"I don't even know how to respond to that. I'm here, aren't I?" Holly finished the last bite of her potato salad.

"How about you? What are you second-guessing?"

"Hmm, besides wondering why I never asked Mom and Dad for a pet reindeer as a kid?"

"Besides that."

"I'm second-guessing if I have what it takes to be a children's book author. I guess I haven't even tried yet, but what if I fail? What if the idea I have to help Claudia falls flat? Or it doesn't translate effectively?"

"It'll translate all right, probably into Spanish, German...and French." Nik rubbed her hand, looking up at her from his reclined position.

"That's not what I meant, but you're sweet." Holly pressed her lips to his forehead.

Crash!
Snap!
Grunt.

A reindeer galloped toward them at a decent clip.

"Dasher! Come back!" Two employees on an ATV sped past them, yelling through a megaphone at the runaway reindeer. They held out a willow branch, trying to entice the runaway reindeer back to pasture.

Nik and Holly watched the comical chase that ensued from their front row seat on the picnic blanket.

"Never a dull moment with you, Nik. You're pretty fun."

"Only pretty fun?" Nik rose. "You're pretty *and* fun, Holly

Noel Brigham." He offered her his hand. She stood.

"It's not every day you get to witness a runaway reindeer, especially while in shorts and a tank top. I'm getting spoiled with these back-to-back dates. We've gone so long without any, I could get used to this."

"About that…" Nik put his hands in his pockets.

"Oh dear, is the strenuous hike next?"

"Not yet. We'll go to church tomorrow if that's okay, but come Monday I have to work overtime for the next several weeks. Our tourist firm has been tasked with a major element of the Christmas in July Festival and, with it being a little over three weeks away, we're scrambling."

"Wait, what?" Holly flung out the picnic blanket several times before folding it.

"I didn't want to ruin the moment, but there's not really a good time to say it. 'Hey, work is crazy right now and even though you came all this way, they're not letting me have the additional time off I requested. In fact, I have to work more.'" Nik finished loading the picnic basket with their used dishes and cups.

First, work wouldn't let Nik use his stored-up vacation time to fly out to see Holly, and now work was keeping them from seeing each other even though she rearranged her life to be here? Gladly, of course. But Holly was not up for playing any sort of Glad Game in the wake of this fresh disappointment.

Holly wondered how Nik would feel about her lips now that they were pursed in a ball and serving as a gatekeeper to keep unfiltered words from escaping. Like dear Dasher crashing through their romantic picnic, Holly's expectations felt trampled on.

What would Elaine say to her in this moment? Probably something like, "This totally stinks, but it's going to be okay.

Don't try to fix it, see how it pans out."

If Holly asked her mom for advice, she would probably say Nik's work ethic was one of his best features and Holly should be grateful about that. But right now, Holly was not a fan. How were they supposed to take things to the next level if Nik was going to be at work most of the time during her visit? Sure, she had work to do remotely for Heart Turn, but it wouldn't take all day, each week day. Was this foreshadowing a life with a significant other who put work first? That probably wasn't a fair evaluation. Nik was anything but selfish.

But Holly had come all this way so she and Nik could connect, not so she could feel cast aside. She wanted to experience his corner of the world, but she didn't think that meant she'd be left to explore Leavenworth solo. She thought they'd been on the same page about what their time together was going to look like, but presently, it seemed like the intent of this trip was lost in translation. She wasn't expecting them to be together every waking minute or anything, but now it sounded like they'd basically only see each other on the weekends. Had Nik already forgotten how he'd felt when Lena, his ex-girlfriend, was so preoccupied with her job? Holly knew Nik was a hard worker, but people had always come first for him, not projects. Maybe people still came first but not in the order she preferred or expected. Co-workers shouldn't trump significant others. Especially when the significant other had flown thousands of miles to spend time with him.

Holly was second-guessing more than her decision to put herself out there as a prospective children's book author.

※

When Holly entered her A-frame rental that evening the screen door slammed behind her. She flopped on the couch and cuddled the blue velvet throw pillow. She didn't have the emotional energy to peek out the window to watch Nik's tail lights driving away.

Adulting felt hard today...in the wake of unmet expectations...of herself. Why did Holly do what she didn't want to do? Why did she say what she was thinking? Why did she hurt the one she cared for most?

Nik's jaw flinched when she had let her unedited thoughts fly. Why was she so hard on him? Why was she so hard on herself?

Having a fight didn't mean their relationship was going to crash and burn, it meant they were human. Maybe the tension was a sign they were getting more comfortable with each other, and even closer? Holly wasn't sure if she was making up philosophical nonsense to feel better. She had a hunch her expectations might crush them both if she didn't get a grip. It wasn't like she had it all planned out. Holly had learned not to do that. But apparently, she had fleshed out the next four weeks more than she realized—not down to the specific details of their dates or anything, but that they would have lots of time together. That was it. Holly didn't want to feel the distance between them while living and breathing in the same town. They felt that enough. This was supposed to be different.

Holly pressed play on her summer playlist. She kicked off her sandals and laid down on the couch. An emo version of "Leaving On a Jet Plane" led her deeper into all the feels and questions she hadn't fully released in front of Nik, while she had fought for danged decorum. Slow-moving tears streaked her face as if her cheeks were runways. She was too stubborn and smitten to leave Leavenworth. Besides, it would be childish to run away at the first sign of conflict. She'd have to check her disappointment at the door in order to make the most of her time here and not drive Nik out of his mind or out of her life.

Maybe the jet lag affected her more than she cared to admit. Or, like her counselor often said, gently yet clearly, maybe Holly's strong reactions had more to do with past trauma than current reality? Holly had come a long way on many levels, yet Nik's unpleasant news pinpricked past hurt from a myriad of circumstances—unrelated to him. He had delivered the disappointment, and she reverted back to fight, flight, and freeze. All three, in rapid succession. It wasn't the ending to date number two she had envisioned.

Holly resisted the urge to grab the pint of ice cream in the freezer and reached for her sketch pad instead.

The cozy cottage was a haven for her hurt feelings. If she was going to dabble in writing and illustrating a book, this was the place to do it. Apparently, she'd now have more time to work on it, now that her schedule was "freed" up.

A couple from Nik's church owned and managed the A-frame and when they'd heard Holly was coming to visit, they discounted the rate to nearly nothing. Due to the summer heat, Holly wouldn't be using the wood stove in the living area, but it added to the ambiance. The walls were lined with pine paneling and the ceiling was supported by dark wooden beams. Trendy area rugs and a smattering of house plants made Holly feel like she was living inside one of her mom's home decor magazines she used to thumb through as a girl. A wooden ladder led up to the loft bedroom. The outer wall was mostly glass, reaching up to the peaked ceiling. A small desk and chair were positioned by the bedroom door that led to the second-story balcony. It was like living in a treehouse. It was evident God had hand-picked this rental for her. The view from the bedroom into the woods took her right back to cherished memories when she used to draw, while precariously situated in the treetops in her parents' backyard.

Outside the A-frame was a stone patio. Overhead, a string of outdoor lights glowed against the jet-back sky, creating a fairyland setting. Holly's favorite feature of the outdoor area was a cedar barrel hot tub. She slipped on her tankini and took her sketch pad and drawing pencil into the steaming water. Determined to wrangle her anxious thoughts, she breathed in and out slowly. After several minutes, she started drawing her little cottage in the woods from the backyard view. It was better than feeding her hurt feelings or drowning her sorrow in a tub of ice cream. Holly turned on the jets. The surge of hot water swirled and bubbled around her, soothing her tense muscles. Her head cleared as she breathed in the crisp mountain air, a slew of diamond stars twinkling above.

She was going to be okay. Tomorrow was a new day.

CHAPTER FOURTEEN
What are your pet peeves?

IN THE RUSH OF GETTING TO Washington in a hurry, Holly hadn't realized she would be at Nik's church on Father's Day. This was somewhat of a complicated holiday for her. Perhaps it was those pesky expectations again or the sting of having to face what was no longer a simple reality. She set a reminder in her phone to call her dad later.

The congregants at church flocked around Holly as Nik introduced her to them.

"We hear you're quite the artist."

"Any friend of Nik is a friend of ours."

"What do you think of our dear Bavarian village?"

"Have you hiked yet?"

"Not yet," Nik gently squeezed Holly's waist, "but we're planning on it."

Thankfully, Holly had slept well the night before. Maybe it was due to the hot tub lowering her blood pressure, or the full day of reindeer games, or the comfy bed in the loft that cocooned her.

During the service, when the small choir starting singing, "How Deep the Father's Love for Us," Nik leaned over and whispered, "I'm glad you're here. I'm guessing this might be a tough day for you. If you want to, we could try and FaceTime your dad later—if you want me to be there—and see how he's doing. I'm sure he misses you."

Congregants in the pew ahead of them turned around.

Holly wrote down her response on the bulletin, "That'd be great. Thank you. I'm sorry I overreacted yesterday about your work schedule."

"I'm sorry too." He draped his arm around her and rubbed her shoulder gently.

Come Monday, Holly woke up early. The birds serenaded her with their morning song, while she spent several hours on the balcony, working on details for the Heart Turn grant.

Satisfied with her efforts of getting work done before fun, she put the final touches on her ensemble—sporty black shorts and a red boxy tee. She decided to leave her wavy hair down in case Nik wanted to run his fingers through it during a passionate goodnight kiss later on.

Holly opted for sandals instead of her tennis shoes or hiking boots. Today was more about leisure than exertion. More about making the most of pre-date time instead of sulking that her man was tied up at the office. It was a change of plans. A pivot not a pothole. No big deal. Everything would be fine. Holly filled her backpack with everything she might need for the day—water bottle, a healthy snack, gum, journal, fine-tip pen, a few art supplies, sunglasses, phone, and wallet.

Nik pulled into the gravel driveway. He rolled down his window and lowered his sunglasses. "Well, hello, Beautiful."

Holly couldn't help but smile.

Nik leaned out the window to greet her with a quick, minty kiss. Holly could get used to this. She wondered how they'd ever go back to their long-distance arrangement after the thrill of in person togetherness.

They drove the few miles between her A-frame rental and downtown.

"I'll meet up with you as soon as I can," Nik said, from the driver's seat.

"I'll be okay. I've got a plan. I'm going to plant myself

downtown and pretend I'm a serious author plotting out her debut best-seller. By the time you're out of work, I hope to have most of the story mapped out. If I'm not too distracted by the glorious landscape."

"Can't wait to hear more about it. Thanks for understanding." Nik drove with one hand, his thumb rested on Holly's knee. As he brushed it back and forth, it sent a shiver up her leg. Gosh she liked him. Not just the way he looked, although he looked very nice. Not just the way he made her feel, which was electrifying at times. But the way he cared for her. Nik Beckenbauer was her best friend. She wanted to be a supportive girlfriend. She didn't want to make things harder for him during this stressful work season. She tried not to think about the fact that his co-workers were getting to spend all day with him, while she'd be served the leftovers.

"I'm planning on you meeting the crew tomorrow. I wish it could be today, but Mondays are staff meetings, and the CEO will stop by to hear our progress on the concert update for the Christmas in July Festival."

"Who will you guys bring in?"

"I didn't tell you? You didn't you see his face plastered around town?"

"My eyes have been on you." Holly hooked his thumb with hers.

"Well played. I can't believe we haven't talked about this...it's Harry."

"Stiles?"

"No silly, our Harry. *The* Harry."

"Connick Jr.?" Holly nearly whipped Nik in the face with her hair as she spun her head toward him.

"That's the one. It was a long shot, but Marina pulled some

strings with a distant relative of hers who used to play in his band and Harry happened to have an opening. We also happened to have the budget for such a headliner this year, thanks to a generous donor from Cali."

"Nik! That's incredible."

"Right? I'll be working the event, so we'll have a chance to hear him live, together."

"I can't believe you didn't tell me." Holly flicked Nik's bicep. "You know...I would have gotten here much faster had I known the news."

"I'll bet you would have." Nik rubbed his arm where she had flicked.

"Let me know what I can do to help. I could make sure he feels right at home in Leavenworth. I should know it like the back of my hand then. I could help run his merch table or bring him bottled water or…"

"Easy, girl. I know you have a crush."

"Do not!"

"Then why are you blushing?"

Holly laughed. "You're a fan too."

"Guilty as charged." Nik turned on his hazards. "It'll be great. I only have to knock a zillion things off the list before we get there. Here's your stop."

Holly hopped out of the car with her full backpack.

"See you tonight." Nik waved out his window.

Holly walked toward the outdoor patio of Bertha's Bavarian Pretzel shop. On her way, she noticed poster after poster advertising the town's annual Christmas in July Festival, with *The* Harry Connick Jr. front and center on every one.

Holly was soon armed with a giant-sized pretzel, dipping cheese, and a freshly squeezed lemonade that might float her right down the Wenatchee River. She retrieved her journal, determined to storyboard her kids' book idea while she waited on Nik.

Drawing inspiration from her latest project with the clients at Heart Turn she had decided to go with a stained glass theme. She jotted down title possibilities for her book on the back of napkin.

Your Stained Glass Window
The Colors that Make You
Light through the Dark Window
Beautiful, Broken Pieces
Tiny Bits of Glass

Holly chewed on her pen. She thought and overthought each syllable. She hummed along to the karaoke hits playlist Elaine had created for her so she wouldn't get rusty while absent from their weekly ritual. Holly stared out at the mountains, trying to garner fresh inspiration. This author stuff was harder than she expected. Although she'd only been at it for a few hours.

Holly figured she'd better buy another pretzel or something if she was going to keep occupying the patio table at the popular tourist stop.

She bent down to retrieve cash from her backpack. On her way back up she almost knocked over her lemonade with her elbow. The cup wobbled near the edge of the table.

"I got you." A lanky arm swooped in to set the cup upright.

"Frank?" Holly yelped. "What on earth are you doing in Leavenworth?"

"Surprise!" He posed in one of his awkward gestures of welcome. "Granddad flew me out to scout out a possible partnership with a local business. The VP was supposed to do it, but he got sick. So, here I am. Small world, eh?"

"For real." Holly felt as off-kilter as her drink had been a moment ago. Frank in Leavenworth? Elaine would never believe her.

"I heard you finally made it out here. Sounds like it was quite an ordeal."

"You don't know the half of it."

"While this whole town is not much bigger than Neumann's, I didn't expect to find you, err, run into you, so quickly."

"How did you locate me? Drone, tracking device, phone app?"

"I have my ways. Can I treat you to a pretzel or am I interrupting?"

"Pretzel would be great, thanks."

Frank got in line. Holly tidied up her slew of papers and tried to organize her thoughts.

What in the world? Frank belonged in the Falls, at the mile-long Christmas store, running the family business, not invading her creative process and personal space. And certainly not showing up on her vacation, with her boyfriend, who unfortunately was very occupied with work. Yes, Frank was her friend, but it felt so out of pocket for him to be here. Here, of all places.

Frank eventually returned with the promised pretzels.

Holly wondered if she'd regret devouring a second bread snack.

"Whatcha working on? Isn't this supposed to be a vacation?" Frank stared at the folded papers Holly was trying to shield.

"It's a work in progress, and the rhyming pattern is off, and—"

"Stop making excuses. Spill it."

Holly cleared her throat, "It's a…book? Not yet, but I hope it will be, one day. The working title is *Your Stained Glass*

Window and the idea is to help children understand that the different parts of their life—the good, the hard, the confusing—can work together somehow."

"Can I hear what you have so far?"

"I don't know. It's not finished yet and—"

"I really want to hear it." Frank leaned his bony elbow on his knee, propping his fist under his chin.

Holly read the following:

Each piece of glass tells a story. A story of dark or of light.

The colors work together to make up your beautiful life.

Joy reflects bright yellow and the tears drip deep blue,

Your wonderings and questions are dyed in an evergreen hue.

There's a pattern forming and forging, even though it's not yet clear

There's more to this delicate story, so hold on tight, my dear

You're not only one thing you're many—bold, complex, unique.

Your window is being assembled, for now, you just get a peek

What remains left unfinished is a part of the artist's plan

The missing piece that's hidden is held in the palm of His hand

One day you'll view the full picture, but today you just see a part

Broken pieces fit together to create a mosaic of art.

For once Frank was silent. Had Holly wowed him so much that he had no words for the sheer genius of it?

Frank sat up straight. "I don't get it. I mean I kind of do, but isn't this a kids' book? Will your niece understand words like 'hue' and the metaphor of the stained glass and all that?" Frank used his pointer finger to push his glasses up the bridge of his nose.

"Not the feedback I expected." Holly resisted the urge to wad up the paper before her.

"You wanted me to be honest, right? No offense, but it's kind of confusing." Frank reached for a swig of Holly's lemonade.

"Ugh, you're right. It's terrible."

"I didn't say that. But it does need work."

"More like a complete overhaul." Holly massaged her forehead. Her art hadn't made its way into a museum display but maybe her kids' book would, with a shiny Newberry Award seal on the cover, announcing to the world that she had finally done something worth noting. Now, after Frank's honesty, she wasn't sure she had the courage to try again. What started out as a grand idea in her mind translated to an idiotic attempt on paper.

Holly folded the piece of paper several times, trying to tuck away her vulnerability in an orderly fashion.

"In the marketing office at Neumann's, we have a saying that might help, 'Keep it clear and dear.' Don't overcomplicate the message you're trying to get across. What is the message exactly?" Frank brushed stray salt flecks off the round metal table.

"To view the good things and hard things in your life as different colors that the artist puts together to create an interesting, beautiful work of art. By itself the piece may feel jagged or out of place, but when strategically arranged by the one who can see the whole picture, it works together somehow to create beauty."

"That's really good. But it still might be over the head of your target audience. Is this book for parents or kids?"

"Kids...you're right, it's confusing. Thanks for being frank with me."

"Ha, ha."

"I guess I'll go back to the drawing board and try to clean up this mess."

"What color might you assign to this mess?" Frank finished off Holly's lemonade.

"That's easy, Electric Lime. It's the trying-too-hard neon green that doesn't match the rest of the crayons in the box. Sour to the taste and sore on the eyes."

"You've tried eating it?"

"No, trying to be poetic again, but apparently it's not a good look on me."

"You always look good, Holly."

"Ha, ha. Flattering Frank strikes again." She tucked a flyaway hair behind her ear.

"It's my specialty. Speaking of, there's something I want to run by you."

"What's that?" Holly shifted her weight, wishing for a cushion to ease her discomfort.

"I have to work up some courage first." Frank tapped a drumroll on the patio table.

"You've never been one to lack courage."

"Typically that's true, except in this instance I'm feelin' more like the Cowardly Lion."

"What's got you squirming, my friend?"

"You'll see. There's a lot on the line. It could change everything and I don't want to ruin what we have."

"We?" Holly squeaked.

"I'll tell you more later, but for now we need a lively diversion from this little therapy session of ours. I think your case of the morbs might be contagious."

"The morbs?"

"According to the dictionary of Victorian slang that my seat mate was reading on the plane, 'got the morbs' means you have temporary melancholia."

"Don't most artists?" She shrugged.

"You have a point."

"It's the fuel we need to run into all our feelings and retrieve the inspiration we need. Sometimes it's our Achilles' heel, tripping us up when we overuse it."

"The morbs might work for you from time to time, but on me, it's about as uncomfortable as the Speedo I had to wear for swim meets. I'm no doctor, but I'm prescribing you a dose of fun to shake off this funk of yours."

Holly decided against confessing that her funk wasn't only because her story was apparently terrible but also due to the fact that Nik was going to be MIA for a majority of her time there.

"Hey, what's this?" Frank spied the mason jar sticking out of Holly's backpack.

"Oh, that's nothing. Just a little something that Elaine suggested Nik and I try to—"

"Let me at it," Frank crammed his fingers in the jar, fishing for one of the slips of paper.

"What are your pet peeves?" Frank read, trying on an Irish accent for dramatic effect.

Holly's serious expression cracked into a grin. Leave it to Frank to drive her crazy and also distract her from her current predicament.

"Wee lassie, do you need me to repeat the question?"

"Okay, okay. I'll give you my top five—loud chewing, turning without signaling, passive aggressive comments, spoilers—especially during a movie I haven't seen yet, and people speaking about themselves in third person."

"Now we're getting somewhere," Frank said, still Irish.

It felt itchy to let him ask her the IOU question of the day, instead of Nik. The questions that were supposed to improve communication and deepen the connection between girlfriend and boyfriend.

"Frank agrees with you," Frank waggled his eyebrows.

"Nice one. Your turn. How about you?"

"Oh, you know me, I'm pretty chill. Not much riles me up." Frank leaned back, crossing his hands behind his head. "But if you insist, I'd say, when people complain about the weather in the Midwest. Wait five minutes and it'll change, people. That pet peeve might be directly related to having a dad who is a meteorologist." Frank stretched his arms overhead and yawned loudly.

"The Weather with Walker on Channel 5." Holly checked the time on her phone. Nik was only halfway through his morning shift.

"I guess I could come up with a few more. Since I recently flew, it's not my favorite when people put their seat all the way back without consideration for the person sitting behind them. I'm all legs and don't like feeling like a caged rabbit unable to wiggle free."

Frank scooted his patio chair closer to the table as the line for Bertha's grew. "As a young boy I used to be in charge of wrangling stray carts from the Neumann's parking lot. You'd think I would have liked the adventure and challenge of it, but it's nearly impossible to push carts through slush and snow. That's my third one...not returning shopping carts to their rightful place."

"Two more?"

"When people don't answer my texts in a timely fashion and when they take themselves and life too seriously."

"I'm going to pretend those last two aren't directed at me?" Holly twisted a bit of her salty pretzel into the remains of her cheese sauce.

"I'm feeling generous, today. You get a pass, Holly Noel."

"Oh, yeah?"

"Looks like I have about three hours until I present my proposal. Enough time to go have some fun. You in?" Frank stood, offering a fist for her to bump.

Holly returned the bump but kept her tush glued to the uncomfortable seat, her feet planted.

"It's up to you. You could try to untangle your story with your current method and mood or you could take a break and let me entertain you. A change of scenery can unlock the breakthrough, right? Besides I'm not here long, just today and tomorrow, and I'm no good at sitting still. What do you say, buddy? Ready to paint the town red?" Frank offered his lanky hand to Holly.

Leave it to Frank to try and pull her out of 'the morbs' with his antics. It would help pass the time until Nik was free. Frank wasn't wrong, sometimes a person needed to step away to see things more clearly.

"All right, what's first?" Holly unstuck the back of her legs from the patio chair as she stood.

"It's a surprise!" Frank clicked his key fab twice as if to punctuate his words.

Holly's wavy hair was an untamed mess due to the top being down in Frank's rental, a purple Jeep Wrangler. Electric lime might have been a more fitting choice. They sped out of town toward the Cascade Mountains. Sunshine beamed from above like a massive spotlight on Chelan County. Frank passed Holly a carbonated flavored water. She took a sip. A hint of peach and lavender were overpowered by a blast of fizz. The beverage paralleled her racing thoughts. On one hand, the spontaneity of her and Frank's excursion tasted exhilarating. Getting out of her head and into nature was exactly what the doctor ordered. On the other hand, regret jostled around in her stomach, causing her to question her current choices. What would Nik think about her galavanting on his home turf, with Frank? But then again, he was tied up at work and unavailable. Besides, Frank was a good friend, to both of them. Hopefully Frank's 'I want to run something by you' wouldn't complicate things. Holly swallowed hard. Frank twanged along to a top hit on the country station, called, "The Songs Will Take Me Back."

Holly held her hand out the window, and like a wing it rose and fell with the flow of the wind. The air cooled for a moment as they passed a waterfall on the mountain side. The drive itself was a treasure hunt.

"I spy an eagle." Holly pointed. The majestic creature glided overhead.

"I'll take your word for it." Frank navigated a sharp turn on the mountain road.

"Can we slow down a little? I want to make it to wherever we're headed in one piece." Holly gripped the edge of the passenger's door.

"I spy road kill."

"Lovely. Hey! I spy an apple orchard in the valley down there."

"This place is full of them." Frank offered the Jeep wave—

a quick hand raise and nod—apparently the universal greeting for those who drove Jeeps—to an approaching vehicle in the other lane.

"Are we touring an orchard? That'd be fun."

"Good guess, but nope. Bigger thrill ahead."

"I think it'd be interesting." Holly retrieved her sunglasses from her backpack.

"What's next will be interesting all right, depending on how you feel about heights and speed."

"Haven't we already experienced both on this drive?"

Frank accelerated.

"Show-off." Holly put on her sunglasses.

Frank eventually eased off the gas. Their game of "I Spy" continued.

A roadside fruit stand.

Wildflowers.

A truck in front of them with an Alaskan license plate.

Had Holly insisted on brooding over her manuscript, she would have missed this. Holly tipped her head back. She welcomed the warmth of the sun. She conceded to let this spur-of-the-moment adventure play out, as evidenced by her current 'Jeep hair don't care' look.

CHAPTER FIFTEEN
What is your most embarrassing moment?

HOLLY CAUGHT A GLIMPSE OF A puff of dust kicking up behind them in the rearview mirror. Frank turned sharply into the gravel parking lot.

"Close your eyes." Frank pulled into a spot under a massive pine tree.

"Bossy, bossy." Holly tried to smooth down her wild mane, but it proved a lost cause. She grabbed a hair tie from her wrist and put her hair up in a ponytail.

"I want to surprise you." Frank turned off the music and the ignition.

"I should add 'being surprised' to my list of pet peeves." Holly released her buckle, keeping her eyes shut. She felt for her backpack near her feet.

"Oh, you won't need any of that. Hands free."

"Let me grab my wallet and phone, at least."

"Won't need those either. I'll lock 'em up in the back."

"What are you up to?" Holly crossed her arms.

"Where's your sense of adventure? You'll thank me later. Unplug and enjoy the moment. That's my motto." The driver's door shut with a thud.

Frank exuded a West Coast vibe even though he was born and raised in the Midwest. He was easy-going with a heaping dash of thrill-seeking, yet also responsible enough to manage massive ornament orders for the family business. When he wasn't working, he was playing and dragging others into the fun. Holly hoped she was headed for fun and not something unpleasant or too rigorous since she was wearing sandals.

Slam.
Thump.

Holly flinched. It was probably Frank putting their stuff in the back of the Jeep for safe keeping.

"Keep those lashes locked until I say so." Frank opened the passenger door and helped Holly out of the vehicle.

"I'm sure I look ridiculous." Holly resisted the urge to open her eyes while she stood next to the Jeep, helpless to know what direction she should go now. She straightened her sunglasses, as if that would help.

"Cute as can be." Frank put one hand on the back of her shoulder and with the other he cradled her elbow. He led her forward.

Holly heard other vehicles pulling in and people talking not far from them.

"They're going to think I'm hungover, with you leading me around while I shuffle next to you."

"Or they'll think you're a famous Hollywood actress enjoying down time in the mountains away from the fans and fast pace, hiding your identity from gawking onlookers." Frank teased. "When you first started working at Neumann's, before I knew you were a local, I had you pegged as a Princess Kate or Zooey Deschanel stunt double. Zooey in 'New Girl,' not 'Elf.'"

"That's laughable."

"You don't see the resemblance?"

"Can't see anything at the moment, remember." Holly held out her left hand trying to make sure she didn't run into anything. Frank still held her right elbow, steering her toward wherever they were headed.

"You're doing great, by the way. Thanks for being a good sport."

"I don't know why I agreed to this. I could be writing my manuscript and gazing at Leavenworth's beauty instead of the back of my eyelids. Another thing, I don't think Princess Kate has a stunt double...although, not a bad idea, right?"

"For real."

"Famous people often visit the mile-long Christmas store, but they don't often work there." Holly stopped to shake a pebble out of her sandal.

"Come on, 'Frank from the Falls' is totally famous."

"And he's speaking in third person...my favorite." Holly tried to elbow Frank but he swerved out of her way, almost taking her with him.

"Easy does it." Frank steadied her.

"Besides, why would a stunt double choose to work at the ornament personalization counter when they could sign up to be one of the costumed reindeer who zip line across the rafters of the store, announcing Santa's arrival?"

"You have a point." Frank readjusted his grip on her elbow.

Voices belonging to various ages and dialects crescendoed around them. Holly heard excited chatter, but she could only make out bits and pieces of multiple conversations.

"Are we there yet?"

"I hear it's better than..."

"Is it dangerous?"

"Wait for me."

"Children, stick close to mama bear."

More people crowded in around them. Almost as quickly as the surge of energy had descended upon her and Frank, it dissipated. Whatever was up ahead seemed to draw people in like a magnet.

"I'm not sure why I let you boss me around. I'm on vacation

and I'm supposed to be sightseeing not being led around like an unruly toddler...or drunken solider." Holly resisted the urge to stop walking altogether.

"Or a famous stunt double—"

"Who has two left feet." Another swell of voices surrounded them, pressing in, then tapering off ahead of them. "Are people staring?" Holly was convinced she was making a scene.

"Don't worry about it. Besides, any temporary embarrassment will be worth the risk."

"You're lucky I agreed to go along with this ridiculous idea of yours. I'm about to open my eyes if you don't give me more info."

"Hang in there...only a few more minutes until you can open your eyes, but you'll have to walk faster, slow poke, or I'm giving you a piggy back ride."

"I'd crush you." Holly picked up the pace.

More than a few minutes later, Holly reached for her phone in her back pocket, then remembered she had stupidly agreed to leave it behind. She was about done with Frank's mysterious outing. This was definitely not what she thought her day would look like. Being led around in Leavenworth by her hometown buddy was not on her summer wish list. However, Frank had a knack for showing up and creating memorable experiences for Holly when she floundered. Even here, across the country. It was like he had a Spidey sense when she was in danger of feeling sorry for herself.

"Are we there yet?" Holly whined, pulling her arm away from Frank's cradling.

"Fine, missy. Have it your way." Frank let go and walked away, his voice becoming more distant, "Good luck going solo on this last incline."

"Okay, okay. I'll cooperate for one more minute, then I'm opening my eyes."

Frank returned to her side, "That's my girl. It's gonna be great. Hang on a little while longer."

"Sixty, fifty-nine, fifty-eight." Holly counted down the minute, holding Frank to his word.

Click, click, click, click.
Click, click, click, click.
Rumble. Roar. Swoosh.
Ahhhhh!
Wheeee!
Help!

"Frank? What in the world?" Holly's voice rose above the roar of the crowd. "I'm done in fifteen, *fourteen*, THIRTEEN…"

"Stop! We're here, my dear. Open your eyes."

Holly's eyes flew open behind her sunglasses. She quickly tried to orient herself to her surroundings. She instinctively took off her sunglasses and instantly regretted it as the noon sun assaulted them. She put them back on.

"Ta da." Frank posed in front of her like a circus ringmaster. His stance resembled Hugh Jackman in "The Greatest Showman," although his looks were more Davey Jacobs from the 1992 version of "Newsies" that Holly and her brother Gabe watched incessantly as kids. Frank's right hand was extended into the air, holding a walking stick he must have acquired on the way.

Rumble. Roar. Swoosh.

The waiting crowd went wild, *"Oohh, aahh!"*

Frank pointed up to the great beast in the center ring, suspended above them. But it wasn't a lion, and they weren't at the circus. A massive metal roller coaster jutted out from the mountainous landscape.

"Come one, come all. Experience Leavenworth's famous alpine coaster. It's the latest, greatest attraction for your enjoyment. Step right up, little lady." Frank offered his arm to a shocked Holly.

She slugged his scrawny bicep and took the lead toward the winding line for the coaster.

Fifteen minutes later it was their turn to ride. Thankfully, each coaster sled was only big enough for one adult. Holly was still slightly annoyed with Frank's theatrics on the way to the coaster, and the last thing she wanted was him whooping and hollering in her ear all the way down. Frank agreed to go first. The coaster attendant counted him down, "Three, two—"

"Woo-hoo!" Frank pumped his fist into the air as his bright yellow sled rolled forward.

Soon it was Holly's turn to get situated in her sled. She was thankful she didn't have to manage her backpack or phone now.

The attendant tugged on Holly's shoulder and lap buckle, "First time riding?"

"The maiden voyage. How fast does this thing go?" Holly leaned back against the seat.

"That's up to you. Pull the side brakes back for a leisurely ride or push 'em forward to zip down the track. Depends on what you're in the mood for. Slow and scenic or lickety-split. You choose."

Holly's sled thrust forward. Had this outing been her idea she'd probably be a bit more relaxed, but because Frank had chosen it for her, she felt slightly off balance—guarded yet willing. Although the off balance thing could be due to the fact that her car was now *click, click, clicking* up the steep incline.

The alpine coaster had been built into the side of a mountain cliff, near the entrance to Tumwater Canyon—according to the sign at the entrance. Scenic overlooks of the canyon, Icicle Ridge, the Wenatchee River rapids, and downtown Leavenworth could be observed from the coaster—if you were brave enough to look around and down while you rode. Holly glanced at the expanse of land and river below, then decided against it. Her pulse quickened. Her eyelids begged to be closed, but she bossed them open.

Experience this. The fear, the thrill. Don't retract, extend. Click, click, click, click.

Holly breathed in deeply and breathed out even longer. She redirected her attention to the blue sky and cotton ball clouds. The rocky hilltop ahead was partially frosted in lush green grass, the tops of evergreens jutted into the air, resembling candles to nature's celebratory cake. Thankfully, no wildfire was currently present to set the tree tops ablaze.

The crest of the first big hill inched closer. Holly would soon zoom past the National Geographic-like scene at breakneck speed. She clenched the side handles of her coaster car, still uncertain if she was ready for lickety-split. Holly could pull against gravity or push into the speed and let her rip. Time was running out for her to decide.

Holly let go for a second to tighten her seatbelt.

She imagined Frank taunting her, "I spy a scaredy cat."

"Not a chance!" Holly answered out loud, raising her hands in a V overheard The sled clicked into place at the top of the steep incline. She grabbed the brake handles and thrust them forward to maximize her speed. She raced down the first hill.

Rumble. Roar. Swoosh.

As the coaster accelerated so did her heart rate. Holly's hands vibrated against the metal handles. She pushed down into the untamed, speeding down the track. Then all of a sudden, it felt like all the fresh air was sucked into a vacuum. Shallow, quick pants gave way to heightened anxiety. Holly had enough wherewithal to shift from pushing to pulling. With a white-knuckled grip on the brakes, she yanked back with all her might, trying to pull herself out of her nosedive of panic. Her hands slipped from the sweat on her palms. Holly couldn't scream, her vocal cords wouldn't cooperate. The bright yellow sled was safe and secure on the track but with each unpredictable turn and twist, up and down, Holly felt wildly out of control. Her grip was weakening.

Holly's sled slowed before making a sharp turn, then sped up again. A flash of light from the coaster's camera alerted Holly there would be witnesses to her wide-eyed fear. It felt like the cotton ball clouds had taken up residence inside her ears. But even with her muffled hearing she could make out the *Ahhhhh!* and *Wheeee!* up ahead and behind her.

Was Holly the only one on the ride who started out brave then plunged into panic within 7.5 seconds? This wasn't her first rodeo, she'd ridden many coasters. She recognized this was more than a momentary aversion to adventure. Her death grip response to the unpredictable was a signal flare. This wasn't her first bull ride with anxiety, but she hadn't yet reached pro status. The bull's aggressive charge often came out of nowhere. Holly couldn't duck out of the way, she had to ride it out.

Her sled swayed down the track. She caught glimpses of beauty racing past but her main priority was trying to steady herself on the inside. Flashes of painful memories popped up as they often did when she experienced a panic attack. Different sounds rang out in her mind, symbolizing her various pain points. *Broken glass shattering after her brother Gabe heard the news of Dad's aneurysm.*

An eviction notice ripping apart Holly's dream of a collaborative art space in Chicago.

Piercing sobs slicing through the quiet apartment as her sister-in-law Monica wept for her unborn baby.

Shock, rejection, loss.
Glass, paper, tears.
Rumble, screech, thump.
The ride was over.

Next came the dismount, the trembling muscles, the exhaustion, the defeated steps out of the ring and into the bleachers while the judges prepared to rank the rider's efforts.

"You all right, ma'am?" A concerned coaster attendant reached out her hand to Holly.

"I will be." Holly received the help as she exited the coaster. She stood slowly to see if she could trust her wobbly legs to hold her up. She could use a stunt double about now. Holly was sure her face was blotchy and it would soon give her away to an awaiting Frank. Where was he?

As if on cue, a peppy Frank peeked around the corner of the gift shop. He was sporting a denim bucket hat with a patch on the front that said, "Coaster with the Moster." He looked ridiculous. Even in her post-panic state, Holly cracked a slight smile.

"Was that rad or what? Turning frowns upside down is my favorite past time." Frank trotted over to her.

Holly didn't have the heart to burst his bubble, but she wasn't sure how long she could hold herself together. While her panic attacks were fewer and farther between, they weren't non-existent. She often couldn't predict when they'd rear up, but the aftermath was pretty much the same. Embarrassment had already slithered in and extreme fatigue would barge in next. That's how it went for her. Her counselor, Nina, had given her numerous strategies for coping. One of those being to go gentle on herself after a panic attack. Gentle thoughts, gentle words, gentle actions. "I barely had time to purchase this hat before your ride was done. Let's go back into the gift shop. I have a few more surprises for you." Frank walked over to the counter. The cashier retrieved a branded enveloped and handed it to him. He trotted back over to Holly.

"I pre-purchased our photos from the ride." Frank grinned.

Gulp. Holly didn't have the strength to explain why this was a terrible idea.

"How's that for living my best life?" Frank pointed to a photo of himself doing the Superman pose at the crest of the hill. "Look at this one." Frank had his tongue out and one hand was flashing the hang loose sign.

"Classic Frank," Holly mustered.

"Look at you, Holly Lou. I spy someone cured of the morbs." Frank held out a photo of her. Holly was surprised to see an expectant, happy woman with her hands raised to the heavens. It looked like she was shouting "holly lou." Except Holly knew it wasn't a shout of praise she had raised in that moment, it was her "Not a chance!" response to Frank's imaginary taunting. She hadn't realized two photos had been taken. She remembered the one flash, mid panic. But the image before Holly captured anticipation of joy. It must have been taken earlier, on the crest of the hill.

"Oh man, this photo tells a different story though. You look terrified." Frank studied a second photo before showing it to Holly. In it, her eyes bulged, her tanned complexion was ghostly white, and her face contorted. She was holding on for dear life.

"You're not wrong. It scared the fun, instead of the

melancholia, right out of me." She offered a weak shrug.

"You okay?"

"I'll be fine. It wasn't the coaster though. I can't often predict when...maybe it was Father's Day...maybe it was...I don't know..." Holly voice trailed off.

"It wasn't my intent to stir stuff up. I was trying to help you relax but looks like that backfired." Frank shoved the pictures into the envelope. He tucked it under his arm and pulled on the sides of his "Coaster with the Moster" hat.

"I appreciated the effort." Holly didn't add what she was thinking. *I'm certainly the friend with the moster issues. Just when I seem fine, I'm not. Sometimes the panic comes out of nowhere. Pieces of broken glass from my past are still being excavated. Handle with care—that's me. Strong and weak. Assured yet second-guessing. Ready to take the bull by its antlers yet sometimes tempted to throw in the washcloth. Wait—horns not antlers. Towel not washcloth. Stupid idioms.*

"Let's find some shade before all the picnic tables are taken." Frank elbowed his way through the gift shop, clearing the way for Holly and her large case of 'the morbs.'

Once outside, they scoured the area for a spot in the shade. It did not look promising until they heard, "Yodel-Ay-Hee-Hoo! Over here." The yodeling mother from the airport, with her crew of kiddos with neon green 'Leavenworth or Bust' t-shirts, frantically waved to them.

Frank hurried over. Holly tried to, but her jello-y legs protested the pace.

The mama bear sprang into action. "We're almost finished, just got to scrub these kids down with wet wipes then we're gonna skedaddle. I even have a spare disposable tablecloth you can use. Here ya go." Holly took the tablecloth and expressed their thanks.

Frank volunteered to buy their lunch at the taco food truck in the parking lot. There was a long line forming.

The yodeling mother and company soon left and Holly spread out the plastic tablecloth. She sat down, thankful to be alone to collect her thoughts while Frank was occupied. She rubbed the top of her hand softly with the back of her palm in a circular, soothing motion. She used to pinch herself repeatedly after a panic attack subsided, as if that would prick the fear out or scold it into submission. But Nina, her counselor, had helped Holly recognize that type of approach was punishment-driven instead of patient, gentle, and kind.

These sincere phrases, spoken over Holly throughout therapy sessions, were on repeat as she processed, at the picnic table:

Redirection not rejection.
Restoration not disqualification.
Reorientation not regression.

After a counseling session this past spring, Holly had gone home to her apartment and penned her own version of these phrases, hand-lettering them into her journal.

Shift gears. Take the detour instead of the dead end.

Count yourself in, not out. You're not done, you just might need a nap and a snack.

Celebrate how far you've come. You're not going backward, you're scaling a new part of the mountain.

She had drawn little illustrations around each one—an arrow, a clock, a party hat. Thankfully her grown brother didn't still try to find and read her diary. She'd be embarrassed if he found her childlike, motivational processing. It was space reserved for her and God. Holly knew He was always with her, but somehow God felt closer inside the pages of her journal.

Room to reflect on her highs and lows, her questions and her "ah-ha" moments were housed in a 5x7 hardbound journal. Tucked away for safe keeping.

Frank returned with the food and two pops. After he straddled the wooden seat, he opened two paper bags. The aroma of chilies, cilantro, and lime permeated Holly's nostrils. She felt more settled now that she'd sat and had time to reflect, and she realized she was hungry.

"Let's dig in, then I want to run something by you. It's a confession, or declaration, of sorts. If you're up for it?" Frank chomped a salsa-dipped tortilla chip and then another.

"What's it about?" Holly reached for her carbonated beverage, a preemptive strike to further soothe her stomach before the spice kicked in and Frank's pending announcement hit.

"I think you probably know." He winked. "But first, tacos."

Gulp.

CHAPTER SIXTEEN
What do you want to save, and what do you need to toss?

IT WAS ALMOST ONE O'CLOCK IN THE afternoon when Frank, Holly, and the purple Jeep returned to downtown Leavenworth. Frank miraculously found a metered spot a few blocks from where they'd started, at Bertha's Bavarian Pretzels. Frank's confession/declaration during lunch had been interesting—somewhat surprising and not at all surprising at the same time. Holly was too tired to process anymore. She needed a nap, but no snack. The tacos had been tiny but mighty. The pickled onions were still going strong, despite the two mints she'd popped in her mouth on the drive.

Frank needed to change clothes before his meeting. He ran to the back of the Jeep and retrieved Holly's backpack and phone. Due to the disorienting nature of their outing, she had forgotten about them.

Holly exited the passenger door, stepping onto the busy sidewalk. Frank hurried over and returned her items. She stuffed her phone in her back pocket. She would check messages in a sec. She flung her backpack over her shoulders. That's when Frank wrapped his rubber band arms around Holly *and* her backpack. He swayed her back and forth several times before patting her head.

"What was that for?" Holly tightened her disturbed ponytail, now that her hands had been freed from Frank's spontaneous hug.

"For today. For your willingness to hang with me while you're on vacation, for never turning down tacos and for your listening ear and positive feedback when I confessed my affections—" Frank's smart watch alarm went off. "Gotta go!"

Frank grabbed the strap of his cross-body briefcase. "It's been real." He darted off.

"Let me know how it goes." Holly waved. She gasped as Frank nearly knocked over an elderly couple as he barreled down the crowded sidewalk.

◈

Holly felt like she had run a marathon over the last three hours, with Frank as a loyal yet obnoxious trainer, shouting encouragement, and barely breaking a sweat. She had hoped to use the rest of the afternoon to try again on the kids' book, while she waited for Nik to get off work, but she was spent.

Holly dragged herself over to the bench near the plaza, where she and Nik had sat and smooched on her first night here. She set her backpack down, then plopped on the bench. Some college-aged students threw a frisbee back and forth while a dog tried to intercept them. Children swung and slid on the playground while parents and grandparents watched over them. An elderly couple fed breadcrumbs to the birds. No one seemed to panic, except for one mother who was trying to stop her twins from climbing up the slide. They squealed as they ran away from her, going back up the slide, nearly being taken out by other children who were going down the slide.

Holly checked her text messages. Five from mom, the typical 'I raised you right but wonder if anything stuck', 'did you remember to pay your bills while you're on vacation' and 'hope you're having fun and drinking enough water' kind of thing. Three from Elaine, the usual best friend banter. One of only emojis from her niece, Claudia. Upon closer examination the line-up included a purple heart, sunflower, baby girl face, a broken heart, and a crying emoji. Holly wished she had the creative energy to tackle the kids' book manuscript that might comfort her sweet niece somehow. Instead, she sent her a red heart and texted: I'm sorry, Claudia Ann. This is really hard. I'm proud of you for letting me know how you feel. When I get home let's go on an ice cream date to Sugar Shock.

Holly ended the message with an ice cream emoji.

She sighed, realizing her feeble attempt to perk up her niece would fall short. It might provide a distraction or a temporary pick-me-up, but it wouldn't glue the pieces of Claudia's broken heart back together. There are difficulties in life that can't be fixed with a Band-aid or a bowl of ice cream. Holly knew that full well. She swiped her phone screen.

Shayla had sent photos of the Heart Turn students' progress on their stained-glass paper projects. Their faces beamed with pride as they held up their colorful conglomerations. Holly responded with double exclamation points and gushing praise. She also texted Shayla about her progress with the grant paperwork.

She saved the best for last. Nik had sent two texts:

Miss you. Hope the book writing is going well. Thanks for coming all this way. Can't wait to kiss those perfect lips of yours after work.

Holly hearted his message.

The second one said:

Not sure where you are? I sneaked out of the office at lunch for a minute to surprise you but didn't see you at Bertha's. Tried to call but you didn't answer. Hope everything's okay? Let me know.

The timestamp on his message said noon. Which was about the time she was processing at the picnic table, waiting on Frank to bring back tacos. Holly checked her recent calls. Sure enough, she had missed one from Nik.

Sorry I missed you. That was sweet of you to sneak out to see me. I'm at 'our bench' in the plaza now. Text or call when you're out.

She'd also missed a call from Betty Jo. Holly wasn't sure if, in her current state, she could absorb the exuberance of her former manager, but she also wondered if there was an update on Betty Jo's application to Kris Kringle Academy. Maybe the call would serve as a healthy distraction.

"Hulllooo, Holly dear! So nice of you to return my call. How do you like Leavenworth? How's Nikolaus?" Betty Jo cooed.

"Leavenworth is lovely and Nik is fine. Although he doesn't get out of work soon enough." Holly glanced over in the direction of town, secretly hoping Nik would get off work early.

"Normally, I'd still be at Neumman's for a bit longer, but I took the afternoon off. I had a dentist appointment with Doc Rasmussen and some top-secret business to attend to."

"I hope it's good news?" Holly witnessed the frazzled mother from the playground scooping up her twins under her arms as they flailed in protest.

"Looks like your old girl is going to need dentures in the not-too-distant future. So that was not such good news, but it's not like I'm lip-smacking the geriatric bachelors in town on a regular basis."

It was hard to stay down in the dumps while listening to Betty Jo's animated commentary.

"I meant, is there good news about your application to the Academy?" Holly said.

"Oh, there is, indeed. Special thanks to one of the more attractive of the geriatric bachelors."

"Do tell." Holly scooted forward so aggressively on the wooden bench she nearly gave her caboose a splinter.

"I guess the older you get, the more unfiltered you become. Can't believe I blurted that out. He and I go way back. He almost took me to prom, my junior year, his senior year. But his mother had arranged for him to take someone else. That someone else became his steady, then his happily married wife. So what almost was, never was. And that's that. *However*, his out-of-the-way kindness to me the last few days has me all stirred up, awakening what has laid dormant for decades upon decades. The problem is he doesn't know exactly what I have up my sleeve and it could be a major deal breaker."

"Who, Betty Jo, who?" Holly insisted.

"First, we've got to clear the air and talk about Frank."

Holly wondered how Betty Jo had already heard about her and Frank's outing, and maybe even his confession/declaration? She knew word traveled fast in Bavarian Falls, but did it here too?

"It was just two friends and a thrill ride…oh, and tacos." Holly reached for another mint out of the front pouch of her backpack.

"What are you talking about, dear? I meant you're going to have to keep those lips locked and not talk about this with your buddy, Frank. What I am about to disclose to you may come as a shock. You can tell Nik though, he's not related."

"I won't tell, Frank. Wait, what? Related?"

"Yes, yes. Frank's grandpa."

"Mr. Walker or Mr. Neumann?" Holly was horrified to think it was Frank's paternal, married grandfather.

"Mr. Herald Neumann, Jr." Betty-Jo sighed like a swoony schoolgirl. "My boss and *almost* beau from eons ago."

"I had no idea!"

"Oh, you wouldn't, I've kept my feelings under wraps. Tucked 'em right up nice and tidy so they wouldn't ooze in an embarrassing display of pining. But soon after his darling Mrs. Neumann passed away—about five years ago now, God rest her soul—those buried feelings for Herald had a resurrection. Straight out of the grave, more alive than ever."

"Wow. I remember you confiding in me, at the Neumann's Christmas party, about your almost fiancé from Wisconsin."

"Yes, yes, Clark Köhler, the vet, from Milwaukee."

"But I had no idea you once had a thing for Frank's grandfather."

"I didn't tell a soul. However, Herald's giving me such special attention lately, that it's got me all worked up. It's complicated having a thing for your boss. Yes, he's a widower, but I still don't want to blur the lines between work and pleasure. Oh goodness me, did I say pleasure? Behave yourself, Betty Jo, I meant work and affection. There, that's better."

Holly wished Nik could hear the whole hilarious confession straight from Betty Jo's mouth. How would Holly do her antics justice in the retelling?

"It's even more complicated because dear Herald doesn't know I want to retire from Neumann's—his store, his family's legacy, the empire of Bavarian Falls. It might break his heart clean in two if he caught wind of his reliable, boisterous, store manager *retiring*." Betty Jo whispered the last word like it was a curse word. "Although, if I wasn't under his direct supervision anymore, I might have a fighting chance of being the gal on his arm, one day. Dare I dream? Dare I dream!"

"This is a lot to take in. How does Mr. Neumann come into to play with your Kris Kringle Academy application?"

"I ran into him at the post office when I was trying to get my paperwork re-notarized and overnight shipped. I had an appointment at the end of the day all lined up, but the notary had the stomach bug and had to go home early. I was at the post office counter blubbering like a baby when Herald tapped me on the shoulder and offered to help. I panicked at first because I was afraid he'd put two and two together and figure out that me applying for Mrs. Claus training meant I'd likely retire from my store management position. Which in hindsight was silly because why would he think that unless I spelled it all out? He happens to be a notary. Add that to his long list of attractive qualities. Not to mention that pure white hair that crowns his head and the adorable way he combs it over, just a touch."

Holly wasn't sure she could stifle giggles anymore. She munched on the last bit of her mint. "Let me get this straight. Mr. Neumann notarized the paperwork for your Kris Kringle Academy application?"

"It doesn't get much more romantic than that. Except it does. He insisted on taking me out for lunch afterwards. We talked for hours. We reminisced about high school, we talked a little about work and how well the new additions to the Christmas village are selling. We enjoyed one another's company talking about almost anything and everything."

Holly imagined that Betty Jo did most of the talking.

"When it was time to leave, we stood there staring at each other by the booth. He reached over and squeezed my shoulder and said, "Betty Jo Wilson, you are remarkable. Let's do this again soon.""

"My knees about gave out at his touch. I didn't want to wash my shoulder for a week. How am I supposed to tell him I am *retiring* in the not-too-distant future? Will that change anything?"

"It might make it better somehow?"

"How?"

"I'm not entirely sure, but like you said, maybe you could

be *The* Mrs. Claus at Neumann's. So you'd be retired from your management position, but not out of Neumann's entirely, and not out from under Herald's loving gaze. Maybe he could replace Doc Rasmussen as the resident Santa Claus?"

"Oh, Holly. I'm blushing at the thought! That's what I hope for, but time will tell if all pans out. First, here's praying the Academy accepts my resubmitted application. It's going to take a miracle, Holly Noel."

"Praying it works out. Keep me posted?" Holly shooed her hand at the birds that had come over to see if she had breadcrumbs to feed then.

"Oh dear, I was a jabber jaws the whole time and didn't zip it so you could tell me all the wonderful things about our sister city out there."

"It did me good to hear your news. I'm really happy for you and these exciting possibilities for your future. Let's have frozen cocoa when I get back and I'll have even more to share then."

"It's a date. Go enjoy yourself, sweet Holly. Drink it all in. Ba-bye!"

"Bye!" Holly felt quite a bit better. Betty Jo had that effect on people. Apparently, Frank's grandfather was one of them. Resurrected affection, indeed.

Holly had caught up on the news from home, window shopped downtown, and snacked on creamy hazelnut fudge. The bakery blew the intoxicating smell into the air and, although she had resisted it the first three times she walked past it, she was human and gave in, indulging in the sweet, toasty goodness. She also learned more about the history of Nutcrackers than she ever thought possible, at the local museum.

Five o'clock Pacific time finally arrived. Holly tempered the urge to find Nik's office and jump out at him like a crazed stalker the second he exited the building. She also shot down the idea of perching herself on the hood of his car. Instead, she waited impatiently next to his car, casually posing against the driver's side door.

"The best part of my day." Nik strode toward Holly. She threw her arms open and welcomed him in. Nik turned his face toward the top of Holly's head. She heard him breathe in. She was thankful she'd washed her hair that morning. They lingered in their embrace/hair smelling stance until a *honk* startled them.

"You coming or going, lovebirds? There's no parking for blocks," barked a weary-looking man driving a vintage mustang that was the color of split pea soup.

"Going. Hang on, you can have our spot." Nik opened the passenger side door of his car for Holly before running over to the driver's side and getting in. Even in a rush Nik didn't compromise thoughtful gestures. He waved to the weary traveler as he and Holly entered the bumper-to-bumper traffic down main street at dinner time. They kept the AC off and rolled down the windows. The whirl of the village provided a layered soundtrack of wonder, impatience, and indulgence. For a while they listened in comfortable silence, transitioning from their time apart to their time together.

"Can't wait to hear about your day. Is it all right if we pick up sandwich stuff and eat on the patio at the A-frame? Town is crawling with tourists this time of night and I want to give you my undivided attention."

Holly's cheeks warmed. A quiet evening, just the two of them, sounded perfect.

"Same scene, different Bavarian village. Summer tourists plus dinner time equals a migration of the locals to the outskirts of town. Except for those who are serving the tourists." Holly wondered how Elaine was holding up without her. She missed their nightly walks around the park.

"It's tempting to complain about the influx of tourists yet they butter the bread and feed the economy with their appetites. Wait until the Christmas in July Festival. They come in droves and with Harry as the headliner we may reach an all-time high."

They stopped at the grocery store outside of town and quickly located the items they needed.

On their way over to her rental, Nik said, "Are you opposed to us asking our question of the day in the car. I don't want to rush it, but there's more I want to talk about later."

"Fine with me. Hang on." Holly reached for her backpack on the floor and retrieved the glass jar, still safely intact. She reached her hand in and drew out a question. Holly didn't tell Nik that Frank had snagged one of the questions from the jar earlier and asked her about it.

"Lay it on me."

"What do you want to save, what do you need to toss?" Holly read. "That's kind of a strange one. I wonder how Cash and Everleigh Rae answered that?"

"He probably said, 'I want to save our B & B, Baby, but we've got to toss out the debt or we're sunk.'" Nik twanged.

"Or, 'I want to save my sanity, Cash, so we need to toss our differences aside and start getting along. We need that spark back and yelling it out ain't working." Holly tipped her imaginary cowgirl hat toward Nik.

"Can we either save this question for another time or toss it out? It is kind of weird."

"Nik, I'm shocked. We're not playing by the rules?"

"Look who's talking."

He didn't know how right he was. Not only had Holly pre-read one of the questions on her way to Leavenworth, but another guy, namely Frank, had asked her one of the questions earlier that day.

"Fine, fine, how about this one? What's your most embarrassing moment?" Holly read. "Too many to count. But if we're starting with today I have several examples. But, why don't you start?"

Nik clicked on his blinker, finally able to pass the pokey car in front of him. "If we're focusing on today, I was so busy at work that I accidentally poured the liquid from a sourdough bread starter into my iced coffee, instead of creamer.

"How did that happen?" Holly scrunched her nose.

"They were both in a glass jar and I reached for it and dumped it in my drink. I was getting ready to take a swig when I was stopped by my co-worker, the maker of the gooey bread starter, who had witnessed the mix-up."

Holly was relieved this work story wasn't about Marina too, since she was gluten free and all.

They had arrived at the A-frame. They parked and walked up the short path to the cottage, side by side. Nik carried the bag of groceries.

"Did you drink the coffee?" Holly asked, picking up their conversation where it had left off.

"No, I was stopped in the knick of time. She nearly fell on me, she ran so fast to save the day." Nik laughed.

"And who is *she* exactly?" Holly didn't laugh.

"Marina, of course. She always has my back. She often sees what others miss. Which comes in handy when we're poring over contracts for the Christmas in July Festival."

"If Marina is so observant, how did she miss the fact that

sourdough bread has gluten in it?"

"Not this batch, Aunt Claire sent her a recipe without it."

"How delicious." Holly felt sick to her stomach.

"Needless to say I threw out the coffee and settled for water. I'm excited for you to meet everyone at the office tomorrow." Nik squeezed her shoulder as they reached the stairs to the deck. It did not have the same impact that Mr. Neumann's squeeze had on Betty Jo. But it had in the past. Nothing to worry about, right? Just a more guarded response to his touch, after hearing another Marina story from work.

"Uh, huh." Holly entered the code to the front door.

They emptied the contents of their grocery bag on the counter and worked together to make a basic charcuterie spread.

"Your turn to answer the question." Nik sliced the Havarti cheese nice and thin.

Holly maneuvered the salami in a flower shape while the grapes drained in a colander. Food art at its finest.

Where should Holly start? Should she tell Nik about the spontaneous outing with Frank? Of course she should, there was nothing to hide. Would she include her panic attack on the coaster? She knew Nik cared for her, but she did not like admitting her weakness at every turn. Or should she keep it more light-hearted and re-enact Betty Jo's hilarious cell phone confession. Or would she broach Frank's confession, first?

Holly decided to toss out the ones about Frank, for now, and save the one about the panic attack for another time. The tale of Betty Jo and Bavarian Fall's most eligible, geriatric bachelor won out. No need to kill the mood with the 'morbs.'

CHAPTER SEVENTEEN
What's one of your biggest fears?

THEIR LAUGHTER EVENTUALLY SUBSIDED AFTER HOLLY'S attempt to impersonate Betty Jo. Holly and Nik took their culinary creation out to the picnic table on the back patio. Over fresh fruit, crackers, and cheese, Holly informed Nik about Frank's unexpected appearance in Leavenworth and their alpine coaster outing. "That's why I wasn't at the pretzel stand when you sneaked out of the office to surprise me."

"Why didn't you text and let me know what was going on?" Nik's laughter lines had disappeared.

"For some reason I agreed to let Frank hold my phone and backpack hostage in the trunk of his rental, because he was trying to surprise me." As soon as the words were out of her mouth, Holly realized the sting of the irony.

"So I was trying to surprise you at the same time Frank already was surprising you." Nik looked stung.

"Something like that," Holly mumbled. She brushed cracker crumbs off the picnic table.

"Wonder why Frank didn't text me to let me know he was in town?" Nik looked out into the woods, past Holly.

"Sounded like he was on a pretty tight timeline. He had a work meeting and then needed to get back to Bavarian Falls before a big ornament shipment was scheduled to arrive." Holly stared at Nik, who was still staring into the woods.

"But enough time to surprise you." Nik said almost inaudibly.

"Dessert?" Holly stood up, clearing the dishes from the table.

"I'll help." Nik grabbed their glasses and they headed back inside to enjoy strawberry shortcake.

The ground beneath them felt a little shaky, so Holly didn't venture further into the waters of vulnerability and disclose about her panic attack. She felt like she knew Nik well enough to know her admission wouldn't phase him too much. He'd probably be concerned but understanding. Then again, she didn't anticipate that the spontaneous outing with Frank would be a big deal, so could she really be sure how Nik would respond?

Nik left the A-frame around nine pm. It had been a roller coaster of a day, literally and emotionally. Holly couldn't fall sleep, so she binge-watched episodes of "The Office"—laughing a lot, crying a little—before finally giving in to exhaustion.

The morning light hit the upper window of the loft before Holly was ready. On cue, the birds started whistling their symphony, beckoning sleeping beauty, with the dragon breath, to rise.

Take-your-girlfriend-to-work day had arrived and Holly didn't want to look like she had just rolled out of bed. Today was a new day and she was determined to remain optimistic. Finally, she would be able to put names to faces and enter a part of Nik's life that felt out of reach. What was Nik like at the office, more laid back or more intense? More Jim Halpert or more Dwight Schrute? She would soon find out.

⁂

Holly held back a yawn as she and Nik strolled, hand in hand, toward his office building. Nik looked like he had slept like a baby, plus he smelled fresh and clean.

"I wish there was more time available, but it'll be a fairly short meet 'n greet with our small but mighty crew, then it's back to the grind as we tie up the loose ends with the Christmas in July

Festival. Everyone's excited to meet you." Nik kissed Holly on the cheek. "You look stunning. Don't worry, they already love you."

"They don't even know me." Holly pulled at her dress that was sticking to the back of her legs. She was embarrassed to admit how much time she had overthought her outfit. She hoped the navy knit dress with the green belt would communicate casual sophistication, like 'I'm put together but not too fussy.' Although Holly had never felt all the way put together in her life. It was like there was a tiny snag that, if pulled hard enough, would unravel.

"Here we are." Nik swept his arm toward the exposed brick and stucco building. The wooden flower boxes underneath the arched windows boasted a fragrant, cheery welcome.

Holly gave herself a pep talk as she entered the revolving door of the office. *Be more chill and less uptight. More Pam Beesly, less Angela Martin.*

But this wasn't an audition or an interview. It was a natural progression in the next stage of Holly's and Nik's relationship.

They entered a spacious, circular lobby with a high ceiling and skylights. Modern touches met alpine aesthetic. A set of white and Bavarian blue checked upholstered chairs, with a bourbon barrel endtable between them, provided an inviting sitting area. Snake plants in stucco pots completed the classy yet comfortable feel of Nik's place of employment. A mural of downtown Leavenworth wrapped almost all the way around the lobby. Holly was excited to examine it closer. She had never seen this part of Nik's office building when they video chatted. He met her kid-in-a-candy-story, or more accurately, her art-degree-student-in-a-museum, expression with a knowing smile.

"I've kept a few surprises, hoping you'd be able to see this in person one day." Nik took Holly's hand and lifted it into the air. On cue, she ducked under their clasped hands, slowly spinning in the exquisite space. The skirt of her navy dress spun away from her in an elegant *swoosh*. She took in the mural as she twirled. It told a layered history, beginning in untamed nature and moving to the conventions of modern life, with brushstrokes of saturating colors and intentionality. This was the stuff that drew Holly in, and drew her true self out. Out into a wide, open space.

Holly felt Nik studying her, enjoying her. She spun slowly once more, free to be herself.

Nik knew her. Not everything, not every inch, not yet. But he knew Holly well enough to understand the type of beauty that would welcome her back to wonder.

"There you are!" Someone shouted from the upper level.

Holly stopped mid-spin. Nik dropped his hand. Outwardly, the tender moment ended abruptly. Yet the sweetness and lightness of 'knowing and being known' floated above them.

A small group of men and women of various ages, shapes, and sizes noisily rushed down the stairs toward Holly and Nik.

"We don't have much time to spare but it's nice to meet you. I work in HR." A middle-aged gentleman shook Holly's hand firmly. He extended the typical niceties but Holly was pretty sure, based on his stern expression, that he'd rather be having a root canal than participating in a meet 'n greet with his co-worker's girlfriend. Holly felt like she was in trouble as HR man surveyed the room and gave her the side-eye several times. No wonder Nik hadn't been able to get away, this guy was as cuddly as a porcupine.

"Pleasure to meet you, Holly. I brought loads of snacks from the local deli for this special occasion. They're in the conference room, help yourself after the tour." A cozy grandmother type looked like she wanted to hug Holly but opted for a gentle hand pat. She reminded Holly of her late Grandma Bea.

There were a few more introductions before Nik's co-workers scattered to their workspaces, except for one, who had been on a phone call, until a few moments ago.

"Holly, meet Marina. Marina, meet Holly." Nik introduced his girlfriend to the co-worker who always had his back.

Marina bounced over and hugged Holly as if they were summer camp friends. Marina smelled like mango. Holly wasn't sure if it was her hair product or lotion, or both.

Marina let go. Holly straightened her green belt.

"Jazzed to meet you!" Marina's eyes twinkled. Her smile radiated from her like sunshine.

Holly took a step closer to Nik. It wasn't lost on her that Marina kind of, sort of resembled Karen Filippelli from "The Office" mockumentary sitcom. Except Marina was shorter and her head was crowned with gorgeous shoulder-length, dark ringlet curls.

"We've heard so much about you." Marina's presence filled the room. She couldn't be ignored, even at only five foot and a few inches. Her raspberry-pink and lime-flowered blouse and black pencil skirt complimented her tawny skin.

Was this firecracker of joy part of the reason Nik couldn't manage a trip to Bavarian Falls, or was it solely mopey HR man who was probably already back at his cubicle?

Holly's mind whirled. She sorted out reality from her late-night binge watching of "The Office." On the episode she had dozed off to, the character of Karen was Jim Halpert's girlfriend. But she was his *temporary* girlfriend, not his soul mate. They shared some history. History that Pam—his true love—hadn't been a part of. And vice versa. But at the end of the day, dreamboat Jim and front-desk Pam went together like peanut butter and jelly, or as Betty Jo would say, 'corn beef and sauerkraut.' That was a fact.

Move out of the way, Karen.

"Yeah, same." Holly blinked, thankful her inner thoughts weren't being projected on a TV screen behind her.

"I heard you had quite the adventure at Dasher's Reindeer Resort?" Marina swayed. The girl didn't stand still. Holly wouldn't have been surprised if she started cha cha-ing around the lobby or bursting into a version of the theme song from "Encanto." That was it! Marina was the mid-twenties version of the animated character, Mirabel Madrigal, who had had a bit of a glow up. Too bad Frank wasn't still in town, Holly could introduce him to Marina Schmeena. The energy between them would be enough to power a whole Bavarian village, or at the very least create electrifying sparks.

"I hope you don't mind, but after our boy Nik told me all about your date gone wild, I took it upon myself to commemorate the experience with a….hang on!" Marina bounced over to the reception area and retrieved a cardboard tube from behind the counter. She presented it to Holly. "Open sesame."

Holly unscrewed the plastic lid and turned the tube over to empty its contents.

"What is it?" Nik looked over her shoulder.

Holly unrolled an 11 x 14 collage poster of the staged photos of her and Nik, in costume, with the reindeer. One was of them smiling at the camera, another one captured Nik rubbing his sore cheeks while Holly laughed at him, another showed baby Blitzen eating Holly's apron while she shooed her away and Nik adjusted his sliding fedora, and lastly, there was one of Nik and Holly gazing lovingly at each other, oblivious to the fact that one of the baby reindeer was relieving himself in the foreground.

Marina had added a caption in the center: In Reindeer of Shinedeer, I'm glad you're mine, dear.

"Get it?" Marina elbowed Nik and waggled her full eyebrows at Holly.

"You're so punny." Nik elbowed her back.

"That was thoughtful. Thank you, Marina." Holly studied the poster. It definitely represented the various dimensions of her and Nik's relationship.

"I toyed with another caption, but it didn't land as well as that one. In good times, or stinky, you're wrapped around my pinky."

"Oh, dear." Holly groaned. She could be punny too. She carefully rolled up the poster.

"Exactly!" Marina elbowed Holly.

Nik laughed, putting his arm around them both. It was almost a group hug, but not quite.

Before grouchy HR man could break up the silly banter in the lobby, Marina got a call from Harry Connick Jr.'s people to finalize the details of his contract rider. She shimmied out of sight.

Holly wondered what Harry required on his rider. Room temperature carbonated sparkling water? A spread of fancy appetizers from renowned local chefs? Or did it include something strange like five perfectly ripened organic cherries from the Yakima Valley, dipped in chocolate, or gold—simply because he could? *Nah.* Harry seemed down to earth and humble. He probably wasn't high maintenance. The room temperature carbonated sparkling water was probably likely though.

"Ready for the rest of the tour?" Nik offered his arm to Holly. "You did great by the way. Our little crew can be a lot."

They walked up the stairs. When they were almost to the top, Holly turned back to see the impressive lobby from higher up. It would make the perfect backdrop for a book launch party or a fundraiser–or an engagement party.

On the second level, Nik pointed out the conference room with the panoramic view of the mountains.

Holly gasped. "I don't think I'd be able to get anything done if I worked in a place like this. I'd get lost in the endless inspiration outside the window and forget all about deadlines. Don't tell me you're used to it?"

"It's a stunner for sure, but you eventually learn to work alongside it." Nik handed Holly a clear plastic plate. She set down her phone and the cardboard tube that held the poster.

A robust spread of snacks from the local deli was set up in one corner. They each filled a plate to take with them, then Nik led Holly to his office area. His desk was tidy, except for a large stack of papers with numbers, scribbles, and diagrams on them. Next to the stack there was a framed, commemorative photo from the winter carriage ride he and Holly had taken in Bavarian Falls this past Christmas Eve, her birthday.

"This is where it all started." Holly picked up the picture.

"We're still going strong." Nik briefly ran his fingertip down the back of Holly's arm before straightening the stack of papers and setting his plate of food on top of them.

"Mr. Beckenbauer, I'm blushing." Holly nibbled on a melt-in-your-mouth goat cheese cube.

Nik stacked his cracker high with pepperoni and cheese, "I don't know how I'm going to focus on my work with all this distracting beauty in front of me." Nik winked at Holly before taking a bite.

"What are you working on today?"

"The list is a mile long."

"Anything I can do to help?"

"You're supposed to be writing the next Newberry Award winner, remember? Or drinking in all Leavenworth has to offer. Or finishing more of the grant work." Nik half-talked, half-read an email marked URGENT.

"If I didn't know better, I'd say you're trying to get rid of me?"

"Hang on." Nik swiveled his chair toward his computer, both feet under his desk, his eyes glued to the screen.

Holly busied herself with a perfectly ripened cherry, not dipped in chocolate or gold. It tasted like heaven.

Nik was immersed in the URGENT email. "What did you say, again?" He started typing a response.

Holly answered the back of his head. "I'm in good shape on the grant work, and still trying to untangle some of the words on the manuscript, but I can't stare at it anymore. As far as Leavenworth goes, I may explore some of the shops later on."

"Uh-huh." Nik typed feverishly.

Holly could have told him she had decided to join the circus to become a tightrope walker and he would have nodded and kept working.

"I don't want to be in the way, but I'm serious about my offer. Is there anything I can do?"

"How do they expect us to add that to the mix?" Nik started massaging his temple.

"What is it?" Holly gingerly rubbed Nik's back trying to comfort him.

Marina barged in. Holly dropped her hand.

"I wish I could help, Nik, but I'm tied up with a new glitch in the contract." Marina pointed to her phone. They must have both received the same email.

"Thanks for offering." Nik stabbed a toothpick into a slice of pepperoni.

"I'm surprised that we're responsible for that part too, but like our company motto says, 'We handle the stress so you can explore, play, and rest.'" Marina acted out the last three verbs with pizazz and a hint of sass. "Gotta get back to putting out this fire. But I'll check back in when I'm done." Marina hopped on her phone and exited with a wave to Holly.

"I don't want to be in the way. You sure there's nothing I can do?" Holly shifted her weight from one hip to the other.

Nik swiveled toward her. "I sincerely want you to go explore, play, and rest." One side of Nik's mouth lifted in a partial, yet defeated smile. He didn't offer any hand motions to punctuate the slogan, like Marina had.

"While you handle the stress?" Holly cupped his shoulder. Then in a moment of playfulness she spun him around. He grabbed her waist and pulled her on his lap as they spun together. Their legs nearly knocked over the water cooler behind Nik's desk. They tried to minimize their giggles.

"What's going on in here?" Grouchy HR man barked from the doorway.

Holly stood, the room wobbling. She reached for the corner of Nik's desk to steady herself.

"Sorry, Holly's leaving now. I'm working on a solution to our signage problem." Nik busied himself with the papers on his desk.

"Good. We don't want to mess this up. I don't have to remind you, there's a lot riding on this." He nodded at Holly and left.

"I think he needs a nap and a snack." Holly whispered in Nik's ear.

"I love having you here, Hol. But I've got to tackle this signage problem, the team is counting on me. Plus, I want to get out of here on time so you and I can maximize our time together."

"Signage, huh?"

"Yeah, apparently we need a massive Christmas in July sign for the festival, to hang above the outdoor stage. It needs to have each business that is sponsoring the event represented on it. However, there are more specific stipulations. They want it to somewhat resemble the mural downstairs. That thing is a work of art, it took months to complete, and we only have two weeks and some change until the concert. Such an impossible ask so late in the game. We're hard-working and reliable, but we're not miracle workers." Nik crinkled his forehead.

"If only you were dating an artist who had overseen a mural before and is caught up on her work back home and is looking for a way to meaningfully spend her time while she waits for her dreamy boyfriend to get off work?" Holly took a sharp breath and blew it out after delivering her playful run-on sentence to her stressed-out boyfriend.

"I'm sure that's not how you want to spend the rest of your time here." Nik rifled through his papers trying to locate something important.

"Close to you? Being creative? Helping you out? Yeah, sounds terrible." Holly put her hands on her hips.

"It might work...I'll text Marina and see if she can set you up with supplies in the conference room. That way you can spread out."

"Have you seen my phone?" Holly realized she must have lost it along the way on their tour.

"Maybe it's in the lobby? Or maybe you set it down in the conference room when we were getting snacks?" Nik said, not looking up from his computer.

"I'll bet that's it. I'll check when I set up shop."

Nik was busy texting back and forth. Holly waited.

"Marina is going to drop off supplies in the conference room for you. You sure you're okay with this?" Nik swiveled toward Holly.

"Glad to help alleviate some of the stress. Besides, it'll be fun."

He reached for her hands and kissed them both.

✥

Holly researched and sketched out rough ideas for the mural for a few hours. Nik poked his head into the conference room. "You're the best, you know that?"

"Happy to help. Besides, it's giving me time to think through the kids' book too. Sometimes inspiration for another project strikes as I'm living life and doing the next thing in front of me." Holly set down her drawing pencil and stood back to assess her work.

"Unfortunately, I only have about ten minutes for lunch today. You okay with us loading up on these snacks and eating in here?"

"Can't complain about the view, the company, or the food." Holly joined Nik at the fridge. He pulled out a colorful fruit tray and cream cheese dip.

"How about we ask one of the questions now?" Holly grabbed two plates and napkins and brought them to the table.

"If you want to. We don't have much time, but we'll take what we can get, right?" Nik sat down.

"Communicating in the cracks, that's what we do. The poster children for making a long distance relationship work despite the challenges." Holly took the seat next to Nik. She pulled out the paper she'd slipped inside her dress pocket when she was getting ready that morning. She handed it to Nik.

"What's one of your biggest fears?" Nik read as he dipped his grape into the fruit dip.

"Forgetting to apply deodorant. It's the worst." Holly did a quick, discrete sniff to confirm today wasn't one of those days.

"You have nothing to worry about. But even if you're ever stinky, you're still wrapped around my pinky." Nik didn't elbow her.

"Ha! Glad to hear that. In all seriousness, one of my biggest fears is losing what I've gained. Unless it comes to the extra five pounds I'd like to lose, then my fear is gaining back what I've lost."

"You're perfect just the way you are."

"Far from it, but seriously, my biggest fear, which probably is no surprise, is messing things up or not being able to fully recover after an unexpected loss. And I'm not talking about misplacing my phone." Holly reached for her water, thinking about her dad. She could feel Nik's gaze on her.

"One of my biggest fears is letting people down." Nik didn't expound. His words hung in the air. Holly turned toward him. He looked out the window. She waited, giving him room to share more if he wanted to. Was he referring to his parents, to work, or her? Nik reached for another grape.

"I wanted to run something by you. When we started the IOU questions we asked each other two questions a week, from across the miles, but, in person, we've been doing a question a day and we're about to run out, and I still have three weeks left of my trip." Holly refolded the paper with the question on it.

"I'm fine with slowing down the questions." Nik wiped his hands with a napkin. His watch *dinged*. He read and swiped a notification. "I hate to cut this short. Duty calls." Nik stood abruptly and tossed the rest of his uneaten plate in the trash. "I'll try and check in later. Thanks again." He rushed off.

Holly had made a lot of progress in not always seeing the glass half empty, in life, and in their relationship. She worked hard to take Nik at his word and not read between the lines. But something about the way he'd answered made her question. *Was Nik actually saying he was fine with them slowing down their relationship too? Was it too much with his current workload? Was she too much?* Holly tried to order her rogue thoughts to time out. Nik had spun her slowly in front of a mural, for Pete's sake. It didn't get much more romantic than that. Weren't they past second-guessing and entering into the sure thing stage?

What was Holly's problem? Something felt a little off, but she couldn't put her finger on it. Nik still hadn't said 'I love you.' Maybe that was it? Was he not sure or was Holly putting too much expectation on those words and on him? Or was she reading him wrong? Maybe he had a Jim Halpert surprise up his sleeve and that's why he was preoccupied? And maybe Karen—err, Marina—was going to be transferred to another office? One could hope. Although Marina was likable which complicated things. But she wasn't Pam. No one could replace Pam—err Holly.

However, this was real life, not a sitcom. And Holly didn't have a copy of the script that spelled out what happened next with her and Nik.

A *tap tap* on the hallway window startled Holly as she pored over drawings. "Hey, Holly, found your phone." Marina held it up. "It was in here earlier, so I picked it up for safe keeping but didn't have a chance to check back until now."

"Thank you. I appreciate that."

"You're really saving the day taking over the mural." Marina said.

"My pleasure. Having your boyfriend's back is what girlfriends do." The sweet-sounding comment with the sassy undertone flew out of Holly's mouth, marking her territory, making sure Marina knew Nik was off limits. She stared at Marina, determined not to blink.

"That's the goal." Marina replied flatly. Miss Pep-in-her-step was not smiling. Apparently, the Christmas in July Festival had sucked the joy right out of the office.

※

The streetlight turned red and Holly hurried across the pedestrian crosswalk. She needed a break from the mural prep, and because she was not on the clock like the rest of Nik and his co-workers, she left the office for a little while to renew her inspiration.

Holly wandered into a gift shop a few doors down from Nik's office building that housed a variety of treasures and trinkets. The perfect distraction from over-analyzing the office interactions. She probably should pick out a few things to take back home with her.

From large paintings to greeting cards, the work of local artists was on display around the store. Oils and watercolors, sketches and mosaics of the surrounding mountains and of the downtown area enticed Holly. She plucked several cards from their designated holders to take a closer look. The local art on the front depicted notable scenery from the region. On the inside, German phrases tied a sentiment to the scene on the cover. One particular card stood out from the rest. Indigo, sapphire, and maroon squares came together to create a mosaic mountain, but one of the squares was missing near the middle of the mountain. It looked unfinished. Holly wondered if there had been a mistake made in the art transfer process—from paper to digital scanning. She contemplated it further. Maybe the void was intentional, maybe it was supposed to represent a cave?

Holly opened the art to expose the sentiment, and maybe more of an explanation, inside.
Its contents read:
Es fühlt sich an, als würde etwas fehlen.
It feels like something is missing.

Etwas fehlt mir und wird mir immer fehlen.
Something is missing and I will always miss you.

Holly touched her hand to her mouth. It said little, but much. She closed the card and studied the front again, like she had in art school, considering different angles, untapped discoveries.

The mountain was still standing. It had not crumbled, even though a large stone had been removed. Had it fallen or been excavated? The mountain was altered from its intended design. The picture was incomplete. The colors royal, the void felt. The eye of the beholder was drawn to both—the beauty and the missing piece.

Holly walked up to the counter and purchased a stamp and the card. It was just the right gift, a combination of local art, Leavenworth scenery, and a message of understanding. She filled out the card and envelope at the counter. She affixed the stamp, sealed the envelope, and slipped the letter into the mailbox outside the gift shop. She prayed the whimsical art and the simple message she had jotted inside to her sister-in-law would deliver comfort across the miles.

Dear Monica,
To our missing piece—never forgotten, forever loved.
Thinking of you,
Holly

CHAPTER EIGHTEEN
What makes you angry?

FOUR DAYS HAD PASSED SINCE HOLLY volunteered to take on the signage project for the Christmas in July Festival. She had made significant progress on the grant work and her manuscript in the mornings. If Ernest Hemingway could garner literary inspiration from his family cottage on Walloon Lake, then maybe Holly could pen a children's classic in the charming A-frame near Leavenworth. It was quite the quintessential writing experience.

Around noon each day, Nik left work and picked Holly up from her rental and they munched on a simple lunch and caught up on the drive downtown. She accompanied him back to the office so she could work on the mural in the afternoons. Holly had pretty much taken over the conference room. The massive sign was slowly but surely taking shape, and the staff was grateful for her help. Even grouchy HR man had expressed his thanks. Holly didn't see much of Marina, but Nik reported she was knee-deep in logistics for the concert.

After working their tails off during the work week it was finally Saturday and time to explore, play, and rest. Holly would hardly call a three-and-a-half mile hike up Cascade Trail restful, but she had assured Nik she was ready for the challenge. She didn't tell him that her resolve had intensified when she caught wind that Marina had led the way on the trail during a work bonding excursion. Ready or not, Holly was geared up for their much-anticipated date, complete with Elaine's snug hiking boots, her backpack, and an ice cold water bottle.

Nik was unusually quiet as they stood at the base of the trail. Maybe he was tired? Or maybe their break from asking each other the IOU questions had left them with little to say? Could it be they'd reached the point where their default was contented silence because they were more secure in their relationship?

Bright blue sky served as the backdrop as evergreens stood at attention, pointing to the rocky gray mountain peaks with a dusting of snow high above them. The sign at the trailhead gave a warning to stay on the marked path and not disturb the wildlife. It promised a spectacular view at the top. There was a lot of trail between the parking lot and their end goal. Holly tightened her backpack straps. Step by step, she could do this.

"Ready?" Nik broke the silence and they began the trek.

Three-and-a-half miles had sounded doable, but Holly quickly realized the hike would require more out of her than she expected. They navigated switchbacks, a log bridge over a creek, and loose rock along the way. The heat, the steep incline, and the need to watch her step carefully, so she didn't faceplant into the dirt, slowed down the process. She suspected Nik was holding back from his usual clip up the trail in order to stay with her. Holly hated being an amateur at things. She'd been on only a few hikes in her life. It was probably a rookie move not to have broken in her footwear ahead of time. Holly had walked more than a mile in her friend's boots and her feet were killing her. But she was set on not complaining and proving she could hike like the best of them.

They rounded a sharp, narrow corner on the trail. Holly was determined not to lose her balance on the loose rock. She hummed nervously, trying to focus on the rising and falling melody more than the steep drop off. Her heart rate quickened. She quietly tried to steady her breathing.

In and out. In and out. Just take the next step and then the one after that.

She was going to be okay. They had made good progress.

Nik stopped ahead of her. "I hate to interrupt our momentum..." Nik put his sunglasses on top of his baseball hat. He bent down on one knee to retie his boot's shoelace. "But there's something I need to ask you." His serious steely blue eyes homed in on her, while his fingers kept tying.

Holly was sweating from the exertion of making it three-fourths of the way up the trail, according to the mile maker they'd recently passed. She blotted her neck and face with the bandana. Nik turned his attention back to his shoelace. He sure was taking a while to say whatever it was that he wanted.

A squirrel darted through the woods behind Nik, startling Holly. Nik didn't seem to notice, but the peripheral movement alerted Holly to the present and pulled her out of her head. All of a sudden she realized that Nik was stalling and he was still on one knee! Was he about to propose? Here? Three-fourths of the way up the trail? Is that why he had been so quiet? He was probably nervous. Holly wished she wasn't sweating so much.

Since she was a tween, she had dreamed of what this moment might be like, when the man she loved would ask her one of the most important questions of her life. Would he choose a public or private location? Would he shout it from a rooftop—or mountain top—or whisper it in her ear? Would he use many words or few? Holly had hoped it wouldn't be at a sporting event on the jumbotron. Would it be as sweet as her dad's proposal to her mom? Or as amusing as Gabe's proposal to Monica? Would Holly see it coming or be surprised?

Nik was working on the lace of his other boot. "Hang on."

He was clearly stalling. Holly took a quick drink of cool water and patted her forehead again with the bandana. Ever since she'd arrived in Leavenworth Nik had been anticipating this hike. No wonder! He must have had it all planned out. It seemed like he would have waited until they reached the top of the trail, with the spectacular view, but maybe he was so excited and nervous he couldn't wait any longer?

"Holly?" Nik brushed off his knee then looked up at her, still crouched down.

"Yes, Nik?" Holly's voice grew quiet, and she took a step closer to him.

"About the next question..."

Oh my goodness! He's going to use the next IOU question to ask me to marry him?! This is the sweetest.

"I noticed the other day there's one question missing. I only saw three left in the jar, but should there be four? Where is the other one?"

Holly racked her brain, trying to recall what happened. Had it fallen out? It took her several seconds to remember that Frank had asked her one of the questions at Bertha's Bavarian Pretzels, on the day of their outing.

"You'll never believe this. I don't know why I didn't mention it before." Although Holly knew why she hadn't mentioned it because she felt like she had betrayed Nik inadvertently when Frank had asked her one of her and Nik's questions. Not to mention that Nik was less than enthused about her and Frank's surprise outing together. "Um...remember when Frank appeared out of nowhere? Well, he grabbed a question out of the jar while I was sitting there working on the kids' book at Betha's." Holly backpedaled.

Nik stood up, no longer on one knee. "You and Frank did one of the questions together?"

"I didn't mean to. It kind of happened before I could stop

it." Holly fumbled with the sweaty bandana in her hands.

"Like the kind of, sort of date to the Alpine Coaster?" Nik grabbed the straps of his backpack.

"That's not fair. It wasn't like that." Holly shifted her weight. This was not a good segue into a proposal.

"He's had a thing for you for a while."

"We're just friends. I've made that clear, although I thought I was going to have to set him straight yet again. But it wasn't like that—"

"Set him straight?" Nik repositioned his baseball hat.

"He wanted my opinion about something."

"You sure that was it?" Nik looked over Holly's head to the trail behind them as if he was surveying the distance that they had already climbed.

Holly opened her mouth to react, then stopped herself. She probably looked like a puffer fish, sucking air. What had gotten into Nik? Insecurity was her kryptonite, not his. It didn't suit him. Holly wanted it to stop. But what ground did she have to stand on, besides the precarious section of trail where her feet were firmly planted in borrowed boots? She was often quick to think the worst. But why was Nik? His steadiness seemed to be crumbling like the loose stones on the edge of the cliff. What was the root?

"It seems like every time you face something difficult, Frank appears. Swooping in like a wealthy benefactor to take your mind off your momentary troubles and give you the time of your life."

"What on earth, Nik? That's a complete exaggeration. Besides, I would hardly call nearly wetting my pants from being scared silly on the coaster as having the time of my life." Holly threw her hands up.

"What *was* the question?" Nik crossed his arms.

A rustle behind Nik interrupted Holly's train of thought. The squirrel was back. It darted up a tree. She watched it climb higher and higher, confidently navigating a narrow branch.

Nik cleared his throat as if trying to redirect her attention back to the heated conversation and away from the squirrel.

"What are your pet peeves?" Holly asked, while the brave little squirrel risked his life for his next meal.

"Since you already shared them with Frank, why don't you go first, since they're still fresh in your mind."

Holly glared at Nik from behind her sunglasses. She rattled off her pet peeves, "My top five are: loud chewing, turning without signaling, passive aggressive comments, spoilers—especially during a movie I haven't seen yet, and people speaking about themselves in third person."

"Interesting." Nik pulled down his sunglasses, positioning them under his baseball hat.

"There's one I should add though."

"What's that?"

"False accusations are also a pet peeve of mine." Holly reattached her bandana to her backpack strap. She tied the knot tight. Two could play this game.

"Oh really? Could have fooled me. You're a pro at them." Nik cinched her backpack straps.

Nik had been on the receiving end of Holly's false accusations and now she was the recipient of his. Her pulse throbbed in her ears. What a pair they were. The walking wounded. Sticks and stones weren't breaking bones, but the sharp jab of words were hurting them. Would they bleed out from the careless communication hurled between them?

Nik drank from his water bottle. The excess splashed from his mouth. "Let's go take a hike." He turned away from her and started walking up the trail.

"My thoughts exactly." Holly muttered around her breath, yet loud enough for Nik to hear.

Nik and Holly walked in silence the remaining fourth of a mile. As they trudged forward, navigating sharp turns around boulders, Holly replayed Frank's declaration at the picnic table, near the base of the alpine coaster.

"I guess this is as good a time as any." Frank had scarfed down his second taco. "I don't know why I'm making such a big deal out of it. Maybe because it feels like there's a lot riding on the answer?"

Holly swallowed hard. Was Frank about to confess that his romantic interest in her had not waned? Holly wished she could freeze the conversation so she could call Elaine or text her discreetly to ask for advice. She didn't want to hurt Frank, but what was he thinking? Holly had a boyfriend whom she adored.

"We've been friends for a while now and well, I'm gonna blurt it out. I really like—"

"Don't say it." Holly thrust her hand forward to intercept his declaration. "I thought we've been over this before, Frank. I don't want to hurt you."

"Wait, what? Did you think I was going to say I liked you?" Frank laughed, a little too forcefully.

"Sure sounded that way." Holly clasped her hands and put them in her lap.

"It's Elaine. I like Elaine. Your best friend. I don't like her because she's your best friend. Although you have good taste in friends." Frank pointed at himself. "I like her because she's fun and easy-going. Okay, okay, and her three-point shot only adds to the attraction. Shall I go on?" He washed his confession down with swig of pop.

Holly waited a few beats before responding. She felt relieved she was not the recipient of Frank's current affections, just his friendship. Holly also felt embarrassed she had assumed Frank was talking about her instead of someone else. Of course Frank had a thing for Elaine. They were good friends, a powerful duo at karaoke and on the basketball court, and they were both committed to Bavarian Falls for the long run.

"She's really great, Frank. Solid choice." Holly sipped the last bit of drink through her straw. It sputtered in protest.

"If I work up the courage to tell Elaine how I feel but she's not into me, then I'm concerned it will mess up our friendship. We've got a good thing going." Frank finished off the last few tortilla chips.

"That is a risk, but maybe she feels the same way?" Holly didn't want to set Frank up for possible hurt, but she also didn't want to discourage him from moving forward if this was supposed to happen. Holly honestly didn't know how Elaine felt about Frank. Did she see him as more than a friend? What about Andy? How did he fit into the picture, if at all?

"Not sure. I hope so." Frank turned his attention to the *roarrr* from the coaster above. "Too bad we don't have time to ride it again. That was epic!"

Holly picked up their trash and discarded it in the waste basket.

Frank stood and stretched his legs and arms. "Are you okay with it?"

"With the possibility of you and Elaine becoming more than friends?" Holly tightened her ponytail.

Frank nodded. "Yeah that."

"You don't need my permission. You're both adults."

"But I don't want it to be weird."

"It'll be fine, my friend. And weird." Holly laughed, assessing the boy-man before her, taller than most, young at heart, and likely the future CEO of the massively successful mile-long Christmas store.

Frank tried to push his bucket hat down on Holly's head, playfully teasing his friend—not his love interest. Holly dodged his attempt.

Frank and Elaine, indeed. Time would tell, but all was well.

The friends walked toward the path that led to the parking lot. Holly had her eyes wide open on the way back down.

Holly slipped in her earbuds as she walked behind Nik toward the next incline. Normally she preferred the birds' song to manufactured tunes, but she craved some sort of shield between Nik's silence and the birds' happy song. She pushed play as the songs started shuffling on her summer playlist. "Deep End" by Birdy started playing. The lyrics paralleled reality, beckoning introspection.

The last stretch of trail was steep. They had to watch their step closely or they'd fall. Step by step they inched forward. Holly resisted the urge to ask, "Are we there yet?" Instead, she scanned the side of the trail for the next arrow or mile marker. *Surely we're almost to the good part, to the reward for all the hard work we've done to get this far?*

"There's more." Nik stopped again, and turned toward her.

"More what?" Holly paused her music.

"More questions about you and our good buddy Frank."

"Seriously? What more can I say?" Holly pulled out her earbuds.

"When Marina found your phone in the conference room the

other day there was a notification that caught her attention." Nik's shoulders were slumped, maybe from the weight of his backpack or the weight of his words. Or both.

"What in the world? She was snooping on my phone?" Holly tried to keep her tone in check but her words had a life of their own, speeding toward a Road Closed sign, despite the warnings to take another route. She breathed in sharply but couldn't get a deep breath. The air was thin up here.

"I'm sure she didn't mean to but—"

"What notification?" Holly scowled.

"It was from Frank and it said something like, 'Thanks for hearing out my declaration of affection. Your favorable response meant more than you know."

"It wasn't worded like that and Frank was talking about Elaine, not me!" Holly groaned. "But you didn't know that so I can see why it sounded bad."

"They're dating?"

"No. I mean, I don't think so. Elaine hasn't said anything. Frank was weighing whether or not he should risk their friendship by telling her he's interested in more."

"Sounds like he wanted your permission to date your best friend." Nik muttered.

"Let me assure you, this isn't like Alexander Hamilton with Angelica and Eliza Schuyler or Theodore Laurence with Jo and Amy March. Frank is not settling for one of the people closest to me, in order to keep me in his life."

"Maybe." Nik took off his baseball hat and swiped the sweat from his forehead with the back of his arm before replacing it.

"I have a question for you, besides this one burning a hole in my pocket, that I thought we could ask each other once we reached the top."

"What's that?"

"Do you have a thing for Marina? Does she have a thing for you?" Since they were clearing the air, Holly asked the question that she had tossed around in her mind for a while. It hung between them.

"Marina's rooting for us in more ways than you realize, so of course she was ticked when she saw that notification on your phone."

"Are you deflecting? Downplaying? What kind of response is that to my question? I was hoping for some assurance like, 'Of course not, Brigham. There's no one else I'd rather be with. Your quirky, artsy, emotional, visionary, messy self doesn't scare me away. I choose you, even when we're living 2000 plus miles away from each other. You're the only one for me.'" Holly instantly regretted how she had made it sound like she was the main character in this imperfect love story.

"Holly, come on, Marina is like a kid sister or a cousin. She's an enthusiastic co-worker with a gift for managing myriads of details for high stakes events, like the concert." Nik unclipped his backpack and set it down.

"Upbeat, administrative, adorable, and in close proximity to you." Holly sighed, taking off her pack and plopping it down into the dirt.

"Is that what this is about? The long-distance thing?" Nik leaned against a boulder.

"It definitely requires a huge amount of trust." Holly sat down on another boulder a few feet away from him, then immediately shot up as the heat from the rock burned the back of her leg.

"For both of us."

"Yeah."

"Is there more to this?" Nik tossed her an extra shirt from his backpack.

"There's more to it, although mostly unrelated to our mutual jealousy for our opposite genders friends who live closer to us that we do to each other." Holly placed the shirt on the boulder before sitting down on it.

"I'm not sure I'm ready for more." Nik raised his hands partially, in surrender.

Holly decided not to read into that statement, although the hinges felt like they were coming off the door to their future. The whiplash from possible engagement to major conflict threatened to sabotage the rest of the hike. Holly decided to go all in and lay it out there. It would either put a nail in the coffin or strengthen whatever foundation was left that they'd worked to build. Holly removed her sunglasses. "I had a panic attack on the coaster. They have been fewer and farther between, but sometimes they still come out of nowhere."

"Why didn't you tell me that either?"

"I don't know." Holly willed her eyes to stay dry.

"That's what I'm here for." Nik took a step closer.

"To feel sorry for me and my baggage that I can't shake off completely? I guess I didn't want to annoy you or burden you or scare you off. I didn't tell you because it seemed like too much. Too many issues. Too much sensitivity. Too big of emotions. I feel like too much for you." Holly heaved the words off her shoulders and out into the open.

Nik removed his sunglasses and tucked them on the collar of his t-shirt. Holly resisted the urge to put hers back on.

"You're just right." He moved closer.

"Not too great, not too bad, just mediocre, that's me." Holly tried to wiggle her toes but they'd gone numb.

"Don't talk about my girlfriend that way." Nik bridged the gap between them and sat down on the boulder next to Holly. "Since we're unloading, it's probably time I told you that I feel like I don't bring enough to our relationship. Not enough excitement. Not enough money. Not enough bold vision for the future. I feel like I'm not enough for you." Nik stared at his hiking boots. They looked broken in and more comfortable than Holly's.

"Not a chance. You're the better half of this relationship. You're steady, you're patient. You're a hard worker, you're generous. You'd drop anything to help someone in need. Not to mention you give the best bear hugs and make me weak in the knees with your dashing good looks." Holly grabbed Nik's arm. They locked eyes. She lowered her voice. "Too much and not enough. No wonder we've been off balance. I guess we've been viewing our relationship through our wounds."

"Wrongful assumptions strike again." Nik sighed.

"Doesn't feel great, that's for sure." Holly didn't add how she thought Nik was going to propose earlier and then hadn't. A well-placed 'I love you' would help about now.

Nik reached for her hand and pulled her up. They lugged on their backpacks and walked side by side up the remaining section of trail that led to the scenic overlook. Within minutes they rounded the last corner.

"Close your eyes." Nik whispered. "This is the best part." He placed her hand on the loop of his backpack and led her, carefully.

"My life is literally in your hands at the moment." Holly shuffled forward.

"Trust me."

After a few minutes of silence, Nik said, "Here we are. Open your eyes."

Holly slowly opened them. She gasped as darkness transformed to vivid color.

A glassy aquamarine lake spread out before them. The jagged mountain rock faces, with snow dusted peaks, served as guardians around this Narnia-like corner of the earth. Overhead, the clouds danced slowly like a kaleidoscope shifting against endless blue sky. There was so much to take in. The grandeur and the details overwhelmed Holly's senses.

Holly and Nik stood in close proximity, hushed by the breathtaking wonder around them. Holly could have stayed there for hours, taking in the boastful beauty surrounding them. They lingered for at least a half an hour, enjoying the fruit of their labor and bearing witness to their smallness in the presence of majesty.

Before they collected their gear for the demanding hike back down, Nik leaned over, "Dare I ask what the question was supposed to be for today?"

Holly reached for the slip of paper tucked in her back pocket. She unfolded it and read, "What makes you angry?" She showed Nik the paper as proof that the questions really were mirroring real life.

"Naturally." Nik shook his head.

"Care to answer?" Holly tucked the question in his T-shirt pocket, above his heart.

"It seems like we established our answers quite firmly on the way up."

"True." Holly put her hand on his shirt pocket. "I know you were looking forward to this hike. I'm sorry it didn't go as planned."

"Definitely not as expected." Nik placed his hand on hers.

"What now?"

"Let's take a picture of this incredible view. I don't think we'll ever forget it or what it took to get here." Nik pulled Holly toward him, wrapping his arms around her. He held up his phone and clicked. The pristine lake was behind them, the mountain peak extended above them toward the heavens—like an arrow pointing upward.

They had covered a lot of ground on the climb, over two thousand feet in elevation. Holly wondered if it was too much, not enough, or just right?

CHAPTER NINETEEN
Why do you love me?

A WEEK HAD PASSED SINCE THE hike and the fight that nearly took out Holly and Nik. They only had two Saturdays left together in Leavenworth but most of this second-to-last Saturday was devoted to ironing out the remaining details of the mural and finishing up concert prep for the Christmas in July Festival.

Nik had agreed to pick Holly up mid-morning from her rental so she could tie up some loose ends before coming into town. She had finished working on the grant to free up mental space to focus on her kids' book proposal. It hung over her head, equal parts dread and delight. She'd tried several different approaches with the manuscript after Frank's feedback. However, after multiple restarts, and hours and hours of word smithing, Holly decided to offer what she had poured out originally.

Nik peeled into the driveway. He hopped out to greet Holly as she exited the A-frame.

"Thanks for giving me some extra time." Holly locked the door behind her. "I submitted my book proposal to my top three publishers. We'll see what happens."

"I'm so proud of you!" Nik drew Holly in for one of his bear hugs. She tucked her head into his chest, letting herself be shielded by the world for a few moments.

"I'm trying to stay calm but putting your baby out there for the world to see and asking others if they think she's good enough is nerve-wracking and heart-wrenching." Holly whispered into Nik's chest, as if depositing a precious coin into a treasure box.

Nik held Holly a little bit longer. "I could stay like this forever, but we need to get back to the office. It's crazy-town over there."

They hurried to his car. Nik opened the passenger door for Holly. She sat down and buckled up. She tried not to think about the fact that she'd soon fasten her seatbelt on an airplane, headed back to Bavarian Falls, far away from Nik.

※

Once she'd settled into her workstation in the conference room, Holly picked up her brush and dipped it into black paint. She began outlining an enormous 'L' in "LEAVENWORTH." Holly had already painted a row of buildings on the banner to represent each business that had sponsored the festival. Now she was outlining the town's name right on top of the downtown scene so that the businesses looked like they were inside each over-sized letter. Each letter was about three feet in height. Holly had lifted the idea from a style of postcard that Grandpa Dale and Grandma Bea had often sent her from their travels around the country.

At lunch time, Marina bounded into the conference room. "Ooo! The mural looks fantastic. You saved the day, Holly. I don't know how we would have managed this on top of everything else."

"I hope I can get it done by the end of the day. It's supposed to go up ASAP."

A few moments of awkward silence passed before Marina said, "We've all been running around so I didn't get a chance to say this earlier. I'm sorry about checking the notification on your phone. I didn't mean to, but it caught my attention. It sounds like it didn't mean what I thought it did." Marina fidgeted with the bangles on her wrists.

"Thank you. I know what it's like to think something is one way but it's really another. I owe you an apology too. I assumed a lot about you and I didn't even know you." Holly wiped the excess from her paintbrush on the edge of the paint can.

"Sounds like we need a fresh start?" Marina extended her hand.

"Deal." Holly set down her brush and shook her hand.

"How's it going in here?" Nik entered the conference room with two bags of takeout. He looked from Holly to Marina as if trying to assess whether or not it was safe to enter. "Ready for a working lunch?"

―※―

The rest of the day was a blur for Holly, and her paint-stained fingers were the proof. While she washed up in the office bathroom, she recalled part of the conversation she'd had with her counselor, Nina, during their Telehealth appointment earlier in the week.

Holly had filled her in on the panic attack and the fight she and Nik had.

"That sounds like growth to me. You're going forward and walking through challenges, and you're not trying to write yourself out of this story and into another one." Nina's kind tone comforted Holly.

"It's tempting to want to run away from the imperfection of it all, but I'm more the imperfect one. Why Nik hasn't jumped ship, I'm not sure. He keeps showing up." Holly had been snuggled under a soft blanket on the couch in the air-conditioned rental during the appointment.

"So do you, Holly. You keep showing up to this relationship and to your life." Nina leaned in, toward her computer screen. "Forward progress is not flawless progress. Focus on one step, then the next step, the way you did on the trail." Nina smiled.

Holly was quiet.

"What if instead of the flaws you traced the lopsided beauty in this story, Holly? The three dimensional, the shading, the contrast, it's all there. Those elements keep things interesting and can contribute to a healthy relationship. You're not sunk. You're learning."

"Can't I learn faster?" Holly laughed.

"We often want that, don't we? Yet I wonder what you'd miss if you rushed through the growth?" Nina's question lingered.

A *knock knock* on the bathroom door brought Holly back to the present moment. She had scrubbed off as much excess paint as she could, and what remained would serve as a badge of honor. The mural definitely wasn't flawless, but it was finished. It had to be. Time was up.

When Holly opened the bathroom door, stern HR man was waiting. Just her luck. She sidestepped him.

"Nice job on the sign. Looks good." He said, before entering the facilities.

"Thank you." Holly turned toward him. The bathroom door closed in her face.

Holly was certain he didn't often give out compliments. She took it as a win.

It was nearly dark by the time Nik and one of his co-workers hung the mural at the concert venue. It said, "Christmas in July Festival in LEAVENWORTH." The hoisting of it had been quite a chore, involving extension ladders, climbing harnesses, and power tools. Holly's job was to tell Nik if it looked straight. While she waited for them to secure the mural, Holly sat down in the empty venue. She pulled out her journal from her backpack and started doodling. She drew a map, a heart on Bavarian Falls and a heart on Leavenworth. She connected the hearts with a dotted line.

Holly thought back to the beginning of this summer adventure. The disappointment of Nik not being able to visit

Bavarian Falls. The wildfire that caused her commercial flight to Leavenworth to be canceled. The news that Nik would be working most of the time while she was in town. Holly stopped herself. While those things were true they weren't the whole truth. She reset her thought pattern and tried again.

Nik not being able to visit her had opened the door to Holly experiencing the beauty of Leavenworth. The canceled flight caused Mrs. Rasmussen and Pastor and Mrs. Meyer to rally together so Holly could get to Leavenworth another way. Nik having to work much of the time allowed Holly time to complete her manuscript and although she missed that time with him it freed her to pursue a new dream that might be a part of her future—and maybe their future?

This love story wasn't only about her and Nik, it was about a community of people who loved them well. Under the map she had drawn, Holly started writing down the kindness shown by many.

- Elaine's creative efforts to help Holly and Nik improve their communication through the twenty IOU questions.

- Shayla letting Holly work remotely so she could be in Leavenworth for a month.

- Mrs. Meyer paying for Holly's plane ticket to Leavenworth.

- Mrs. Rasmussen orchestrating an alternative, last-minute plan to get Holly to Nik.

- Pastor Meyer dropping everything and flying Holly across the country in the puddle jumper plane.

- The couple from Nik's church discounting the rental house for Holly.

The list could go on and on.

"How does this look?" Nik yelled from the rafters.

"Can you raise it a little bit higher?"
The mural inched upward.
"Like this?"
"Yes! Just right." Holly nodded. The artist was satisfied.

Moments later Marina appeared, skirting down the aisle, yelling something in Spanish. Holly could not decipher the flurry of words.

"I can't hear you from up here," Nik called down from the rafters. "Hang on!"

Holly walked over to a pacing, frazzled Marina, who was texting wildly on her phone and murmuring under her breath, still in Spanish.

Soon Nik ran over, "What's going on?"

"Sounds like our guest of honor won an award or something and can't be here. I'm working on a quick replacement, but I'm not sure how it'll to go over. Everyone was so excited about Harry." Marina hadn't stopped typing as she lamented to Nik and Holly.

"Wait—what?" Nik ran his fingers through his hair. "Who did you get instead, at this short of notice?"

Marina stopped, took a deep breath and said, "He's from Vegas. His positive reviews are off the charts. I've been assured he's the next best thing to having Harry."

"Vegas?" Nik cocked his head.

"Vegas." Marina nodded as if trying to convince herself things were fine.

"Oh dear," Holly involuntarily said out loud.

"It gets worse," Marina whispered.

Holly couldn't imagine how it could get any worse. Yet another dream dashed before it became reality. She should have known that it was too good to be true that she'd meet Harry.

"It's his name."

"His name?" Nik drummed his fingers on his legs, clearly nervous about what this unfortunate turn of events meant for the festival and their jobs.

"Are you going to repeat everything I say?" A slight glimmer returned to Marina's face for a moment. But it left as soon as she shared the impersonator's name with Nik and Holly.

"You can't be serious!" Holly blurted. "That's his name?"

"We'll be the laughingstock of Leavenworth." Nik massaged his temple.

"You can imagine my shock when I first heard it too, but what choice do we have? They've reassured me we'll be pleasantly surprised." Marina didn't look convinced. "It's going to be okay…somehow. It has to be."

Marina's phone rang. "I've gotta take this." She hurried back up the aisle, leaving Nik and Holly to process the ordeal.

Holly turned toward Nik. "Barry Cronnick Sr.? What in the world? This is going to be a disaster."

Nik, who had been clearly shocked throughout Marina's frantic admission, started to chuckle.

"Our musical hero is not coming, and we've landed a senior citizen from Vegas to replace him?" Holly tried to stay stern, but Nik's laughter was contagious, and she found herself joining in.

They laughed so hard tears ran down their faces. The whole situation was so ridiculous. What else could they do but belly laugh their way through the disappointment and the fact that tomorrow night might be a huge flop. Time would tell if impersonator Barry would save the festival or it would be an epic fail.

The Christmas in July Festival started yesterday with a parade,

Art in the Park, a caroling contest, and a fruit cake bake off. The quaint alpine village buzzed with tourists from all over. It was now Saturday, July 4th, the night of the big concert. Holly and Nik agreed to arrive several hours early to help out with last minute details before the main event. They hurried to the venue, dressed in red, white, and blue. Nik was soon wrangled into catching the parking attendants up to speed on how they would manage all the extra traffic. They expected record numbers even with the last-minute change of the concert's headliner. Maybe everyone wanted a front row seat to the disaster that might be coming their way? At least they might get a viral video out of it.

Holly helped set up the remaining props on stage. She hung red, blue, and gold ornaments on evergreen trees dusted in fake snow. After that, there wasn't much for her to do. She wandered backstage and called Elaine.

After Holly told her that Harry wasn't coming after all, they chatted about the news back home, Elaine asked how Holly and Nik were doing.

"I kind of feel like I'm failing at this love thing. I haven't been very patient, kind, trusting, or hopeful. I've been jealous, insecure, easily annoyed, and selfish in many ways." Holly kept her voice down so as to not disturb the sound check that was underway. The technician was testing each mic on stage. "Maybe that's why Nik hasn't said the l-word yet." Out of the corner of her eye Holly noticed movement to her right. She turned to the left and tried to blend into the scenery housed offstage.

"I'm sure that's not it. He's crazy about you." Elaine sounded out of breath.

"Or driven crazy by me." Holly lowered her voice. She heard shuffling behind her. She turned but couldn't make out the figure in the shadows.

"I don't think you realize the good thing you have going. Stop overthinking things. Go easy on yourself, *and Nik*. Enjoy your time there." Elaine breathed sharply into the phone. "It doesn't get much better than a Christmas in July concert with one of your favorite entertainers, in a picturesque Bavarian village, with your smokin' hot boyfriend as your date. Not to mention your artwork hanging loud and proud for all to see. Sheesh, girl! You've got it going on." Elaine had a way of helping Holly see the bigger picture, when she was lost in the particulars.

"Thank you. I needed that." Holly looked up at the giant mural hanging above the stage. Nik and his co-worker had added a weighted piece to the base to keep the banner in place. "Hey, are you at basketball or something? You sound winded?"

"Running!" Elaine shouted.

"Is Frank with you?"

"Why do you say that?"

"Just curious." Holly knew she shouldn't push the issue further. They'd have plenty of time to talk next week when she and Elaine resumed their walks in the park. Hopefully her best friend would fill her in on whether or not Frank had made a move.

"Have fun tonight with Nik. Promise me you won't pick a fight at the festival."

"Yes, mother." Holly groaned.

"See you soon!" Elaine sounded like she was running again.

"Sounds good. 'Bye." Holly hung up. Elaine was right. Tonight was not the time for Holly to fixate on the missteps in her and Nik's relationship. They'd come so far. Time in person had amped up some issues but had also intensified the joy. Holly was embarrassed to admit that sometimes she'd approached her and Nik's relationship with 'a fixin' kind of love'—pointing out what was wrong, homing in on the flaws more than giving thanks for what they already had. Unrealistic expectations and unspoken hurts between them had translated into their "too much and not enough" collision on Cascade Trail. Nik and Holly weren't trying to transform a fixer upper into a B & B, like Cash and Everleigh Rae did, from Elaine's rom com. But they were trying to strengthen the foundation of their relationship and build upon it.

In the process of building, some restructuring and even some demolition was required. The walls of insecurity and jealousy needed to be torn down. New pillars needed to be raised so that Holly and Nik's relationship wouldn't topple under the pressures of life. Pillars of trust and hope, patience and perseverance, securely set on the foundation of faith. Faith that this relationship could work—no matter the distance, no matter the cost. Holly realized that although the twenty questions seemed to work against them sometimes, and read their minds at other times, their communication had improved. They definitely knew each other at a deeper level thanks, in part, to the questions.

Holly thought back on her latest counseling session with Nina. She tried to look at things from a different perspective. What if her and Nik's fight on the hike wasn't a setback but a sign they were moving forward, together? They were excavating and seeing what was really beneath the surface. They had broken past the shallow barrier to deeper ground.

Maybe they could embrace a different 'fixin' kind of love'? Not a love that criticized or hid but one that sought understanding and rose above? A love that was fixed on the only One who could repair and restore what, and who, was broken. A love that would stick it out and see things through, whether in sickness or health, moments of misunderstanding or clarity, in person or online, in Leavenworth or Bavarian Falls. A love that was unmoving, no matter what.

A huge gust of warm wind blew across the venue.

"Watch out!" Someone yelled.

Holly's banner, with the weighted base, swung from the rafters and nearly took her out. She ducked out of the way just in time.

"Are you okay?" Nik rushed over to her.

Holly's heart raced. "Hopefully that's not a sign that everything will fall apart tonight."

"I don't know how that happened. We had that baby securely fastened." Nik accessed the damage. "Thankfully it's still intact. I'm going to call in for backup."

Holly was relieved the banner hadn't ripped. She'd invested so much time in it. She dusted it off while Nik went to talk to the venue workers.

It was almost time for the concert to start. The mural had been successfully repositioned. The white lights on the evergreens had been plugged in. People of all ages were filing into their seats. Marina had assigned Holly backstage, on the right-hand side, to make sure all went according to plan. Holly was armed with a clipboard that contained a detailed spreadsheet with the cues for everyone's entrances in case anyone forgot or had a question.

"Great turnout tonight."

Holly froze. She turned to confirm what she suspected. The elderly man of the hour had spoken to her. "H-h-hello, Mr. Cronnick. I'm Holly. Thank you for agreeing to headline the festival on such short notice. We're so excited you're here." Holly tried to make it sound like she wasn't trying to convince herself. A tan, white-haired, grandpa type, in a stylish suit, stood before her, with a welcoming smile.

"Pleased to meet you, Holly. What song do you most hope

to hear in the set?" Barry reached to shake her hand. His kind eyes put her at ease.

Holly cleared her throat. "That's easy, 'Make You Feel My Love' from the "Hope Floats" movie. My Grandma Bea loved that one. She'd watch it many times a year. She cried every time that song came on. I didn't understand why back then. But I'm beginning to."

"That's a great one. It pretty much lays out how to stay married for forty plus years and counting." Barry smiled wide, pointing to his wedding ring. "I still get butterflies when my wife walks into the room."

From the stage the opening chords of "It Had to Be You" swelled from the band, which was Barry's cue.

"I have a new song I'm trying out tonight that I think you might like as much as that one. Hang tight. You'll see." Barry smoothed the collar of his black suit jacket. He wore a crisp white shirt underneath with a thin black tie. "If I can offer one piece of advice for you and the guy I overheard you talking about on the phone earlier, it's this: Don't keep a record of wrongs, Holly. Love speaks volumes, often without words." He slipped in his inner ear monitors.

"Thank you." Holly's cheeks warmed. She would never forget this for the rest of her life—when none other than Barry Cronnick Sr. gave her hard-won relationship advice. You couldn't make this stuff up. It would be a story she would tell her grandkids one day.

Barry strolled onto the stage with a surprising amount of swagger. He was met with cheers, whistles, and thunderous applause.

"I feel the love in Leavenworth tonight. I know you were expecting a younger fellow, but I hope you're pleasantly surprised by the good time we'll have tonight as I sing the crooner's beloved songs and a few of my own. Who's ready for amore?" He pointed to the band. The horns, sax, strings, and drums all contributed to the wave of jazz flooding the stage. Barry sat down at the red piano, center stage. His skilled fingers danced along the keys.

The high energy concert continued for almost an hour with familiar favorites and a few new tunes. Barry shared stories throughout the set, some funny, some touching. Holly watched from stage right. She hoped Nik was almost done with whatever had him tied up so they could watch the concert together. She tried texting him again.

Barry adjusted his microphone. "My wife and I have been married for over four decades. While me serenading her with love songs helps keep the romance alive, people often ask what the secret is to us staying together all these years. Sometimes they assume we don't fight. Which is not true—but we're in this for the long haul." Barry played low, slow jazz chords on the piano as he talked. "She's stuck with me and I'm the luckiest to be hers. Plus, we're stubborn and we're committed to seeing this marriage through, even when we face choppy waters that threaten to capsize us." Barry mimicked the sound of something being capsized on the keys. "One night we went out on our boat to watch the sunset. It had all the elements for a magical evening, except we started arguing about something stupid that I can't even remember now. The sun went down and we were still irritated with each other, so I retreated to my music room and tried to communicate through lyric and melody that I wasn't going anywhere, even when we didn't see eye to eye. Most of the song flowed out easily, except I got stuck on the bridge and it wouldn't unravel. No matter what I tried, it wasn't right. So I called a dear young friend of ours, whom you've probably heard of, and she graciously agreed to co-write with me. My friends, if a storm is raging around you, and you and the one you love feel like you're sinking tonight, I invite you to stand up in the boat and Raise the Sail."

Barry began playing a progression of haunting chords. "Ladies and Gentlemen, all the way from Nashville, Tennessee, let's give a warm welcome to Miss Lauren Golden. The voice of an angel, with hair of gold and eyes of blue and such a generous heart, Lauren helped me put the finishing touches on this song and I've invited her to duet with me. Is that all right with you?"

The crowd went wild. Lauren Golden had recently had a breakaway hit on the country music charts. Before tonight, most people hadn't heard of impersonator Barry from Vegas, but they most definitely knew Lauren—unless they lived under a rock. She entered the stage from the other side and positioned herself next to the piano in a gorgeous gold-sequined gown. Lauren's surprise appearance must have been one of the secret contract details Marina had been working on behind the scenes. Holly was proud of all the work Nik, Marina, and their co-workers had done to pull off such a huge event in Leavenworth. Holly was honored to play a small part in the incredible evening.

Barry's and Lauren's voices crescendoed in perfect harmony as they sang. Barry played the piano and the other instruments in the band layered in their contribution to the masterpiece. Holly held on to every word.

Raise the Sail
We were fine
Smooth sailing over time
Now we're upside down
Lost at sea

Want to repair
The damage that's there
Exposed by wave and wind
Pulling you from me

So much between us
Out here in the deep
So many reasons
We won't sink

Raise the sail
Brave the dark
Chart the course
To your heart
I'm not giving up on us
Not giving up on us

Don't you fear
Thunder crashing near
Flashes of lightning
Our signal flare

We'll get through
Gonna face this storm with you
Not going under
We'll cross this sea

So much between us
Out here in the deep
So many reasons
We won't sink

The tide is rising but I'm not gonna bail
The struggle makes us stronger
Sink or swim we're tethered
So let's raise the sail
And hold on…hold on…a little longer

Raise the sail
Brave the dark
Chart the course
To your heart
I'm not giving up on us
Not giving up…on us

There weren't many dry eyes in the crowd. Holly's certainly weren't. The lyrics could have been written about Holly's parents and the way her mom faithfully stood by her father's side, post aneurysm. They could have been written about Betty Jo patiently waiting in the wings for Mr. Neumann for years. The lyrics also pointed the way forward for Holly and Nik. They could make it through if they hung in there. If they were anchored in what was true and not just perceived or assumed, they could make it. What would it look like to raise the sail and brave the dark, together?

Lauren and Barry took a bow. The crowd clapped their approval. He started the next song, a rousing rendition of the classic, "Sleigh Ride" mashed up with "Christmas in July."

"There you are." Nik slipped his arms around her waist from behind.

"Here I am." Holly leaned back as they swayed to the next song.

"I'm all yours now that the concert is well underway. Can you believe we're here, with Barry Sr. crooning away while we make out off stage?"

"Is that what happens next?" Holly hugged her clip board, a coy smile on her lips.

"I hope you don't mind, but I took it upon myself to write my own question to ask you tonight." Nik released her waist.

"You did?" Holly spun around to face him.

Nik reached for the slip of paper in his pocket. He handed it to Holly. "Would you do the honors?"

"Why do you love me?" Holly read.

"Let me count the ways." He held his finger to her lips. "One." He pressed gently down on her lips. His fingers warm to the touch. "Two" Nik held up both her hands in his and squeezed them. The piece of paper was folded into Holly's palm, pressing into her skin.

"But you haven't even—I mean, why this question?" Holly nodded to her hand.

"I didn't want to chance another fight due to whatever question we'd draw out of the jar. With only two left, I decided to take matters into my own hands." He smiled looking at their hands still clasped together.

"Yeah, at this rate, the question was probably, 'What's the most annoying thing about me?' Can you imagine how well that would go. I mean, that's a set-up for sure and—" Holly flailed their clasped hands.

"I love you." Nik's declaration shut Holly right up, in the best possible way.

"Love?" She tilted her head to the side.

"What? Did I not say it right?" Nik let go of their hands.

"I've been screaming those three words to you in my head for months."

"Screaming them, eh?" Nik rubbed the back of his neck.

"You know what I mean—thinking them very loudly but not

audibly. I wanted you to say it first." Holly had to raise her voice as the stage music grew louder. Barry was really bringing down the house. Holly locked her eyes on Nik's. She'd waited a long time to hear these three little words. She put her arms around Nik's neck.

Nik wrapped his arms around her waist.

Holly thought back to Barry's advice, "Love speaks volumes, often without words." That's when she realized that Nik had been shouting his love to her for months, through all the ways he cared for her, preferred her, was patient with her.

Nik leaned closer and tipped his head down until their noses were touching and their lips almost met but didn't. "I'd walk more than five hundred miles for you, Holly." Her breath caught as he referenced one of her favorite love songs. "I'd walk 2,167.3 miles to prove my love for you."

Holly believed him.

CHAPTER TWENTY
Where do you see yourself in five years?

THE SOFT, ENCHANTING THEME FROM "PRIDE and Prejudice"—the Keira Knightley version not the BBC version—played from Holly's phone at precisely 5:00am Pacific time on Sunday morning. The song, aptly titled, "Dawn" gently transitioned Holly from sleep to an awakened state. While it was tempting to remain nestled under the airy comforter after the late night at the concert, Holly willed herself to leave the refuge of her cocoon. She only had forty minutes to get into position. She let her alarm tone keep playing as she reached for her tank top and shorts. The notes landed then lifted, like delicate raindrops descending and ascending in a nuanced dance. The mesmerizing melody of the piano was mostly happy, with a touch of melancholy contemplation. It matched Holly's mood perfectly.

Not only was it the last day of the Christmas in July Festival, Nik and Holly were down to their last IOU Question. Holly peeked at the question she and Nik had bypassed due to his replacement question from the night before. It said, "What is something nobody else knows about you?" Holly liked Nik's question much better. She tossed the paper into the waste basket next to the dresser, leaving one lone question in the jar.

Holly was scheduled to fly back to Bavarian Falls next week. This was the last weekend of her visit. She tried not to think about it too much to keep the ache at bay. She had grown accustomed to the charm and majestic views of Leavenworth. She hadn't had as much time with Nik as expected, but she appreciated the fact that he was within reach. How would she get used to the distance again? The first goodbye had been one thing, when Nik had decided to take the job out here. She anticipated the second goodbye would be worse.

Holly had to admit the IOU questions had helped them work through their communication barriers. At times, it felt like those crazy questions were contributing to the problem, but they served as a tool to rototill their relationship and help it grow healthier. Part of that growth meant locating the weeds that threatened to choke out life. In their case, the weeds of insecurity and inadequacy had to be uprooted. They might sprout back here and there but the source had been exposed so they wouldn't have the same stronghold they once did. While Holly wasn't ready to tackle a fixer upper farmhouse and turn it into a B & B with Nik, like Cash and Everleigh Rae did in Elaine's rom com, which started this whole thing, Holly knew her and Nik's relationship carried more depth and a stronger bond after the summer they had.

Holly retrieved the lone piece of paper from the mason jar on the dresser. She kept it folded, slipping it into the back pocket of her jean shorts. She hoped she and Nik could read it together during a quiet moment. Although a quiet moment might not be possible with the festival in full swing.

Holly reached for her hairbrush. She'd attempt curls later, but for now a messy braid would have to do. She had early morning plans that included her paint brush and the sunrise.

Holly grabbed her hair tie off the dresser to secure her hair in place. She briefly accessed her appearance. Taped to the mirror was the photo Nik had printed of them at the top of Cascade Trail with the aquamarine lake behind them. She studied it for a moment, equal parts mortified and amused by the bonding experience. Their communication still needed work, but they'd gained sure footing along the way.

A few nights ago Holly had discovered a German book of

idioms in the A-frame among the other books on the shelf. If she couldn't keep the American ones straight how would she do with the German ones? Holly had thumbed through the book, some of the idioms funny, some serious. One was particularly poetic, *'Morgenstund hat Gold im Mund'* which translated to, 'The morning hour has gold in its mouth.' In other words, there's treasure to be found at the start of the day, so don't miss it. She'd written it in her journal. It had inspired her early morning adventure.

According to the guidebook created by the rental owners, there was a trail with a notable view, within walking distance.

Step by step, turn by turn—with her fully-charged phone flashlight lighting the way—Holly hiked the one and two-tenths mile of 'moderate trail with a stunning view—well worth the effort.'

Once she reached her destination, she set down her backpack, took a long drink of ice-cold water, and sat on a wide rock.

In the morning stillness, the sliver of sun permeated the darkness, and the mountain and valley came alive. Piercing light rolled over the darkest of spaces, nothing hidden, nothing untouched. The light changed the landscape.

Holly retrieved her art supplies so she wouldn't miss a thing. She was more skilled in communicating the sacred through brushstrokes than she was through babble—more accustomed to exploring her emotions on paper and canvas.

The increase in altitude brought clarity. Holly had been drawn to capturing the beauty of creation from a heightened perspective since she was young. Treetops, roofs, steeples, mountains peaks, clouds—they rose above the landscape, a part of but away from. Seeing from their vantage point took risk and faith.

A part of, but away from.
Risk and faith.

These phrases, these words, took on form as Holly painted evergreens, cobalt sky, and rocky mountain on the canvas. Her brush was an extension of the view.

Holly listened to the symphony of living things. She watched the gold of the morning roll over the valley and the mountain, transforming all under its warmth and light. She reflected on her trip. The lows, the highs, the in between. The echo of Nik's declaration was the refrain: *I'd walk more than five hundred miles for you, Holly, I'd walk 2,167.3 miles to prove my love for you.*

Their love story was special and it was human. There would likely be future misunderstandings and stepping on toes—without or with intention. There might be words flung in carelessness and relapses back into insecurity and inadequacy. Yet, the risk and the faith were worth it.

An hour or so must have passed but it felt like a blink. Holly put down her paintbrush and let her painting dry. She turned her full attention back to the nature in front of her. High-definition creation, a lavish display of glory, even if she was the only one to bear witness to it. Nothing was held back, it was laid bare to enjoy, delight in, learn from. Unexplored territory spread into the distance before her, with heightened risk and faith-building turns and spectacular sights that couldn't be contained on a canvas.

A bird cawed overhead. A gentle breeze rustled through the treetops. Creation was awake. Holly was still and quiet.

She reached for her Bible, a gift from her Grandma Bea when she graduated high school. She opened up to the dedication page and read what she had many times before.

Dear Holly:
In the wonderings, in the waiting, on the heights, or in the

depths, in the storm or in the calm, whether you stay close or move far away, God is the solid ground beneath your feet.

Psalm 62:2-3, "He alone is my rock and my salvation, my fortress where I will never be shaken."

Love you,

Grandma

After a few minutes of reflecting, Holly turned to Romans 8 and read familiar words, but today they hit differently, more deeply. The last verse of the chapter, verse thirty-nine, stood out to her. She read it several times slowly: "Neither height nor depth, nor anything else in all creation, will be able to separate us from the love of God that is in Christ Jesus our Lord."

Holly contemplated the words anew. No wrongful assumptions, no panic attack, no dwindling bank account, no argument with her man, no sudden loss would be able to separate her from God's love.

Holly slipped her journal out of her backpack. She wrote the verse at the top of a blank page.

She waited.

Soon she heard the whisper. *Love is willing to go the distance.*

"Even when HR tries to interfere?" Holly smiled.

Even then.

"What about when Nik and I fight? When we get it wrong?"

Then too. Fight for one another, not against.

"We still have so far to go with our communication." Holly glanced at the empty space underneath the verse in her journal. It was like a question mark hanging over the unfinished story of her and Nik's future. She thumbed back through her journal, to the page with the folded down corner.

Celebrate how far you've come. You're not going

backwards, you're scaling a new part of the mountain.

As Holly reread it, a new understanding was impressed upon her. *You're crossing into new territory, not just with Nik—with Me.*

She kept listening.

As you move forward, don't confuse earthly love with heavenly love.

One is but a glimpse, the other the full picture.

Will you trust Me when you only see a glimpse?

Holly listened to the whisper more closely and realized that it was shouting. Shouting through the way the light pierced the valley with golden glow, through the breeze rustling the leaves, through the way her heart was thumping in rhythm to the opus of praise.

She tuned into the melody that was often drowned out by her anxiety.

Holly, I have walked more than five hundred miles. I have walked more than 2,167.3 miles. I have walked a million miles to win your heart. I walked to the Cross to prove my love for you.

In the blank space in her journal, underneath Romans 8:39, Holly wrote two words. The only two words that were fitting for this dawning moment.

Thank you.

༺❀༻

A showered, spruced up, and more settled Holly arrived downtown at dusk, by way of an Uber. Nik had been trying to make it work so he could pick her up, but it was too complicated. Holly assured him she'd be fine. Nik needed to be able to focus as he and his co-workers wrapped up the festival.

The driver dropped Holly off downtown. She walked over to her and Nik's bench at the plaza. Unfortunately, it was occupied so she wandered through the crowded park looking for another spot to wait. Holly had exchanged her messy braid for wavy curls, sandals for heels, and tank and shorts for a knee-length black cocktail dress. Her summer tan enhanced the ensemble.

Holly tried not to think about the upsetting email she'd received earlier. She wanted tonight to be the best one of her visit. However, the concert and Nik's declaration of love would be hard to beat. She pushed away the memory of the email. She wanted to be fully present.

Holly's phone started playing the chorus of the "Raise the Sail" song from last night. She had made it her ring tone for texts. She didn't want to forget.

Meet me by the maple tree in the far corner of the park. It's lit up with white lights, like a Christmas tree.

Be right there, Holly typed.

She wandered through the park until she reached the far corner. Nik's face lit up when he spotted her. He'd spruced up too. He wore navy pants and a light blue dress shirt. Holly smiled. He'd worn something similar the first time she met him. Nik stood under the white-lighted tree.

She wanted to rush into his arms but her high heels slowed her down.

"You are gorgeous." Nik kissed her cheek once she reached him. He seemed to appreciate Holly's hour-glass figure in her classic black dress. "Wow."

"You clean up nice as well." Holly laughed.

"I'm trying not to think about this being one of our last days together in person."

"Shh, let's not talk about that." Holly put her fingers to her lips.

"I want to make the most of tonight, so I thought we could start with our last question."

"Really? That feels sad. Like when you're almost to the end of a book and the characters have become your friends and you're not ready for it to end?"

"You're a strange one, Holly Noel. I love you for it."

Holly was convinced hearing Nik say 'I love you' would never get old.

"I love you, Beckenbauer." Holly offered the words she had been holding in.

"I'm so glad." Nik brushed his hand down Holly's cheek. "Now, the question?"

Thankfully Holly had remembered to retrieve the question from her shorts pocket and put it into her clutch. "Here you go."

"Where do you see yourself in five years?" Nik read.

This last question could bring them even closer or produce an irreparable rift. Would they see eye to eye on where they were headed, or would this last question be a deal breaker? Their relationship was in that stage of 'Do I make my own plans and see if they line up with yours?' Or 'Do we start adjusting and merging our plans, heading in the same direction with more intention?'

"Five years? How about five months? I'm thankful my clients have been in good hands while I've been gone. I enjoy the meaningful work with them and yet I'd like to branch out and see where this kids' book takes me. I'm not ready to walk away, but I'm willing to see how I could travel more, reach farther, and this book thing may be the ticket. I guess I have a knack for picking work that doesn't deliver big paychecks, but the meaning is more important to me than the money."

"Whatever you do, Holly you bring beauty and meaning to

it. You have a *knack* for that." Nik folded the question and tucked it into his dress shirt pocket.

"This is probably a terrible time to bring it up, but I received my first rejection today from a publisher. I had barely sent the email when I received a response. I'm not even sure they read my full proposal. Here, let me pull it up." Holly retrieved her phone from her clutch. She'd almost memorized the four sentences, the four blows to the chest. The thrust of the rejection from the publisher would either scare her off, feed bitterness, or forge her character.

Holly turned her phone horizontally and enlarged the size of the text. She cleared her throat. 'Ms. Brigham: If you are serious about being a children's book author, consider taking some classes, joining a writing group, and better understanding your audience. This sounds like it was written for adults, not children. Nice sentiments but confusing language. Say what you mean.'"

"Hol, I'm sorry. I'm proud of you for sending it though. That was a big step." Nik reached for her hand.

"A flailing leap into humble pie. I wrote my heart out in my charming A-frame in the woods, feeling like a real author. I prayed over it. I worked and reworked the words, the syllables, the imagery. Resisting the urge to call off the whole thing, I pushed past the doubt. My intentions were beyond seeing my name on the cover of a book, they were to help Claudia and all those who have lost someone. Those who are trying to make sense of the brokenness that threatens to break them in two. I thought it was hope and light, but it fell short, into a heap of disappointment." Holly knew she was being dramatic, but she needed to verbally process the sting and the thrust of this first rejection, so it didn't eat her alive.

"It's one person's opinion. It doesn't have to be the verdict on your budding writing career, right?"

"Career? You always believe in me so big. I love you for that. Even when I'm failing miserably."

"I see it a little differently. You were brave enough to send it. That's not failing, that's trying." Nik stroked the top of her hand. "Besides, didn't so-and-so get rejected like seventeen times before her first book in the best-selling series was published?"

"Too soon." Holly knew Nik was right, but she wasn't ready to hear it. She stared at her heels, wishing for the comfort of her sandals about now.

"It'd actually love to see your name changed before you become a children's book author and illustrator."

"What's wrong with my name? I mean I get that Holly Noel is a bit much. But Brigham is a perfectly fine name. Wait—what? Are you meaning a pen name? I'm not sure how I feel about that either. I mean it can't be cheesy like Page Turner or Ima Story or, I don't know, Will Reed." Holly let go, and crossed her arms, perplexed by Nik's statement.

"Why would you go by Will?" Nik waggled his eyebrows.

"I wouldn't, obviously." Holly flailed her hands in exasperation. "It came to mind as a terrible pen name. What did you mean about me ditching my name? Do you think there's something wrong with me using my given name?"

"Holly—I mean, you're right. You can keep your last name if you want. It starts with the same letter after all." He offered a tempered chuckle.

"Wait, what?"

"I guess it's fitting that we're fighting again in a moment like this. We have a knack for misunderstandings, don't we?"

Holly's mind raced back to the proposal-gone-wrong-Scavenger Hunt in Neumann's and their big misunderstanding about Leavenworth and Nik's past. Not to mention the more recent example with the whole Frank ordeal and the mix-up with Marina.

"I think I'm the one more guilty of that crime. Let it be known, my knack for assumption dates pre-Nik to the time when the cute yet arrogant Duke Bentley passed me that blasted note in sixth grade."

"Duke is a thing of the past. I prefer to focus on our future."

"Ah yes, back to the future," Holly teased.

"This is for real this time, for keeps...if you'll have me." Nik tucked in his shirt. "You're stuck with me."

"Am I?"

"The stakes are high for heartbreak either way. I'd rather be broken open, pouring out my love for you day after day than have my heart broken in two, trying to live without you."

Holly felt lightheaded, which had less to do with Leavenworth's altitude than with Nik's latest declaration. However, she didn't want to assume his intent.

For a few seconds Holly searched Nik's eyes, wondering if her suspicion was correct. He stood there, steady as usual, an attractive blend of determination and tenderness. She swallowed, bossing herself into silence so as to not make a fool of herself yet again.

Nik bent down on one knee.

Holly closed her gaping mouth with her right hand. Her frustration from moments earlier melted faster than a kiddie scoop of cookies-n-cream on a sun-baked day.

"When I think about the next five years, I see you by my side and me by yours. We can fill in the details later." His steely blue eyes locked on hers. Nik looking up at her was quite the change. She was used to looking up at him.

Nik reached for her hand again. His grasp anchored her.

He smiled. "I mean Page Turner does have a nice ring to it. But I'm not going to lie…" He brushed her hand in his. "I'd love it if you'd take my last name."

Holly willed herself not to look away from the intimate gaze of this man, on one knee, before her.

Breathe girl, pay attention to every detail of this story being written right in front of you. The one you'll be telling over and over. It's happening!

The twinkling lights overhead danced like stars on Nik's chiseled face. The muted sounds of the Christmas in July Festival served as the background track as his rich baritone voice continued.

"I've been searching for the right thing to say. I tried writing a song, but it was lame. Love, dove, above, thug didn't make for very compelling lyrics. I even tried drawing a picture, but I'm sure you're not surprised that was a disaster. Finally, I called Betty Jo, because her German is better than most and, as we've established, she's a romantic at heart. Here's what she taught me and here's what I want to define us. *Liebe ist, wenn aus dem ich und du ein wir entsteht.*" The words rolled off Nik's tongue.

"You can talk German to me, anytime." Holly blushed.

"The translation is even better… 'Love is when you and I form a 'we'.'" Nik spoke the words like a perfectly formed melody.

"I like the sound of that."

Nik placed her fingertips on his lips as he repeated the phrase, in German, slower this time. Holly felt his lips annunciate each consonant and vowel. It was if his words were a paintbrush. Each stroke deliberate, sweeping, and soft to the touch.

"I like the feel of that too." Holly responded, barely audible.

Nik gently held her wrist. He brushed his lips against her fingertips before letting go of her hand.

"In that case, I have one more question for you, Holly Noel Brigham." Nik pulled a small white box from his pants pocket. He opened it. The delicate diamond ring inside it sparkled under the lights. She lifted shy eyes to her one and only.

"Will you marry me?" Nik asked, searching her eyes.

All of Holly's daydreams of what this moment would be like did *not* prepare her for the feeling of her heart bursting into a hundred tiny butterflies of joy when Nik asked her to share the rest of her life with him—as his wife.

"I'm glad I get to practice loving you forever." Holly's eyes glistened.

"Is that a yes?"

"It's an OH YES!" She nearly tackled him, throwing her arms around his neck.

"That's a relief." Nik laughed, swaying her side to side.

Nik stopped their bear hug, "May I?"

Holly let go and nodded fast.

Nik carefully pulled the ring from its slot in the white box. He slid the ring down Holly's finger. Her finger shook slightly. Upon closer examination, the center round diamond was cradled by two diamond leaves, creating a subtle yet elegant holly effect. Holly rotated her hand back and forth admiring its beauty as it caught the reflection of the lights overhead.

"It's perfect," Holly whispered, resting her adorned hand on Nik's chest.

"Relief number two. This is why I was putting in so much overtime...to pull this off. It was one of my goals." Nik winked.

"I sure didn't make things easy on you. I about had it with those goals of yours. But this was a very good one indeed."

"I'm glad you hung in there, Brigham."

"Same, Beckenbauer. I really put you through it."

"Where do we go from here?" Nik smiled, pulling Holly closer.

"I don't care, as long as we're together, in the same zip code." Holly play punched Nik on the chest yet didn't get much leverage because of their close proximity.

"We agree."

Nik put his arms around Holly's waist inviting her even closer. She wrapped her arms around his neck. She touched her engagement ring, assuring herself she had not been dreaming. Holly could feel Nik's heart pounding in his chest. Heat radiated between their bodies, and not only from the summer night. She pressed her soft lips as close to his as she could, cupping the back of his head with her ringed hand as her other hand rested across the back of his neck. Nik rubbed her lower back with his thumbs. Holly tilted her head slightly to the side as Nik's warm lips communicated more than words could. Her kiss responded to his in all caps. YES!

Nik's breathing quickened. A surge of longing ran down Holly's spine.

There was no distance between them.

Book Club Questions for *A Very Bavarian Summer*

Nik and Holly asked each other these questions, and now it's your turn. Answer these in a journal, with a friend, around the dinner table, or at your book group. You can download an illustrated version at: katimreid.com/a-very-bavarian-summer/

1. What's your next move?
2. What are you hiding?
3. What is your favorite childhood memory?
4. What makes you snort laugh?
5. What do you dream about?
6. What makes you cry?
7. What if you had a million dollars?
8. What lights your fire?
9. How can I lighten your load?
10. What would a perfect day look like?
11. What do you run to?
12. What's my best feature?
13. What are you second-guessing?
14. What are some of your pet peeves?
15. What's your most embarrassing moment?
16. What do you want to save, and what do you need to toss?
17. What's one of your biggest fears?
18. What makes you angry?
19. Why do you love me?
20. Where do you see yourself in five years?

Author Note

Dear Reader:

Communicating with those you love is not always easy. Misunderstandings, hurtful words, and lofty expectations can cause the strongest relationships to wobble. In this second book of the Very Bavarian Series, Holly and Nik take steps to improve their in-person communication, through twenty questions.

Which of the questions would you like to ask those you're closest with, or those you're getting to know? If you haven't already, head over to katimreid.com/a-very-bavarian-summer/ to access the downloadable IOU questions. You'll also find music that goes along with the book.

A few summers ago, my friend and I were at a writing retreat, trying to find an open spot to eat our lunch. She sat down at a table in the back corner with people we didn't yet know. Like a good author, I eavesdropped on the conversation happening around me, mining any interesting tidbits that might surface. At the time, I had written about seven chapters of this book. Holly was getting ready to reunite with Nik, but I needed a conflict to keep things interesting. Would you believe that the couple sitting at our table was talking about Fort Leavenworth, Kansas, where they are from? It didn't take long for me to pummel them with questions, "Is there an airport there? Could a commercial plane land at the airfield?" Before long, a plot twist emerged out of thin air. They insisted there is much more to Leavenworth than the military prison and I happily included that fact in the manuscript. What started out as a few intentional questions unlocked the place I was stuck. The same was true for Holly throughout this story.

The Very Bavarian series reminds us, by way of Friedrich Heinrich Wilhelm Körte, and Betty Jo's mutter, *"Anfangen ist leicht, beharren eine Kunst."* Or, in other words, 'To begin is easy, to persist is an art.'

Whether at work, with hobbies, or in relationships, sticking with something and someone requires endurance. Some days it's like a thrilling alpine roller coaster, other days it's like dodging reindeer doo doo, and every once in a while, it's as fulfilling as a tender kiss on a summer night, with diamondy stars overhead.

If you've never traveled to Leavenworth, KS, or Leavenworth, WA, I hope you have an opportunity to visit either one, or both. If you go to Kansas, stop in for a cuppa at the tea house. If you go to Washington, enjoy a Bavarian pretzel and keep an eye out for a runaway reindeer. If you're ever near my neck of the woods, you might stumble into a town like Bavarian Falls. Betty Jo and ceramic Baby Jesus #1 have already rolled out the welcome mat.

> With Hope,
> Katie
> *Psalm 121*

I'd love to connect with you. Be sure to subscribe to my website in order to receive my monthly "Good News-letter" and stay updated on future books. You can also find me on Instagram and Facebook.

Connect with Katie at:
katiemreid.com
Instagram @katie_m_reid
Facebook Katie M. Reid
Listen to the Martha + Mary Show podcast

Acknowledgments

Adam: Twenty-four years of marriage and I love and appreciate you more each day.

Brooke, Kale, Banner, Isaiah, and Lark: It is my honor to be your mama. Remember to fight for each other not against each other. You siblings are God's gift to one another, never forget that.

Pearsons: Thank you for your commitment to fun family road trips growing up. I fondly recall many of the children's books you read to us, Mom, and now read to your grandkids. Thanks for instilling in us the gift of learning and reading. Dad, thanks for introducing us to the Pacific Northwest.

Reids: Thank you for expanding your horizons by adding dramatic creatives to your sports-centric family and loving us for who we are.

Dave Schroeder: Thank you for your encouragement to follow the path through Bavarian Falls and see where it leads.

Jenaye Merida: Thanks for your kindness and enthusiasm about my many projects. Grateful to be represented by you.

Miralee and the Mountain Brook Ink Team: Grateful for your belief in this series and your willingness to go the distance.

Lee: You help keep me grounded and at the same time cheer loudly to "go for it"…thank you.

Viv: You said just the right thing when I needed to hear it. Thank you for understanding me and encouraging me not to put myself in a box or on a shelf.

Kate: Grateful for your friendship, prayers, and understanding on the winding path of this work.

Janyre: Thanks for helping me turn up the heat on the

conflict and unleash the sparks.

Sarah: Barry Cronnick Sr. was the perfect addition to this story, thank you.

Jami: Aloha! Thanks for hosting us in paradise. It was a thrill to write a bit of this in Oahu.

Nicole, Charity, and Dawn: Thank you for your prayer covering and divine perspective.

Real-life Holly Noel: Hope you enjoy the continuing journey of our girl. *Celebrating how far she's come. She's not going backward, she's scaling a new part of the mountain.* You too.

My own "Nina": Thank you for caring and counseling me through my own story.

Prayer Team: Wouldn't want to do this without you. Thank you for every prayer.

Team Holly: Grateful for your enthusiasm and willingness to spread the news about our "friends," I mean characters. ;-)

Jesus: Thank You for lavishly and clearly communicating your love in a hundred million ways. You are worthy and You are worth it. You write the best stories. I trust you.

Made in the USA
Columbia, SC
06 July 2025